Praise for the *New York Times* bestselling
Sunny & Shadow Mysteries

"Small-town Maine hasn't been this dangerous since Jessica Fletcher started finding dead bodies in Cabot Cove! In this debut, Sunny Coolidge, with the able assistance of a 'big kitty' named Shadow, proves she has the skills to make a successful amateur sleuth."

—Miranda James, *New York Times* bestselling author of the Cat in the Stacks Mysteries

"Deftly combines heartwarming humor and nail-biting suspense for a fun read that leaves you looking forward to Sunny and Shadow's next adventure."

—Ali Brandon, *New York Times* bestselling author of *Plot Boiler*, a Black Cat Bookshop Mystery

"A purrfect debut. Four paws up and a tip of the tail."

—Carolyn Hart, *New York Times* bestselling author of *What the Cat Saw*

"A charming, witty, exciting new entry in the genre, featuring the best-realized and most personable fictional character on four legs. You'll love Shadow. And Sunny's fun, too."

—Parnell Hall, author of *NYPD Puzzle*

"With a dandy plot and comic relief provided by Shadow, *Last Licks* continues a pleasing series packed with suspense and amiable characters."   —*Richmond Times-Dispatch*

"A must-read for all ailurophiles."

—Melissa's Mochas, Mysteries & More

Berkley Prime Crime titles by Claire Donally

THE BIG KITTY
CAT NAP
LAST LICKS
HISS AND TELL
CATCH AS CAT CAN

Catch as Cat Can

Claire Donally

BERKLEY PRIME CRIME, NEW YORK

An imprint of Penguin Random House LLC
375 Hudson Street, New York, New York 10014

CATCH AS CAT CAN

A Berkley Prime Crime Book / published by arrangement with Tekno Books

ISBN: 978-0-425-27607-5

PUBLISHING HISTORY
Berkley Prime Crime mass-market edition / May 2016

PRINTED IN THE UNITED STATES OF AMERICA

10 9 8 7 6 5 4 3 2

Cover illustration by Mary Ann Lasher.
Cover design by Colleen Reinhart.
Interior text design by Laura K. Corless.

Penguin
Random
House

For Mom, who always liked dogs,
and Belle, who always loved Jack.

Also, many thanks to Larry Segriff
of Tekno Books for staying the course
in difficult times
and to Michelle Vega,
who inherited me.

And finally, many, many thanks
and a loud purr to all the people
who read these stories and enjoyed them.

1

The wind off the water was frigid enough to cut through the thickest coat. He shivered, hunching his shoulders as his eyes flicked around, searching for someplace warm. Bright winter sunshine was giving way to darkness now. He'd spent the day wandering around town, mooching a bit here and there, keeping out of the cold, and watching . . . always watching.

Somehow, though, he kept winding up back here, unable to make up his mind. Side by side stood the office and the store. Looking through one large window, he could see *her,* all bundled up against the chill, her eyes on a computer screen.

Maybe that was just as well. If she spotted him, there'd be trouble. She'd let him know pretty clearly that she didn't want him around there. But he didn't care. She could say what she liked, he knew he could walk in there and do as he pleased. He almost decided to tap on the glass, but there was the other window, the store. He'd spent a lot of time working on the owner and it had paid off—he'd been generous. But there was generous, and there was more. And he wanted more, even if he had to steal it.

How to do that? He could wait till a customer entered and the owner was distracted. Or. . . he could just do it under the owner's nose and dare him to do anything. Again, he was pretty sure he could get away with it. A quick peek showed that the store looked completely empty right now. If he managed to find a way in, he could take whatever he wanted, no problem.

So—love, or greed?

He never got a chance to make up his mind. The choice was yanked away from him as a hand descended, caught him by the scruff of the neck, and raised him high in the air.

His breath came out in a furious hiss as he dangled helplessly, his tail lashing in frustration. He tried to twist round, but he couldn't bring his teeth or claws to bear on this stranger. All he caught was a glimpse of a hairy face, a smoky stink . . .

And then a new voice started angrily shouting.

*

Sunny Coolidge scowled at the computer screen, sighing. The shopping cart software on the website still wasn't working. And since online commerce was the lifeblood of the Maine Adventure X-perience—MAX for short—failure of the payment system meant big trouble. The upgrade for the shopping cart was supposed to fit in seamlessly, but now it wasn't talking with the rest of the site.

Just like one of those girls in middle school suddenly bullying kids she's known since first grade, Sunny thought. *And with about as much reason.*

She kept poking at the source code, but she couldn't find the problem string. If she didn't make any progress soon, she'd have to roll the whole site back to its previous configuration and hope that didn't leave any exploitable security flaws.

Good thing it's a slow day, she thought. Tuesdays didn't see a lot of tourist action in the dead of winter. Things would pick up a bit later in the week, with people booking romantic weekends in the local bed-and-breakfast scene. That's why she'd taken the opportunity to install the new shopping cart and had spent the whole day trying to get it to play nicely with the rest of the site software—or at least notice it.

Sudden noise outside brought her eyes from the screen to the big plate glass window at the front of the office, just in time to see a furry gray streak taking cover under a parked car.

What's Shadow gotten into this time? Sunny wondered.

Her dad had already called earlier in the day with a missing cat alert. That had become all too common lately, Shadow hitching rides into town with her. Since he'd adopted her more than a year ago, Sunny knew the big gray cat was a wanderer. But the situation had gotten a lot worse since an attractive nuisance had opened next door to the MAX office.

Among his many business enterprises, Sunny's boss, Oliver Barnstable, owned a bit of real estate here in Kittery

Harbor. Specifically, he rented out the row of shops around the MAX office—the New Stores, as the locals called them, although they'd been built back when Sunny's dad was a kid. Names tended to stick in Kittery Harbor—the folks were on the conservative side.

But the space next door to MAX was a symbol of hope and change. Hopeful entrepreneurs opened businesses, failed, and the premises changed hands yet again. It had happened so often since Sunny started working that she had a hard time keeping count.

When Neil Garret opened Kittery Harbor Fish, she'd worried about the smell, but figured it wouldn't last long. Actually, Neil had kept the place spotless and odorless, keeping his stock on fresh ice or in a state-of-the-art walk-in freezer.

Shadow, however, had caught a whiff when Sunny began coming home with fresh fish as a healthy alternative for her dad's suppers. The cat had stowed away to find the source, shamelessly playing up to Neil as the fish merchant's new best friend. Now he often went visiting the fish market in hopes of snagging himself a snack.

When Sunny's father called to say that Shadow wasn't around, Sunny figured he'd snuck aboard her Wrangler for a ride into town—probably while she'd left it to warm up. *Well, he got skunked this time,* Sunny thought. *I haven't seen Neil at all today.*

Kittery Harbor Fish had survived longer than other tenants in that jinxed location, but lately Sunny had been seeing the signs—late openings, early closings. Today, it looked as if the store hadn't opened at all.

It didn't bode well for the business. *And it means that if Shadow hopes to score the occasional piece of fish, he'll have to use his charms on me—provided he survives his latest adventure.*

Even as she thought that, Sunny rushed through the door and outside into the chilly weather to find an upset Zach Judson standing on the sidewalk. "Whatever he did, I'm sorry," she told the shop owner.

Zach turned, a look of surprise on his blunt features. "Nah. Shadow is innocent—for once."

Sunny had to smile. Zach had actually known Shadow longer than she had. Before the cat had settled with Sunny, Shadow often used to turn up at Judson's Market, and probably a lot of other places around town, in hopes of a handout.

Zach shrugged his massive shoulders, the product of years spent unloading food deliveries. "At least I didn't have a problem with him, but somebody else may have. I stepped out of the store and spotted some guy grabbing your friend here."

As Zach spoke, a familiar face appeared from under a salt-splashed Chevy parked at the curb. Shadow still looked skittery and wild-eyed, scanning for possible enemies. But he must have recognized Zach's deep voice. Then Shadow spotted Sunny, and his eyes went wide. She could see the conflict on his furry face, whether to run toward her or stay under the relative safety of the car. Slowly, he edged up onto the sidewalk and slunk his way toward Sunny. About halfway to her feet, he suddenly stopped, swiping out with his paw and hissing.

"Whatcha got there, Shadow?" Zach bent to retrieve

whatever had upset the cat. It seemed to be a piece of string or twine.

"Maybe he's catching a whiff of whoever grabbed him from that," Sunny suggested. But her voice faltered as the string dangling from Zach's fingers fell straight, to reveal a loop tied at the end—a crude but effective noose.

2

Sunny realized she was staring when Shadow came up and butted his forehead against her knee. Almost automatically, she bent and picked up the cat to cuddle him in her arms. "You don't think the guy you saw was going to use that on Shadow?"

Zach Judson frowned, holding out the noose. "It's really short if he intended to use it for a leash."

Shadow twisted in Sunny's arms, snarling and trying to lay a claw on the twine. Usually his response to a bit of string was a lot more playful, a mock pounce rather than a serious attempt at attack.

"I guess you are smelling something there," Sunny said, then shook her head.

It's not as though Shadow is going to give us a brief rundown and description of the creep.

She saw the same thought must have struck Zach. "I didn't get a good look at the guy. All I saw was a raincoat—maybe he had a beard." He dug out a cell phone from the pocket of his heavy coat. "Anyway, I'm calling the cops."

Sunny carried Shadow to her office door. "I've got a plastic bag to hold that noose." She gulped a little on the last word.

Zach came in, and Sunny bagged the evidence. "If anyone comes, you know where to find me."

Sunny nodded. From early morning until closing time, Zach was at his market down on the far corner. She said good-bye to Zach and returned to her seat in front of the computer screen. Shadow immediately squirmed his way free and dropped to the floor, stalking around Sunny's desk and hissing the occasional cat curse to vent his offended feelings.

"I know how you feel," Sunny told him as she began rolling back the MAX site software. It was pretty evident that she wouldn't get the peace and quiet to do anything else.

I wonder who'll end up getting this call—if they send anybody, Sunny thought as she worked at the keyboard. Kittery Harbor was a pretty quiet town. But she wasn't sure the local police would leap into action over someone messing with a cat.

Maybe Ben Semple will turn up if the traffic is quiet in outlet-land. Ben usually patrolled the miles of outlet malls to the north of town. And since he was a friend of Sunny's, he might stop by.

But Sunny got a very different visitor. Her eyebrows rose in surprise when Will Price came through the office door.

"Is this pleasure, or business?" she asked, looking up into his face. Sunny and Will were comrades in arms, dealing with all sorts of mysterious business since she'd returned to Kittery Harbor. And more recently, they'd finally wound up in each others' arms. She knew what Will looked like when he was being romantic and when he was busy being a cop.

"I'm going to go with business, then," she said. "Don't you think it's a bit of overkill, having the sheriff's chief investigator coming out over a case of possible animal abuse?"

"Chief and only investigator," Will said, stepping around Sunny's question. His laugh came a beat too late. "I had some spare time. How's the little guy doing?"

A gray-furred face appeared from under Sunny's desk, staring warily up at Will. Shadow usually got off to a rocky start with the men in Sunny's life. But he'd come to accept Will being around. Now, though, the cat advanced with hesitant steps and dubious looks. But Shadow's basic nosiness soon won out over caution. He went over to Will's boots to give them a good sniff. Will chuckled. "For a second, I thought he didn't recognize me."

"Well, he's more used to seeing you in uniform," Sunny said, smiling. Will's promotion to plainclothes hadn't just given him a new look. It put a strain on his wardrobe. When he took off his parka, Sunny saw he was wearing what she called his big date sports coat—a tweed hacking jacket he usually wore when he was taking her someplace nice. Besides that, he had two courtroom jackets for when he was called to testify and a pair of wedding and funeral/ interview suits. Even though the area was crammed with outlet malls, Will hadn't blown his new raise on additional work clothes. Sunny approved of that. Whenever she made hurried purchases, she usually regretted them.

Besides, a lot of the stuff available in the outlet stores featured so much shiny polyester, Sunny was amazed the items didn't slide right off their hangers. Will only bought some heavy trousers and additional dress shirts there. She'd contributed a new tie that she'd given him as a Christmas present. She smiled as she noticed he was wearing it now—although the smile slipped a little when she found he had already gotten a mark on it.

Will sank into the visitor's chair across the desk from Sunny, smiling when Shadow stretched up to put both paws on his knee. "So you know who I am now, huh, little buddy? What have you been up to that someone wants to string you up?"

He dropped his grin when he saw the look on Sunny's face. "Guess that wasn't as funny as I thought it was."

"I think hearing it out loud finally made the idea sink in," she admitted, reaching into her desk drawer and bringing out the bagged noose. "Here's the evidence."

Inquisitive as ever, Shadow watched as Sunny passed the bag to Will. But he didn't have any dramatic reaction to it. "He just about pitched a fit when we found it outside," she said. "Maybe Shadow smelled his attacker on the string."

Will examined the loop. "No chance of getting fingerprints from this," he said. "And I don't think we can take Shadow around to give the sniff test to everyone in town. What can you tell me about the perpetrator?"

Well, now he sounds as if he's taking this seriously, Sunny thought. *Too bad there's nothing much I can tell him.*

"I was working on the MAX website. Ollie the Barnacle doesn't pay me to stare out the window. Zach Judson was coming out of his store and noticed that Shadow was in trouble."

"They were in front of Judson's Market?"

"No," Sunny replied. "The problem was next door, at the fish market."

That brought another off reaction from Will. He hadn't been delighted to find an attractive older guy setting up shop next door to Sunny's office. Not that Neil had done anything for Will to complain about. He'd been polite and pleasant, not flirtatious at all. But Sunny hadn't mentioned that to Will. She figured possible competition would keep him on his toes. Instead, it seemed to make Will frown and think.

"You don't suppose that Zach and Neil are still mixing it up, do you?" she asked. "I mean, Zach did complain to Ollie when Neil opened his store, saying it was competition."

"The only fish Zach sells comes in cans," Will said. "I thought they'd buried the hatchet—except for the parking space thing."

Sunny laughed. Like a lot of New England towns, Kittery Harbor had a sort of unwritten law when it came to snowstorms. He who clears snow for a parking space has exclusive use of said space for twenty-four hours. If the shoveler moves his car, he can stake a claim to the space with a marker.

The beginning of winter had been pretty mild, but when the first big storm came, Zach had cleared a space in front of his store for himself. Neil, who didn't come from this part of the woods, pulled into Zach's spot after removing the milk crate Zach had left as a marker.

Zach got his revenge though, thanks to a buddy working in municipal street clearing. Several front-loaders full of snow had created a small mountain where Neil's car had usurped the space. When things had been explained to him, Neil turned out to be a pretty good sport, hiring a bunch of local kids to clear the whole block.

"I don't think Neil will go the extra mile if we have another big storm," Sunny said.

"What do you mean?" Will sat up straight in his chair.

"I think the store is in trouble," Sunny told him. "You know that spot has been a revolving door. I've noticed that Neil doesn't offer the variety of fish he used to have. And I notice because I shop there occasionally to pick up something for Dad's supper. Unlike some people, we can't live on burgers all the time."

"Can't help it that I'm not wild about fish," Will said. "And I didn't have a burger last night. I had a steak." He smiled at his joke, but Sunny wasn't buying it. Again, she'd caught something off in his response, something that made her reporter's antenna tingle. Okay, maybe she was an ex-reporter, but she still got the tingle.

"Well, this isn't helping us get a better picture of whoever came after our furry friend here," Will said, changing the subject again. "I'll check with Zach and see if I can find out anything else and ask the other store owners if they saw something out of the usual." He shrugged. "But if you want to keep the little guy safe, you should probably keep him at home."

"Yeah—like I can tell him that." Sunny rolled her eyes. "You know he does what he wants. And these days he wants a taste of fresh flounder more than crunchy tuna treats." She watched as Shadow sat on his haunches, his head swiveling back and forth between them. "Maybe this was enough of a scare that he'll avoid trouble for a while."

As she spoke, Shadow uncurled his tail from around his paws and strolled over to Will, extending his neck in a silent demand for a head scratch.

"I wouldn't bet on it," Will said.

From the glance Shadow shot from over his shoulder, he was thinking the same thing.

*

Shadow leaned against the two-leg's fingers scratching his head. Sunny's He wasn't as good at it as Sunny, but Shadow was willing to try different things. Besides, how was the He to learn if he didn't practice? Shadow kept his head in place until he'd had enough. Then he drew back, stretched, and sat again, watching the humans talk.

From the tone, he figured they were winding down, and he was right. Sunny's He rose to his feet and rested a hand on the big piece of furniture Sunny sat behind, bringing his face to her cheek.

Shadow had seen many humans do that during his travels, but he still wasn't sure what was going on. Was the He sniffing her or licking her? Anyway, it was quickly done, and the human male walked to the door and outside. The blast of chilly air reminded Shadow of what had happened out there.

Too bad Sunny's He wasn't around when that Smoky One tried to get me, he thought. Shadow had seen the He hit a bad two-legs who'd tried to hurt Sunny, and even knock him down. That would have been good, even better than the Big One shouting and scaring the Smoky One away.

Shadow couldn't help unsheathing his claws at the thought. He wanted the Smoky One to suffer for grabbing him and scaring him like that. A snorting hiss escaped from his throat at the thought of being held helpless. He'd keep a wary eye—and nose—out for that one with the stink of smoke all around him. Shadow jerked as he detected movement above and behind him, but it was only Sunny reaching down to pet him. He'd have to remember, though, that was how the Smoky One had gotten him, being sneaky.

That definitely was not a good thing.

*

Shadow sat in front of Sunny's desk, staring out the door after Will, his tail twitching. That should have been the tip-off. When Sunny went to pet him, Shadow spooked, flying up and off as if he were on springs—high tension springs.

Guess I should be glad he didn't scratch me, Sunny thought ruefully. *This little episode must have shaken him up more than he wants to let on.*

A second later, Shadow was back, rubbing against her shins with a contrite purr. Sunny dropped to one knee, opening her arms. Shadow leaped aboard, his purr getting louder as he snuggled close.

"I know, I know," she told him. "At least it can't get any worse."

The phone rang.

"Sunny?" Whenever Sunny heard that tone in her father's voice, she braced for bad news. It was the same voice she'd heard when he'd told her about his heart attack—although it had been a lot weaker then.

She repressed a sigh. "What's up, Dad?"

"Do you think you can get off work a little early today?" Mike Coolidge asked. "Helena has a bit of a situation, and I'm hoping you can help."

Helena Martinson was the lady in Mike's life, and in Sunny's opinion the best thing that had happened to him after recovering from that cardiac scare.

"Got to finish up a little job here." Sunny shot a guilty glance at her computer screen, with the web software only halfway rolled back. "But after that I can make my escape. By the way, Shadow turned up. I'll drop him off at home."

"Good, good." Mike sounded distracted.

"Aren't you going to tell me what Mrs. M. needs?"

"Oh, right." Mike paused for a second. "Helena got a call from Florida."

Sunny grinned. "Is she going down to escape this weather?"

"No, it was a call from Abby. She managed to find a flight today and just took off. She expects to land in Portsmouth in about two and a half hours."

"Oh, Abby! Right!" Sunny had altogether forgotten about Helena's daughter's upcoming visit, maybe because the journey from California to Portsmouth had begun to resemble Homer's Odyssey. Since Abby had taken off two days ago, the polar vortex had sent a sucker punch into America's midsection, cutting the nation in two between the east and west coasts with violent storms. Abby had been stranded in Texas. As the storms blew eastward, they cut travel between north and south, further complicating Abby's attempts to get to New England.

Now she was apparently on the final leg. Sunny looked out the window at the dying sunset, making the connection. "Helena wants to meet her, but she doesn't like to drive in the dark anymore."

"Would you mind?" Mike asked.

"Of course not. Just let me finish a little brain surgery on this computer, and I'll be heading out."

Actually, restoring the system to its previous state wasn't quite as finicky as brain surgery, but it took Sunny a little while. Shadow took up residence on her lap and occasionally tried to "help" with a paw on the keyboard. At last, she finished and set the cat back on the floor. Shadow made a protesting sound at being left, staring up at Sunny as she collected her parka. Then she scooped him up again, killed the lights, and left, locking the door. Sunny carefully deposited Shadow inside her Wrangler, parked at the curb half a block from the office.

"Now stay there," she told him as he sat on the passenger-side seat. "We don't need any more excitement from you today." Sunny got behind the wheel, started the SUV, and off they went.

Kittery Harbor wasn't a big town, but enough people worked there that there was a rush hour, at least on the main roads. Sunny took a more roundabout route, but still managed to pull onto Wild Goose Drive more quickly than if she'd fought traffic. As she approached her house, she noticed Helena Martinson's Buick parked in the driveway.

"Let's get you inside and fed," Sunny said to Shadow. "Looks as though Mrs. M. wants to get her show on the road as soon as possible."

Shadow led the way, tail high, obviously feeling more confident in familiar surroundings. *At least he has the good sense to choose a nice, warm house over fooling around out in the dark and cold,* Sunny thought as she unlocked the door. As soon as they stepped into the front hall, Sunny heard her father call, "We're in here."

Sunny turned to the arched entrance way that led to the living room. Shadow, nosy as ever, scampered ahead. Helena and Mike sat companionably on the couch, the picture of a nice older couple. Sunny's father was on the tall side, with an unruly mass of white curls growing out of his Christmas haircut, his startling blue eyes staring fondly at the lady next to him. Helena Martinson was petite and lovely, dressed in a pants suit that contrasted with Mike's flannel shirt and jeans.

In the old days, people wore suits when they went flying, Sunny thought with a smile. *Mrs. M. wears one to visit the airport.*

"I hope I'm not imposing," Mrs. Martinson began, then broke off. "What's the matter, Shadow?"

The cat stopped his advance, peering suspiciously around the furniture.

"I think he's looking for Toby," Sunny said diplomatically. Since their neighbor had adopted the blond lab pup, he often accompanied her on visits. Toby seemed to grow exponentially, developing into a high-spirited, galumphing presence, convinced that Shadow was his best friend.

Shadow, however, made a habit of disappearing whenever he found Toby in the house.

"Toby is home." Mrs. M. leaned down to pet Shadow. "Saving up his energy for when he meets Abby."

"Well, he hasn't grown enough that he could knock her down," Mike said.

Sunny decided to ignore that remark, even if it was true. "Let me get this guy fed, and then we can go." She opened a can of the better cat food, figuring Shadow had been through enough today, and refilled the water bowl. "Okay, little buddy?"

Shadow kept his attention on the food, daintily lapping it up.

Sunny returned to the living room, where Helena Martinson already stood, holding out a set of car keys. Mike helped her into her coat, then she bent to retrieve a shopping bag. "I brought something along for Abby to wear," she said. "She hasn't been up in these parts in a while."

"You saw her in Boston—right? It was the end of this past summer," Mike said.

"During summer," Helena emphasized. "And it was just a couple of days while she interviewed around for jobs. We scarcely had any time together." She allowed herself a hopeful smile. "Maybe one of them panned out, and she'll be working closer to home."

Sunny didn't know how to answer that, so she stepped ahead to open the door. Mrs. Martinson didn't often talk about her daughter on the other side of the country. Sunny had still been in high school when Abby quit college and headed for California, determined to conquer the movie scene. From what Sunny had managed to glean, Abby had given up on acting and had been working for a law firm.

"We'll find out soon enough." Helena gave Mike a peck on the cheek and stepped through the doorway. Sunny took the package from her and offered an arm.

"I'm not feeble, you know," Mrs. M. told her as they stepped down to the drive.

Sunny couldn't see that discussion going anyplace pleasant, so she stepped around to open the passenger door on the Buick, stowing the bag on the back seat. By the time she got around her side of the car, Helena was already buckled in.

"Off we go," Sunny said, inserting the key in the ignition. Beside her, Mrs. M. twisted around, waving. Sunny turned to see her father outlined against the light in the doorway, his arm raised.

And down at his feet, drawn by the action, was a four-legged figure.

Hope he doesn't make a dash for it when Dad closes the door, Sunny thought.

Conversation went in fits and starts as Sunny merged onto the interstate, heading for downtown Kittery Harbor. "Abby and I talk every week," Mrs. M. said, as if she were afraid Sunny might get the impression that physical distance meant a distant relationship. "Still, I was surprised when she told me she was coming."

"I'm sure it will be good to see her." Sunny followed the traffic toward the bridge over the Piscataqua River. Kittery Harbor, on this side, was Maine. Across the water was Portsmouth, and New Hampshire. She wondered why Abby had scheduled this visit for the dead of winter, rather than, say, the holidays.

When Sunny was a kid, Christmas had always been an anxious time. Not because of worry over presents, but because it was her father's busy season. Mike Coolidge delivered road salt all over the Northeast, and a snowy December could mean that he'd be on the road. Then Sunny's mom had died in a holiday ice storm right at the end of Sunny's college term. It added up to a season a bit thin on Christmas cheer.

But this past December had been a surprisingly warm celebration, a sort of adopted family dinner. Sunny splurged on a ham, with roasted potatoes, green beans, and her mother's secret recipe for onions and raisins. Will cooked the appetizers at his place, scallops basted with maple syrup and teriyaki sauce, wrapped in bacon. The food police had definitely been off for Christmas. Mrs. M. had, of course, provided her famous coffee cake for dessert. Ben Semple, a police colleague of Will's, had surprised everyone by creating mulled wine in the kitchen, and his girlfriend, Robin Lory, supplemented dessert with cupcakes from the bakery where she worked.

It had been a special day with presents and laughter, not to mention good food. Sunny thought that they might have the beginning of a wonderful tradition. Now she found herself wondering if everything was about to change.

Mrs. Martinson checked her watch as they rolled across the bridge.

"How are we doing?" Sunny asked. "The traffic hasn't been too bad."

"No, it hasn't," Helena agreed, but she still looked anxious.

"Why don't you use your phone and check the arrival time," Sunny suggested.

The plane was on time, and so were they.

Sunny continued on the interstate until she reached the airport exit, turned, and made her way along gradually smaller streets to the terminal. Her irrepressible side couldn't help remembering that just beyond the runways stretched a golf course. *It's not everywhere you can fit in a few holes before taking off,* she thought.

She dropped Mrs. M. at the terminal entrance and parked at the short-term lot nearby. Picking up the shopping bag, she set off across the street, still making good time.

The whole area—airport, country club, and a lot of other structures—had formerly been Pease Air Force Base, and still served as an exit and entry point for military flights. As a veteran, Mike Coolidge sometimes came here to greet the troops as they returned home.

"It didn't happen for me when I came back from 'Nam," he explained. "But I want every guy and gal to know that we appreciate their service." He'd talked Sunny into accompanying him a few times, so she knew her way around the terminal.

Sunny quickly spotted Helena Martinson over by the arrivals section and joined her. "They're taxiing up to the Jetway," Mrs. M. reported. "We just made it. Did you—" She spotted the bag dangling from Sunny's hand. "Oh, good."

Of course, there was a wait, but at last passengers began to file past the barrier toward them.

Helena suddenly straightened up, raising a hand. "Abby!"

Sunny stared at the woman approaching. With her winter tan and honey-blond hair, Abby Martinson was hard to miss. Her years in California hadn't left her unrecognizable. Quite the opposite, in fact. Abby had grown into the spitting image of her mother as Sunny remembered her while growing up, when Helena Martinson was the hottest mom in the neighborhood.

Only when Abby got closer did Sunny see beyond the knockout looks and notice the effects of two days of cross-country travel, the puffy skin around bloodshot eyes, the tension in her shoulders even as she hugged her mother.

"Do you need to go to the luggage carousel?" Helena asked.

Abby shook her head. "Nope. Everything's here." She hefted the wheeled carry-on bag she'd been trailing behind her.

"What about your coat?" Mrs. M. looked at the waist-length quilted jacket her daughter was wearing. Sunny remembered having one like it when she was working in New York. It had turned out woefully inadequate when she returned for a Kittery Harbor winter.

"It's lucky we brought something," Helena said, reaching for the bag Sunny held. Catching Abby's glance, she said, "Oh, I'm sorry. I suppose I should introduce you—reintroduce you, I mean. Abby, this is Sunny Coolidge. She drove down with me."

"Coolidge?" Abby said.

"Yes, she's my friend Mike Coolidge's daughter. Sunny, I'm sure you remember Abby."

"Sure," Sunny said, extending a hand. "Welcome back to Kittery Harbor, Abby."

"Of course. Sunny," Abby said, taking a moment to

place her. "You've got to forgive me, Sunny. It's been—well, more years than I like to think." She shook hands. "Good to meet you again."

Once again, Sunny's reportorial instincts gave a little twinge, detecting something not quite right.

Somehow, I don't think Abby is as glad as she sounds, Sunny thought. *Either that, or my antenna needs serious adjusting.*

3

Maybe I can't get a read on Abby because she's an actress, Sunny told herself. Certainly she felt at a disadvantage. Standing beside the two Martinson women, petite, slim, and shapely, Sunny felt hulking and over-upholstered.

Helena drew a parka out of the shopping bag. "I thought you might need this. Looks like it should still fit."

The coat was a deep, almost indigo blue. And however many years old it might be, it was still beautiful.

Why can't I get coats like that? Sunny thought with a rueful look at the mustard-colored parka she was wearing. An unfortunate incident with a nail sticking out of a fence had killed her winter coat, forcing her to look for a replacement when the outlet stores had mainly cleared out their winter stuff. Mustard was the color beggars had to take when they couldn't be choosers. It was warm at least.

"Mom, I'm not a kid anymore," Abigail said, as Helena held out the coat to her.

"You'll thank me when you get outside."

"We're just walking to the car, and then to the house." Abby shrugged out of her jacket and pulled on the parka. It looked great on her, of course.

They pushed their way through the terminal doors to get outside. When Abby shuddered, she wasn't acting. "You think you remember how the weather was, until it hits you in the face."

Sunny smiled, remembering her own rude reintroduction to wintertime in Maine.

"So you think, maybe, I was right to bring the coat?" Helena said as they crossed the airport road to the parking lot.

"Actually," Abby replied, "I was wondering if you were sure you didn't want to move to some place like California."

"Abby, this is where I've lived my life—and you've lived half of yours." From Helena's tone of voice, this wasn't her first go-round on this particular conversation.

Sunny led the way to Mrs. M.'s Buick. She unlocked the doors and opened the trunk to deposit Abby's carry-on bag.

Helena and Abby took the rear seat. That didn't surprise Sunny. When Mrs. M. rode with Mike, they often sat in the back together when Sunny drove. She kept her eyes on the road, giving her dad and his lady friend some privacy. But she couldn't keep her ears turned off as they moved to join the traffic out of the airport.

"When did you stop driving your own car, Mom?" Abby asked.

"I didn't stop driving." A little more testiness crept into

Helena's voice. "But I think it's safer to let Sunny do the driving when it gets dark out."

"I could have—"

"Which would be safer, the old woman driving, or the young woman who's spent most of the last two days getting here from California?" Mrs. Martinson cut in. "I can see you look dead on your feet."

Abby sucked so much air in, Sunny braced herself for an explosion. Instead, the younger Martinson released it all on a long sigh. "I don't think that's fair, considering I had to go by way of Hoppenskip Airlines to find a route that ended up at this airport. I left home for a one A.M. red-eye flight to Texas, transferred to another plane to Florida, and then had to catch a ride between airports to hook up with the flight up here. It should have been a day in the air, but thanks to that storm I spent the night with a choice between a chair or the floor in the Texas airport lounge. I'm sorry I got here late, after dark, and in such a crabby mood."

"At least you're here now," Helena said. "We'll get you home, into a shower, and then to bed."

They engaged in small talk as Sunny headed for the interstate.

"I took my national paralegal certification exam," Abby reported. "Managed to pull a ninety—now I have a credential I can use all over the country."

"Would that help with the people who interviewed you in August?" Helena asked.

"Well, it makes me a better candidate if I try again," Abby said.

Conversation petered out as they headed north. In fact,

Sunny suspected that Abby had dozed off before they had gotten to the bridge.

She drove carefully—it would be a heck of a thing to put a ding in the Buick after Mrs. M. had made such a point of how much safer it was having Sunny behind the wheel.

Traffic lightened up as they proceeded through downtown Kittery Harbor and headed for the northern suburbs of town. Sunny smoothly pulled the Buick into the driveway of the Martinson place.

Abby blinked awake, glancing around in confusion for a moment until she saw her mother.

"We're home, honey," Helena said. "Let's get you in for a nice, quiet night."

Even as she spoke, they could hear Toby's joyous welcoming barks coming through the windows of the house and car.

Mrs. M. sighed. "After we get you introduced to Toby."

Sunny went to get the bag from the trunk as Helena and Abby exited the car. She brought the carry-on to the front door as Mrs. Martinson opened the lock and ushered Abby inside. Helena paused for a moment as she took the piece of luggage. "I know your father thought we might get together tonight, but I think Abby is a little too tired. Maybe tomorrow? I'll give him a call when we've sorted ourselves out in the morning."

"Sure. Get some rest yourself." Sunny called a good night to Abby, getting a sleepy reply, and turned to head home.

As she walked the couple of blocks to Wild Goose Drive, the wind seemed to swerve around, sending a frigid blast right into her face.

Welcome home, Abby, Sunny thought, ducking her head

and wishing she could find a hat that could cover her mop of curls.

Was this the homecoming Abby expected? Sunny wondered. *She seemed really surprised that her mom had me driving. But maybe that's a good thing—a wake-up call. I always thought that Dad would go on going on until the heart attack showed me otherwise. Better that Abby gets a line on how her mom is doing while Helena is still well.*

Then Sunny remembered Abby asking her mother if she wouldn't be better off getting away from Maine winters and moving someplace like California.

Don't know how Dad would like that, she thought.

Sunny arrived home to find her father and Shadow both ensconced in the living room, watching TV. At least Mike was watching. Shadow lay flopped in an odd pose on a chair cushion, half asleep. Sunny came in with a sandwich, putting down a glass of seltzer to tickle Shadow's paw. "You and Abby both, pal."

Shadow twisted around to get his feet under him, eyes wide as he watched Sunny take a bite of turkey and cheese. She ran a hand through his thick fur. "Mrs. M. apologizes, but Abby was pretty much knocked out with her cross-country marathon."

Mike nodded. "Should have figured that. I had the same thing you're eating, with a little soup. I could reheat some, if you like."

Sunny shook her head. "Helena says she'll call tomorrow after they get sorted out."

"So how is Abby doing?" Mike asked.

"Besides being dead on her feet? I don't know. As gorgeous as ever. I have to admit, there was a part of me that hoped she'd put on thirty pounds and would have a secretarial spread. But I don't know if that applies to paralegals."

Mike pulled himself a little straighter on the couch cushions. "She was such a beautiful girl. I don't know why she didn't do better in Hollywood."

"It's hard to throw a rock in Hollywood *without* hitting a beautiful girl," Sunny told him. "It's a case of talent and luck against a whole lot of competition. Fact is, I had a better chance of making the *New York Times* than she had of becoming a movie star." She tried to pass it off with a laugh, but there was some truth in what she said. She'd managed to land a job in the cutthroat New York journalism market, even if it was with the *New York Standard* and not the more prestigious *Times*.

Still, she thought, *if I'd caught a couple of breaks, a few big stories with my byline on them . . .*

Shadow ducked his head so she could scratch him between the ears, and Sunny obliged him, silently laughing at herself. *I wonder if Abby has the same sort of daydreams.*

She scooped Shadow up in her arms and sat in the chair, giving him a good petting and letting the TV fare just wash over her. The cat seemed no worse for wear after his adventure earlier in the day.

"I'll just have to keep a more careful eye out, so you can't go off mooching fishy handouts," she told Shadow.

"Don't know why he bothers," Mike grumbled from the couch. "He gets enough handouts around here."

Sunny stuck with the television until she saw the weather forecast on the late news—what a great surprise. It was going to be cold and windy tomorrow, too. Then she deposited Shadow on the floor, said good night to her father, and headed upstairs to her bedroom.

Shadow followed her, taking big leaps up the stairs.

"I thought you'd be tired after wandering around downtown today," Sunny told him. "But no, you look full of energy."

After a quick detour to the bathroom to wash her face, Sunny arrived in her room to find Shadow sitting at the foot of the bed, waiting for her to turn down the blanket and quilt. "Just wait a second," she said, changing into a pair of flannel pajamas. It was a little chilly upstairs, but that was the way she liked it. She got under the covers, Shadow wiggling in beside her to bundle in nice and tight. He even gave her hand a little lick as she settled her arms around him.

"Yeah, yeah," she gave him a drowsy chuckle. "I know you're going to sneak off to patrol the house as soon as you think I've dropped off."

She didn't feel him leave, though. She was soon fast asleep.

*

The next morning, Sunny rose, showered and dressed on her own, coming downstairs to find Shadow sitting expectantly beside his feed and water bowls.

"Bottomless pit," Mike said from his station in front of the stove, stirring a pot of oatmeal. Sunny set out some fresh food for the cat and then got herself a cup of coffee. "So what's the specialty of the house today?" she asked.

"I tossed a handful of dried cranberries in the pot before the water boiled," Mike said, "and sprinkled in some cinnamon when the oats went in. When it's done, I've got some applesauce and walnut pieces waiting to go on top." He cocked an eye at her. "If the food police approve."

"Sounds good to me," Sunny told him. Holiday feasting had been fun, but she was glad it was in the rear-view mirror. "Nice and healthy."

She put a little milk in her coffee. "How do you think Mrs. M. would deal with the food police?"

"You thinking of making her life miserable as well as mine?" Mike took the question in good humor. "Helena thinks her coffee cake is one of the major food groups."

"I wasn't thinking of me," Sunny said. "But what about Abby?"

"Why would she—?" Mike broke off, groping for words.

I think you're trying to find a polite way of saying "go poking her nose in her mother's business," Sunny thought.

"She hasn't been home with her mom in a while," she said aloud. "Some things could come as a shock—like me driving for Helena when it's too dark out."

"I don't think—" Mike stopped again. "I guess it's less of a shock than getting called home to find someone in a hospital bed with an oxygen thingy under his nose."

Idea planted. Good time to change the subject, Sunny thought. "Are you going for your walk today?" Part of Mike's recuperation involved a daily three-mile hike, not easy to accomplish in the teeth of a polar vortex.

"I'm going to do it indoors, up in outlet-land," Mike replied as he dished out the oatmeal. "That's why I need a good, solid breakfast, so I won't be tempted by all the junk food giveaways."

Sunny ate her breakfast, then knelt to say good-bye to Shadow. "You stay around here and try not to get into trouble," she said as the cat stared up at her. Glancing at her dad, she added, "Can you make sure he doesn't sneak out?"

"He doesn't sneak out because of *me*," Mike responded. "But I'll keep an eye out. Promise."

Sunny kissed him, got her mustard-colored coat, and headed for her Wrangler and the ride into town.

The good news was that she made decent time and even found a spot near the MAX office. The bad news was that the lights in the office were on. Sunny glanced around the block and spotted Oliver Barnstable's Land Rover across the street. *So much for deconstructing the shopping cart software,* she told herself. *I'm not going to try doing that with the boss looking over my shoulder.*

She came inside, calling, "Morning, Ollie" as she walked through the door.

He looked up from the papers spread across the desk to the clock on the wall. There were still a couple of minutes until the official start of the business day. "Hi, Sunny."

Truth be told, the boss had mellowed considerably from the days when Sunny had started out in her job and secretly called him Ollie the Barnacle. He'd been heavier, redder-faced, and often ill-tempered, whether from a hangover or sheer orneriness. The ornery side still showed up every once in a while, but Ollie had gotten a lot better, thanks, strangely enough, to a broken leg. Going through physical therapy in a rehab setting had separated Ollie from a lot of bad habits, and his relationship with an attractive occupational therapist had kept him more or less on the straight and narrow.

Sunny began the usual office chores, starting the coffee machine, booting up the computer, checking emails, and responding to requests for information or reservations.

They worked together in silence until Ollie asked, "Did you notice whether Neil Garret's place was open?"

"The gate was down over the door when I came in," Sunny replied after a moment's thought.

Ollie nodded. "Is he usually this late to open on a weekday?"

"Sometimes."

Ollie nodded again. "I ask because he's also late with the rent this month—unless he gave it to you yesterday."

Sunny didn't want to get into this, but she also didn't want to find herself in the middle. "The fish place was closed yesterday—all day as far as I could tell. Maybe Neil was sick—"

She was interrupted by the metallic clang of a metal door gate being rolled up.

"Sounds as though Neil has turned up." Ollie rose from behind his desk. "I think I'll go over and invite him in for a cup of coffee."

When he came back with Neil Garret, the fish store owner didn't look sick. A little tired, maybe. His eyes were bloodshot, and he stifled a yawn as he came in. In a wool flannel shirt and heavy jeans, he looked like about eighty percent of Kittery Harbor's male population—the folks who didn't wear ties to work. "Hi, Sunny," he said.

Sunny moved over to the coffeemaker. "Milk and one sugar, right?" She was just as glad to put a little distance between them. Neil had a distinct whiff of fish around him today. She filled a cup, glad that Ollie had sprung for a fresh carton of milk, and passed it to Neil, who took a seat opposite Ollie's desk.

"Running late today?" Ollie asked, sticking his nose in his own cup of coffee.

"Early, actually," Neil replied. "I caught the fishing boats as they were coming in, took a couple of captains out to breakfast. I've found it pays to keep up the connections." He took an appreciative sip of coffee. "Much better than the sludge you get at that diner by the waterfront."

"Just checking to make sure you're all right," Ollie said. "There's a little question of rent."

Neil made a face as if the coffee had suddenly turned rancid. "I know," he said a little shamefacedly. "Had to straighten out a couple of accounts. You'll see the whole sum by the end of the week."

"Good to know." Ollie's voice was offhand, but his eyes told a different story. *Give me my money, and don't waste it on a bunch of floating losers.*

When Neil first opened the store, he often met the fishing boats as they came in. Sunny would see him walking past her window with a pair of fish wrapped in newspaper under each arm. "I pay a little more than they'd get in the market at Portsmouth, but you can't get it any fresher."

Sunny wondered if that's where the smell came from . . . or if Neil had come empty-handed from his meeting this morning.

She got distracted when she saw Will walk past the window with a strange woman—a big gal, with shiny dark hair falling to her shoulders and a parka hanging open over a heavy Norwegian sweater. The clothing might be casual, but the woman had the same moves as Will, an easy sense of authority that suggested she was some sort of cop. She caught Will by the arm, nodding through the window. A second later, they came into the office.

"Sunny, Ollie, Neil," Will greeted them, "this is Val Overton."

Val gave Sunny a smile full of gleaming teeth. "Nice to meet you. Will's told me a lot about you."

Sunny gave Will a grin. "Are you bringing in professional help for my poor, traumatized cat?" She turned to Val. "I thought I'd met all the animal control and humane officers roundabouts working with Jane Rigsdale and her adopt-a-pet program, but you're a new face."

That got a hearty laugh from the other woman. "Good guess. Lord knows I've dealt with a lot of animals, but they all walked on two legs." She whipped out a leather case bearing a star rather than a badge. "U.S. Marshal."

"Whoa," Sunny said, impressed. "We don't see many of those in these parts."

God, she thought, *I'm beginning to sound like an old Western movie.*

Val didn't seem to notice. "I'm just a glorified government process server."

Ollie shot Will the look of a man betrayed. *What with the navy yard across the river and all the local pies he has fingers in, Ollie might be afraid of someone dropping federal paper on him,* Sunny thought.

But Val Overton didn't present an envelope. "The sheriff's office lent me Will here as local liaison. As we were walking past, he mentioned what happened to your cat yesterday. I figured he might as well stop in and check if there's anything new."

"After bringing out such big guns for such a small-town

matter, I'm sorry that I don't have anything to report," Sunny said. "The victim ate heartily last night and this morning and seemed to sleep just fine. I was only kidding about him being traumatized."

"Something happened to Shadow?" Neil sounded upset. "He was just in the other day, after a little piece of fish like always."

"Seems as though some nut tried to hang Sunny's cat right outside your store," Val said. "You didn't see anything?"

"I wasn't in," Neil replied. "Had some business out of town." He got up and leaned across Sunny's desk. "I'm really sorry to hear this. Maybe if I had been there—"

"Hey, I was sitting here and didn't realize anything was going on until Zach Judson began hollering." Sunny gave an uncomfortable shrug. "He's the one who saved Shadow."

"Well, I hope your critter stays safe." Val Overton glanced over at Will. "Guess we should get on with our business."

"Me, too." Neil hustled to the door and held it for Val and Will.

On the way out, Val turned back with the thousand-watt smile. "Good to meet you, Sunny. You, too, Ollie. You're cute when you squirm."

4

Ollie Barnstable sat open-mouthed, staring after Val Overton through the window as they set off down the street. Then he chomped his teeth together with an audible click, turning a pink face toward Sunny to reassert his authority.

"Now, about Garret. I want you to keep on him. No way are we letting this turn out like the last tenant."

"Madman Mel's Pillow-Mania?" Sunny asked in an innocent voice. "Who would have imagined any problems with that? Although now that I come to think of it, using 'Madman' and 'Mania' in the name of his store might have suggested he was a bit of a nut."

Ollie was still squirming, but he tried to look like a hard-line executive. "He had a business plan. I didn't see any problem."

He had all his retirement savings sunk into a pillow

store, Sunny silently responded. *And you saw a chance to get rent for an empty property.*

The problem was, Mel wasn't about to give up on his plan—his dream. He fought tooth and nail to hang on even though the public wasn't beating a path to his door. As he fell behind in rent, his publicity stunts got more desperate— like heading off to outlet-land to show the world how poorly made the competition's pillows were. Loudly bad-mouthing the "cheap crap pillows," he tore several open, showering passers-by with chopped feathers or polyester fill. That got him banned from the outlet malls, but it was much harder getting him out of the store.

After the eviction Sunny feared Mel might return to throw rocks through the windows of his former premises— or the MAX office. It made her glad her boyfriend was a cop—she had plenty of police presence on the block. In the end, though, sadder but wiser, Mel went off to Florida to be a greeter for a big box store. And the space next door had been empty until Neil Garret had come along.

"So are you providing me with a cattle prod, or do I need to hire some muscle to scare him off?" Sunny finally asked. "Val Overton looked capable of handling the job— and I think she'd like having you owe her."

She could hear Ollie struggling to silence his usual temper. "Don't blow things out of proportion," he finally said. "Just catch him sometime each day and mention I'm waiting on the rent until he comes across with a check."

Or a rock, that annoying voice in the back of Sunny's head hastened to add.

Ollie turned back to his project, finally gathering up all the papers and locking them in one of the file cabinets lining the back of the room. "I'm off," he said. "Anybody calls, give them my cell number."

Sunny relaxed a little. She probably wouldn't see him for another week.

Ollie stopped in the doorway. "And don't forget about Garret. A gentle reminder—but every day."

"Sure, Ollie." Sunny tried not to sigh her response.

With Ollie out of her hair, Sunny finally got back to work. Troubleshooting the shopping cart software went smoothly after a bit of trial and error. She finally got it to recognize the MAX website and even work properly.

By the time she sat back in satisfaction, it was time for lunch. Sunny got the phone and gave her father a call. "Before I feed my face, I figured I should check in. Do we need to get something for supper tonight, or are we going out with Helena and Abby?"

"Looks as if we're on our own for dinner," Mike replied. "But those Martinson girls are coming over for coffee. Helena said she's baking a cake."

No wonder he sounds so cheerful, Sunny thought. Helena Martinson's coffee cake was one of Mike's favorite things.

"She also suggested that we see if Will would like to come, too," her dad went on.

"You're sure you want to let him glom onto a piece of that cake?" Sunny teased.

"As long as he restricts himself to just one."

She smiled. "Okay. I'll stop off at Zach Judson's and get some chicken." For a moment, Sunny considered going next door for fish instead.

No, she decided. Chicken was quicker . . . less trouble in general.

Sunny said good-bye to her dad and then called Will to check his availability for dinner. He agreed, so she went shopping for three.

The evening meal wasn't fancy—broiled chicken breasts, boiled potatoes, and mixed vegetables, simple fare that could be prepared quickly after Sunny got home. The doorbell rang, and Sunny moved from the kitchen to answer it. She brought Will inside, took his coat, and led the way into the living room. Will looked around. "Wow. Pulling out all the stops."

The house looked great. Mike must have been cleaning up all day. He'd even splurged on some cut flowers arranged in a vase on the coffee table.

It had been a while since he'd gotten some flowers . . . and then Sunny remembered why. A gray form eeled its way along the side of the couch, stretched low to the floor in stalking mode, gold-flecked eyes fixed on the vase and the nodding blossoms as if they were magnetized.

"Shadow," Sunny called sharply.

Her voice must have alerted Mike, who appeared in the entrance to the living room, his vivid blue eyes focusing on Shadow in what Sunny called the laser glare of death.

"Don't even think about it," Mike warned the cat.

Shadow paid the voices no attention, padding away in an elaborate display of unconcern.

*

There's always later, Shadow told himself as he paused at the entrance to the hallway. Sunny and her He sat on the big chair, joined by the Old One who also lived here. Shadow was a little surprised to find Sunny's He at the door. The Old One had fussed around the house all day, driving

Shadow out of several napping places with his dusting and cleaning. He'd never done that for another male before.

And then there were the flowers. During warm weather, the Old One spent a lot of time outside in the yard, digging in the ground and fooling around with bushes—another of those weird things two-legs got up to. Shadow had no problem with bushes. They were good for shade, and when the flowers appeared, they could be interesting. But the only time Shadow played in the dirt was for a specific reason—to cover up things that should be covered. And why should the Old One holler when Shadow tried to play with the flowers on those special bushes?

It was even weirder when the two-legs brought flowers into the house when it was freezing outside. He thought they must be very tough to live out in the ice and snow, but they came apart under a curious paw just as easily as the ones that popped up in summertime. And there was even more hollering when he investigated. Like this time. Both Sunny and the Old One had growled at him.

Then they had sat down right in front of the flowers, so there was no chance after that. Shadow went down the hall to the room where the humans messed with food, got a running start, and leaped to the top of the box that made things cold.

That was another thing that drove Shadow crazy. They had a box that kept things cold, and they'd take food out of that and put it in a box that made food hot. He sniffed appreciatively at the aroma of chicken and spices filling the room. Okay, that wasn't so bad. But if they wanted to keep their food cold, why not just leave it outside where it was cold already?

I suppose the squirrels might steal it. Or the birds, he thought. When he was hungry, he sometimes tried the door of the cold box to find something to eat, but he couldn't get inside. He had to go and herd a human over to the place where food was kept.

Sunny came in and did things on top of the hot box. Then she came over and gave Shadow a gentle scratch between the ears, talking to him.. He closed his eyes in pleasure, then opened them wide to stare at her, thinking, *I'm hungry, too.*

It must have worked, because Sunny went over to the place where his food was kept. She got some of the crunchy stuff and put it in one bowl and refilled the other with fresh water. Then she went to wash her hands and went back and forth in the room, setting things on the table and getting more things to eat.

She went down the hall and called the others, who came in and sat down.

Now might be a good time to go and see about those flowers, he thought as he watched them pass food around. It would be fun to bat at those drooping heads, maybe even give a shove to that glass thing they were in . . .

He pushed up onto his feet, and his stomach rumbled. *Maybe I'll stop off at the food first.*

*

They had a pleasant meal, Mike happily tucking into what he called "good old-fashioned meat and potatoes."

Thinking of all the diner food her dad must have consumed during his years on the road, Sunny thought, *At least here the meat isn't covered in grease, and the potatoes aren't fries.*

She'd gotten skinless chicken, preparing it with lemon slices and herbs. It went down pretty easily, with no complaints from anyone.

Shadow decided to be sociable and eat, too. He came over when Will held down a morsel of chicken in his hand, but after sniffing it he went back to his own bowl. "Most times, he's not interested in people food," Sunny said.

"Maybe if I were Neil Garret with some fish . . ." Will gave her a grin.

"The tidbits Neil serves up are uncooked." Sunny returned the grin. "That's why he wears gloves." She got a bit more serious. "I don't know how much longer that store is going to stay open. Neil's behind in his rent. Ollie wants me to keep reminding him it's due."

"That's a shame," Mike said. "Garret seems like a nice guy. Better than that whacko with the pillows."

"If he starts pulling fish apart up in outlet-land and dumping the insides on passing shoppers, I'll let you know," Will promised. He put down his knife and fork. "So, Mrs. Martinson's daughter is back in town. How is she?"

"You'll have to ask Sunny," Mike said. "She's the only one here who's seen Abby."

"I played chauffeur for Mrs. M., taking her over to the airport to pick up Abby," Sunny said. "After two days of cross-country nonsense, I can't say how she stacks up against Hollywood starlets, but she's probably in the top one percent of paralegals."

"Huh." Will had an odd look on his face.

"Did you know her?" Sunny asked. Will had grown up in the county seat, Levett. While that wasn't exactly the end of the earth, it wasn't Kittery Harbor, either.

"Not really." Will returned to his normal self. "She was in a lot of plays around here."

"I was telling Sunny, a beautiful girl like that, it's surprising she didn't make it in Hollywood," Mike said.

Sunny shot him a look. *It's one thing to say that to your daughter,* she thought, *and another to say it to your daughter's boyfriend.*

"Well, I'm not a Beverly Hills cop, just a plain old Elmet County one," Will said. "From what I hear, it's mainly a question of getting good breaks. Right now, though, the big question for her is: Will there be cake?"

Mike smiled in anticipation. "Helena told me she was baking."

Mrs. M.'s coffee cake was famed throughout the county for its deliciousness.

Better to have the conversation swerve to bake-offs instead of beauty contests, Sunny thought as they finished the meal.

Mike excused himself. "I'm going to go keep an eye on those flowers in case the furball gets ideas."

That left Sunny and Will alone to do the dishes. He picked up the dish towel while she got the sink's spray attachment. "So did you know Abby Martinson or not?" she asked.

"Not really." That odd expression was back on Will's face. "But—full disclosure here—I did have a crush on her. As I said, she was in a lot of plays. I went to an all-boys high school, so if we did a show, we had to import actresses from other schools. She was Kate in *Kiss Me, Kate*, and I was a lowly lighting tech. A buddy was kind enough to warn me that I was punching way out of my weight class."

"B–but—" Sunny sputtered. "You ended up going out with the queen bee from my school. How—"

Will held up a hand. "Yeah, I went out with Jane when *I* was in college. Abby was going out with college guys when we were in high school. It's just the way things were—and one reason why I'd never wanted to be younger than twenty."

Sunny went to work on the dishes. *Yeah, "the best time of our lives"—phooey.*

They finished and headed for the living room to find Shadow in his sphinx pose, his eyes on the vase of flowers . . . and Mike's eyes watching him like a hawk. Back in her youth, Sunny had taken some scorching looks from her father. With the one he was aiming at Shadow, she was surprised that patches of the cat's fur hadn't begun to smolder.

She scooped Shadow and sat in an armchair, depositing him in her lap. Will took the other chair, leaving Mike the couch. After a few minutes of conversation, Mike looked at his watch. "They should be here soon."

"I'll get the coffee started." Sunny rose from the chair, letting Shadow leap to the floor. In typically nosy fashion, he trailed after her to the kitchen.

"Nothing to eat," she told him as she set up the coffeemaker. "And you're probably the only person in the house who's not wild about Mrs. M.'s coffee cake."

The doorbell rang, and Shadow stared up at Sunny. "There's the company," she said, walking down the hall to the door. He trailed along, curious but not necessarily eager to get chummy with the outsiders. Mike was already opening the door, greeting Helena, getting introduced to Abby, and then introducing Will.

"And, of course, you know Sunny," he said as she joined them.

"Nice to meet you now that I'm awake." Abby handed her parka to Mike, revealing a sweater that hugged her curves up top and some mutant offspring of jeans and leggings that were so tight Sunny could see the play of muscles in Abby's thighs as she walked to the living room. Worse, Sunny noticed that Will had noticed. Since Sunny was wearing a turtleneck, a sweater, and jeans cut to accommodate long underwear, she was not pleased.

"What say we get comfortable?" Mike said as they arrived in the living room.

"I'll bring this back in with Sunny." Helena Martinson held up a covered cake plate. They left Abby sitting on the couch with Mike. Will had resumed his seat in the armchair.

In the kitchen, Sunny began filling cups and arranging them on a platter while Mrs. M. cut pieces of cake. "So how was your day with Abby?"

"To tell the truth I'm not quite sure," Helena replied. "We took it easy today, just chatting. But I got the feeling there was something Abby wasn't saying. She still hasn't." She looked up from her work, concern in her eyes. "You don't think she might have lost her job? Could that be why she was interviewing in Boston? Maybe this visit is a way to look into the idea of moving back with me."

"I'm sure if there's something like that going on, Abby will bring it up sooner rather than later." Sunny arranged sugar, sweetener, and a small pitcher of milk on the tray and headed back to the living room. Mrs. M. followed with the cake, plates, and forks.

After passing the goodies around, Sunny took a seat while Helena sat beside Mike.

"This is nice," he said, enjoying a forkful of coffee cake.

"Yes, you and Mom seem very comfortable together." Sunny noticed the edge in Abby's voice. "That strikes me as pretty incredible, considering the way your daughter and Constable Price seem to spend all their time chasing murderers."

Will started to open his mouth but shut it when he caught the look Sunny sent his way.

This is not the time to tell her that he's Chief Investigator Price now, Sunny thought.

"It seems as though my mother has gotten into a lot of things while I was away," Abby went on. "Things she'd never do."

"Like helping a lot of families here in town and all through the county?" Sunny spoke quickly. "Have you heard of the 99 Elmet Ladies? Helena was a founding member and runs their food pantry. If you think we're getting her to do that—"

"Why did you change all the doorknobs in our house?" Abby interrupted. "Putting those handles all over the place."

"That was quite a project," Mike said, still not catching on that Abby wasn't pleased with the change.

"I have to deal with a bit of arthritis in my hands." Helena carefully flexed her fingers. "Turning those knobs was getting harder and harder."

"Mom—" Abby burst out, then made a scrubbing gesture with her hand as if to remove the word from conversation. She started again at a lower volume. "You don't have to kid me along about who the invalid is here. What worries me is that you're setting up our house for him." Abby glanced over at Sunny and Will. "And I guess you'll be setting up house-keeping here when your father goes to live with my mom?"

Helena and Mike looked like a pair of teenagers caught making out on the couch. Mrs. M. sputtered for a moment. "Abigail Martinson," she finally managed to say. "What are you suggesting?"

"Come on, Mom. When I get you on the phone, all you do is talk about Mr. Coolidge there."

"Mike," Sunny's dad said in a faint voice.

"I mean, it's obvious you have a relationship, and I'm glad for that—honestly."

Mrs. M. stared, and so did Mike. "You are?"

"Well, sure. You ought to have someone in your life, and I have no problem with that. But . . ." Abby bit her lip, trying to find words. "When Dad got sick, you took care of him, and I know that was very tough on you." She glanced at Mike. "Are you ready to do that again with Mr. Coolidge?"

Mike and Helena shared a look—and a different kind of shock. They'd been enjoying one another's company, but that didn't mean they'd immediately started on long-range life plans.

Sunny decided it was time for her to speak up. "You know, I've been taking care of my dad."

"From before or after you lost your job in New York?" Abby smiled at the look on Sunny's face. "It's amazing, the resources a law firm offers if you want to check into people."

"Wow, you're a one-woman intervention." Will shook his head in wonder. "Come here to save your mom from our clutches."

"But I think you've been in California too long." Sunny

struggled to keep her voice level. "I lost my job *because* I came up here to help Dad out. But that's what we do here. We look out for our own. I help my dad. Helena helps folks who can't put food on the table. And if she needs a hand, I'm happy to offer one."

Abby looked as if she'd been slapped. "Maybe I have spent too much time in Cali." She looked down at her hands. "You see a lot of bad stuff there, greed, pretense, backstabbing. But I worried about you, Mom." She reached over to take Helena's hand. "I wanted to see how you were doing."

That was the moment Shadow chose to make his entrance. He veered a little to rub beside Sunny's leg, but then he headed boldly to Abby, staring up at her.

She smiled and leaned forward. "Well, hello there, cutey. Who are you?"

*

Shadow hung back, watching as the two visitors arrived. One he recognized, the Old One's She. The other was another two-leggity female, younger. Shadow wasn't sure that was good. Some places he'd been, when there was an extra She, fights began. If Sunny's He got too interested, that might happen here.

That wouldn't be good.

As they sat down to eat, it seemed as though he was right to be worried. Shadow could feel the tension in the air, and it seemed to center around the strange new female. The Old One and his She seemed almost frightened, giving the newcomer hard looks. Shadow thought Sunny might fly from her chair, even though she didn't have much in the way of teeth and claws.

He did, though. And if this strange She started making trouble, she'd have him to deal with.

Sunny spoke sharply, and Shadow got ready to jump into battle. But then the mood suddenly changed. The strange She spoke softly, taking the older female's hand.

Maybe there won't be a fight after all, Shadow thought, padding forward. He stopped to mark Sunny—and to remind her that he was on her side. Then he walked up to the stranger.

She showed teeth in that odd way humans had and bent forward, extending a hand. But she wasn't grabby like some two-legs. She politely held it down so he could give it a sniff. Unlike the older female, who always stank of that big yellow dog who lived with her, this one didn't smell of biscuit eater. He pushed his head against the younger one's fingers, and she began petting and running her claws through his fur in a very well-practiced way.

Shadow glanced around. Everyone seemed to have calmed down. *It's a shame they don't know how to groom one another instead of making noises,* he thought, closing his eyes to better enjoy Good Petter's ministrations.

*

The Martinsons left soon after Shadow appeared. Mike volunteered to walk Helena and Abby home, which suited Sunny just fine. As soon as they left, she turned to Will. "Don't think I didn't see you checking Abby out."

"An investigator has to be alert for any possible evidence," he said in his best Dudley Do-Right voice.

"Oh yeah? And what evidence did you get from her thighs?"

Will shrugged. "That she probably spends a lot of her free time in spinning classes."

His response was sufficiently out of left field that Sunny laughed. "Well, don't go letting that old crush mislead you."

"Are you kidding?" Will said. "A cop falling for someone who works in a lawyer's office? It's unnatural. Plus, California hasn't exactly given her a sunny disposition—or didn't you notice?"

Sunny smiled. "I may have noticed a couple of clues along those lines."

*

Sunny stifled a yawn as she pulled her Wrangler into a parking space near the MAX office. She hadn't stayed up late last night after Mike came back home. Will had left, saying it was a school night, and Sunny had turned in well before the late news. She didn't sleep well, though, and the morning alarm seemed to go off just as she was settling in for some decent rest.

She had to drag herself out of bed and through the morning routine. Throw in some overnight ice, a fender-bender that snarled up traffic, and she arrived late at the office.

Good thing Ollie didn't pick today to drop in, she thought as she crossed the street. She wasn't the only one who was getting in late. The gate was still down over the door to Kittery Harbor Fish. Digging out her key, Sunny went into the MAX office, glad to be out of the wind and freezing weather. *A hot cup of coffee would go down pretty well right now,* she thought as she started the machine.

Sunny was just getting through the morning's emails when she heard the rattle of the gate going up next door.

Better go play rent collector, she thought, putting her cup down. *If Ollie calls, I'll be able to tell him I did my duty for the day.*

It was just a couple of yards between doors, and Sunny was wearing a heavy sweater, but she still felt the cold as she darted into the fish shop's entrance. Neil Garret stood in front of the counter, wheeling around as Sunny came in. "We're not really open—" he began.

Sunny rubbed her arms. "It's almost as cold in here as it is outside," she said. "Are you turning off the heat?"

Her question seemed to shake Neil out of a daze. "No," he replied, heading around the counter. Sunny followed him as he strode to the rear of the store—and an open back door. "Oh, no." Neil ran to the cash register, hitting buttons to open the drawer. Sunny got out her cell phone and hit 911. "I'm at Kittery Harbor Fish," she said, giving the address. "There's been a break-in."

As she spoke, she followed Neil to the door of the walk-in freezer, nearly crashing into him as he suddenly stopped. Then Sunny saw why—the sprawled form on the floor in a puddle of frozen blood.

"And a body," she added.

5

Ben Semple, one of Kittery Harbor's town constables, was the first law-enforcement type to arrive on the scene. When he saw Sunny, he let out a long, "Aaaahhhh, man. I was hoping I hadn't heard the squawk on the radio right—or that this was one of those swatting things." He was a friend of Will's, and knew from experience that if Sunny was involved, there had to be a dead body around somewhere.

Sunny pointed toward the freezer, Ben jumped inside and a moment later came out, keeping his back to the door. Ben was more at home writing traffic tickets for the bargain hunters racing through outlet-land, but he knew how to secure a crime scene. He got on his radio, and the street and store began to fill with people from the sheriff's department. Captain Ingersoll, the number-two man in the department, arrived about two minutes after Will came in, accompanied by Val Overton.

Sunny didn't have any chance to ask about that. Ingersoll immediately buttonholed her. *From the look on his face, you'd think this place stinks to high heaven,* Sunny thought. "You found the body?" he asked, his voice dropping the temperature in the chilly store a few more degrees.

And it's great to see you, too, that flippant voice in the back of Sunny's head answered. Aloud she said, "We found the body," gesturing to Neil Garret.

That didn't make the captain look any happier. He turned to Will. "Why don't you take Mr. Garret here and get a statement. I'll send Ms. Coolidge to the station with Mullen. I called the state police barracks. Their crime-scene team is on the way."

Typical cop procedure, Sunny thought. *Splitting up the witnesses so they can't concoct a story together.* Not so typical was the fact that Val Overton accompanied Will and Neil.

Maybe they're using the same car. She didn't get a chance to check. Ingersoll put her in the custody of a sheriff's deputy she didn't know. He looked at her as if he were afraid she was going to pull an Uzi from under her sweater and try to shoot her way to freedom. Mullen almost refused to let her into the MAX office to get her coat—kind of unfair, considering the way he was bundled up in a green sheriff's parka. But Ben Semple intervened, accompanying them as Sunny got her coat, turned off the coffeemaker and the computer, and locked the office door.

Well here goes a day shot to hell, Sunny thought as they headed to Mullen's car. She knew how long it could take getting out of police clutches. *Good thing there's nothing urgent going on, or Ollie would have a fit.*

Thinking of Ollie reminded her of the whole rent question, which had gotten sidetracked when they'd found the body in the freezer. *It won't be easy to scratch up the money for Ollie if the place is closed,* she thought. Even though the outer door stood open, it was pretty clear no business would be transacted today.

Deputy Mullen offered no conversation during the trip to the sheriff's office in the county seat. As soon as Sunny arrived, she was conducted to an interrogation room and left to marinate. *Well,* Sunny thought, *I expect they'll be busy with the dead guy. And let's face it, considering my popularity with Ingersoll, he'll leave me at the end of his list.*

So she was surprised when the door opened and the sheriff herself walked in. As the widow of the former sheriff, Lenore Nesbit had ridden a wave of public sympathy after her husband's death in the line of duty, trouncing Will in the primary and winning in the general election for the office. What she lacked in police skill she more than made up for with a shrewd sense of politics. In the light of her own painful experience, Lenore had promoted Will, admitting that the county needed more investigative capacity to deal with new kinds of crime. She relied on Ingersoll for administrative matters.

Sunny smiled at the sheriff, but couldn't help thinking, *Either they're really pressed for personnel, or they don't think I have much to offer if Lenore's going to question me.*

"How are you feeling?" Lenore Nesbit asked.

"Not too bad," Sunny replied. "Lucky, I guess, because

I only got a quick look at the body—just enough to be sure he was dead."

Lenore shuddered. "I saw the crime-scene photos on the computer. Don't think I'll have anything with tomato sauce for a while." She paused for a second. "Why don't you take me through what happened?"

"Traffic was bad, so I got to work a little late." Sunny began the story, but Lenore soon interrupted. "You say you got in late, but the fish shop was still closed."

Sunny shrugged. "Maybe the traffic made Neil late, too."

"You're sure the place was closed?"

"The gate was down. I could see that from across the street." Sunny explained that Ollie had given her the responsibility of reminding Neil about the rent. "So, when I heard the gate go up—"

"When exactly was that?"

"A few minutes after I got in," Sunny replied. "I'd gotten a cup of coffee and just started the day's routine. Anyway, I figured I'd get over there and take care of Ollie's errand. I found Neil in front of the display case and asked him why it was so cold." She went on to describe how they'd found the back door open.

"How was Mr. Garret acting?" Lenore asked.

"Spooked," Sunny said. "I guess he knew something was wrong the moment he stepped in. He tried to tell me the store wasn't open yet. Then, when we found the door open, he checked the cash register and then the freezer. That's when we saw the body. I was already on the phone to report the break-in, and added that fact. Then we waited until Ben Semple arrived."

"Neither of you went into the freezer?"

"I didn't see the need, once I saw all that blood. It was like a sheet of red ice on the floor." Sunny took a moment to call up her memory of the grisly sight. "Whoever it was must have been there for a while. The store was cold enough that you could see your breath in the air, and I wasn't seeing any around the guy down there." She stopped for a moment, struck by something else in her mental picture. "The dead man wasn't dressed for Maine weather," she said. "He was wearing some kind of light-colored raincoat, so he must have been half-frozen before he wound up in the freezer."

That sparked another memory. "I didn't get to see the guy's face. Did he have a beard?"

"He was pretty scruffy," Lenore said. "Why do you ask?"

"We had something weird happen outside the office a couple of evenings ago." Sunny described what had happened to Shadow. "I didn't see it, Zach Judson broke it up. But he said the guy with the noose had a beard —and was wearing a raincoat. Maybe if you showed him a picture . . ."

Lenore Nesbit shook her head. "Trust me, Sunny, what's left of that face is nothing you'd want to look at."

The sheriff asked a few more questions, but Sunny didn't have anything to offer. Then she thanked Sunny, saying, "I'll need you to write up a statement—I'm sure you know the drill."

Sunny knew it only too well. She sat cooling her heels in the little room until a deputy finally came with a legal pad and a pen. Sunny wrote an account of what she'd seen and done since getting out of her Wrangler, and waited again until somebody came and picked it up. Then more waiting until it got typed up. By the time she finally got to sign her statement, the day was pretty well shot, and she was starving.

Claire Donally

The day brightened a bit when Will Price stopped by the desk where she was signing off on the paperwork. "I wrangled the job of getting you back to your car," he said.

They went outside and got into an unmarked car. Will pulled out of the sheriff's department parking lot and headed for the interstate.

"Well, it's nice that you're allowed to talk to me again," Sunny said. "Did Ingersoll give the okay?"

Will grimaced for a moment. "He wasn't exactly subtle, was he? But he had a point. My job is to investigate now. And we do have a connection."

"Yeah, we've investigated a lot of things together."

"But now I'm supposed to be doing it officially." Will didn't look happy at the expression on her face. "Have I ever told you how to write stories when you do them for the *Harbor Courier*?"

"No, but then I've read the way you write reports." Sunny looked around the car. "I was almost expecting to see your friend Val Overton in here."

"Why would you say that?" Will said sharply.

"She was at the crime scene with you," Sunny pointed out. "Apparently it was okay for her to be around."

"Val is a trained investigator," Will explained. "We worked together on a fugitive task force when I was with the state police up by the border."

"We seem to keep bumping into people from your past," Sunny said. "First Abby Martinson, and now this federal marshal. Did you have a crush on her, too?"

Will laughed. "You haven't seen Val in action. She's a big gal, and I've seen her take down even bigger guys than me."

"Somehow, that doesn't reassure me," Sunny told him.

"Strictly business," Will assured her.

Sunny decided to change the subject. "So, did you find out who the dead guy was?"

Will shook his head. "No wallet, no ID."

"So you have to go with fingerprints."

He nodded. "Which always takes a lot longer than it does on the TV cop shows."

"I thought of something when Lenore Nesbit was questioning me. The guy in the freezer was wearing a raincoat. So was the guy who went after Shadow."

Will glanced at her from behind the wheel. "You think the two may be connected?"

"I don't know," Sunny replied. "But I do know better than to stroll the streets of Kittery Harbor in just a raincoat during winter." As if to underline her thought, a sudden blast of wind actually made the car shake a little. "Did the body in the freezer have a beard? Maybe you could have Zach Judson take a look at him."

"Zach told me he only got a glimpse of the guy outside your office," Will said. "As for the fellow in the freezer, his face isn't exactly recognizable. He took two shots in the back of the head. The exit wounds—trust me, you don't want me to draw you a picture."

But Sunny was thinking of something else. "Shots in the back of the head. Execution style. In a fish shop? Why break in there in the first place?"

"Well, it's quiet, and the freezer would be pretty much soundproof," Will said. "I hate to tell you this, but the New Stores are hardly Fort Knox. Why did Ollie put the gate on the store next door to your office? Or did Neil do it?"

"Ollie had it installed, hoping to lure a better class of

tenant." Remembering the elaborate shutters protecting stores in New York, Sunny shrugged. "It's window dressing really. Or rather, it only protects the door, not the windows. If anybody really wanted to get into those stores, they could do it pretty easily."

"Yeah, but a broken window draws attention," Will said. "Better to go in the back way. The rear doors are metal, but you could get through them if you were determined."

"I'll bear that in mind in case I forget my key," Sunny told him. "I have to admit, when I saw the body, the first thing I thought of was Madman Mel."

That got a laugh from Will. "From what I remember of Mel, our friend in the raincoat seems a bit on the skinny side."

Sunny nodded. The would-be pillow magnate always looked as if he had a couple of his products stuffed under his shirt. "Maybe he fell on lean times—literally—after he lost his store."

"Well," Will promised, "I'll have Mel checked out, although I think it's a long shot." They were on the local streets in Kittery Harbor by now. He pulled up in front of the New Stores. Sunny gave him a quick kiss and stepped out onto the street. Kittery Harbor Fish had its gate down now, with crime scene tape festooned across the entrance.

Huh, Sunny thought as she turned to the MAX office, *I'd have sworn I turned off the lights.*

As she went to put her key in the lock, she discovered the door was open, too. She stepped inside, her hand going for her cell phone, when she spotted Ollie sitting behind a desk.

"You scared me for a moment," Sunny said, then she realized that her boss had company.

Val Overton sat in the visitor's chair, flashing her brilliant smile in Sunny's direction. "Just sitting here, passing the time with Ollie."

Ollie looked as though he'd have been happier passing time with a rattlesnake. "Seems as though Marshal Overton hasn't tracked down the party she's supposed to serve. I offered to help, but she won't tell me who it is."

Translation, Sunny thought, *I'd do anything to make her go away, but she won't.*

"Now, honey, I explained that," the marshal said in a sweet voice. "How do I know you might not be partners with the fella I'm after?"

Her tone left Sunny wondering which "fella" Overton was after right now—the person to be served or Ollie. Judging from his expression, Ollie wasn't sure, either.

"So I've been trying to get a grip on the general state of business in these parts," Val went on. "Since Ollie seems to be a mover and a shaker, I thought I'd pump him a little." She smiled that high-wattage smile again. "You own all these stores?"

"Yeah, this used to be my dad's—a soda fountain and candy store," Ollie said. Sunny could remember herself as a kid, sitting on a stool and sipping some sugary concoction through a straw.

"When I came back here with a little capital, I was able to buy the whole property. Several of the tenants are long-established businesses."

Like Judson's Market, Sunny thought.

"But the fish store is new—or is it all just refurbished?" Val asked. "When I was in there, everything looked brand new."

"No, it's all newly installed," Ollie said. "Quite an invest-ment for the tenant."

Speaking of which . . . Sunny spoke up. "I didn't get a chance to talk with Neil Garret about the rent—considering what happened."

Val Overton sat a little straighter. "Garret was having problems paying the rent?"

"The fact of the matter is that next door has always been a bit of a problem location," Sunny said, earning an annoyed look from Ollie. "The fish store seemed to be doing fine during the summer months. Lately, though, I think business has been dropping off. Maybe the local folks are eating less fish in the cold weather."

"There won't be any business done with that damned tape across the door," Ollie complained.

Val Overton leaned forward and patted his arm. "Don't underestimate how big a crowd a nice, public crime scene can draw."

Ollie didn't snatch his arm away, but he looked even more uncomfortable.

"And if you're invested in any kind of home security, you might get a bump," Val went on. "Nothing like a good break-in to make people reevaluate their locks and shutters." She leaned back in her chair. "Now, could you tell a gal where she might get something decent to eat around here?"

The reminder made Sunny's empty stomach rumble. "There's a little cafe down by the docks," she said. "It shouldn't be too busy, this time of day."

Ollie's expression was almost pathetically grateful as he said, "Why don't you take Marshal Overton over there, Sunny? I'll finish here and lock up. You can take the rest of the day off. Doesn't look as though we're going to get much work done, anyway."

*

The wind coming off the water was like a freezing cold knife stabbing into Sunny's face, and strong enough to make her stagger. But Val Overton just plowed ahead, apparently unfazed by the weather, until she said, "I'm beginning to see why this place isn't too busy. Do people freeze to death before they get there?"

"Almost." Sunny kept her head down as the wind tore at her curls. "But they've got a hot chocolate that can revive the dead."

They fought their way to Spill the Beans, and Sunny took her usual wintertime table, the one directly under the heater. The waitress brought her a hot chocolate before she even ordered.

"I think I'll have the same," Val said, looking on as Sunny spooned up some thick brown cocoa from under its cover of whipped cream.

"They do a sandwich with home-baked ham and their own hot mustard on farmer's bread." Sunny rolled her eyes as she took a sip of chocolate. "It's not like the shaved ham you get from a deli. They carve slices off."

"Can we get two ham sandwiches, please?" Val asked as the waitress returned with a cup for her. "Breakfast doesn't seem to stretch as long as I'd like when I'm doing cop things."

They sat quietly for a few minutes, shedding their parkas and letting the heat penetrate their chilled faces and hands. Then the sandwiches arrived, mounded high with thick slices of ham. Sunny took a bite, savoring the way the spicy mustard blended with the salt from the ham and the sweetness of the brown sugar glaze.

"Mmmmm," Val Overton mumbled as she chewed and swallowed. "Worth a trek through the Arctic. And you're right about the reviving powers of this chocolate." She took a sip, put down her cup, and sighed. "So, tell me about your boss."

I think she's taking Spill the Beans a bit too literally, Sunny thought. *Is she after one of Ollie's business connections?*

Aloud, she said, "With Ollie, what you see is what you get. He can be gruff, sometimes unreasonable—"

"I'm going to cut right to the chase," Val interrupted. "Is he single?"

Sunny was glad she didn't have a mouthful of chocolate. Otherwise, it might have come spewing out her nose. "Ollie?"

"Yeah. Slightly older guy, reddish hair, blue eyes . . ." Val grinned. "Pink face."

"You're interested in Ollie Barnstable?"

"We can't all get guys like Will Price," Val said. "So, is he taken?"

"I can't speak for Ollie," Sunny said. *Especially about this,* she added silently. "He broke a leg not too long ago and wound up in rehab. I think he's been seeing one of the therapists."

"Good. Then he must be used to taking orders." Val laughed at the look on Sunny's face. "Oh, come on, loosen up. I've got a job that sends me traipsing all over a pretty big state. Unless I want to pick up guys in hotel bars, it isn't easy to meet people. Do you think Ollie might go out with me?"

Sunny took a bite of her sandwich to chew that one over.

"Frankly," she said as she finished, "right now I think you've got him scared to death."

"Yeah." Val looked a little repentant. "I overplayed the whole serving papers thing." She grinned. "But his expression was so priceless."

"He takes this stuff seriously. After all, he is a businessman."

"Okay, okay," Val said. "I promise to be nicer to your boss."

"It could be the difference between honey and vinegar in drawing the fly," Sunny said.

Silence fell as they devoted themselves to their sandwiches, until Val, putting her napkin down, said, "Speaking of honey, does this place do any good desserts?"

Sunny smiled. Here was a person after her own heart. "Do you like whoopie pies?"

"Those cookie things with the whipped cream?" Val asked.

"If you have to ask like that, you haven't had a real whoopie pie," Sunny told her. "But they have them here."

"Oh, really?" Val purred. "You know I'll have to test that."

Sunny nodded. "And maybe another cup of chocolate."

6

Shadow glared down from his vantage point on top of the refrigerator, his tail lashing in aggravation. Usually, this was his place to look down on the world and those crazy two-legs. But today it felt more like a refuge.

The Old One had come home all sweated up, something that always baffled Shadow. How did he manage to do that when it was freezing out? It had looked to be a typical day. The Old One had gone upstairs and washed himself off so that he didn't smell so bad, sitting on the big chair and drifting off into a nap, which was fine with Shadow. He did the same.

But when the Old One got up and fixed himself something to eat, he put the picture box on. Shadow hadn't paid attention. He'd made a nice warm spot for himself, creating a sort of cave with a blanket. The last thing he expected was for the Old One to jump up and run to the box. The sound came louder, killing any hope of a continued nap. By the time Shadow got out to see what the trouble was, the Old One had already turned off the picture.

Usually, the Old One only got this excited when the picture box showed gangs of two-legs running around and chasing a ball. Then the human would shout and shake his arms. This time, though, he sat down but didn't go back to sleep. Instead he picked up the talking thing and began to poke at it.

Shadow was close enough that he could hear some of the voices that came from somewhere inside the device. One sounded like Sunny, although the Old One didn't talk to her. Another sounded like the Old One's She, and they talked for a while. But Sunny's father didn't seem very happy when they stopped. He talked to other humans, male and female, and just seemed to grow more anxious.

The Old One finally stopped talking, but he didn't stay seated. Shadow wasn't sure what to do. He and the human finally got along, but it was more like an armed truce than good feelings. Shadow didn't trust the Old One not to misinterpret any friendly overture. He'd known some humans to kick him away when he'd tried to rub against them and make them feel better.

So in the end, Shadow had tried to follow the Old One as he paced unpredictably back and forth around the room, sometimes looking at his wrist, sometimes looking out the window.

Is he waiting for Sunny? Shadow wondered as he scrambled to keep up with the longer legs. Finally he had to retreat to the kitchen to make sure he didn't get stepped on.

The problem was, the Old One had managed to transfer his anxiety to Shadow. Safely on top of the refrigerator, far away from voices and feet, the cat should have been able to compose himself for another nap, even if he didn't have a blanket-cave anymore. Instead, his tail beat an uneasy time as he watched the shadow of the roving human shift around the hall.

Annoyance made him want to leap down, charge down the hall, and pounce on it, even though he knew shadows couldn't be hurt or even caught. And he certainly knew better than to try and pounce on the Old One when the human was so unsettled.

So Shadow pushed sleep away, keeping anxious watch, hoping it was just some crazy two-legs thing that a cat didn't have to care about—but afraid that it wasn't.

If you kept me up for nothing, you'll pay, he silently promised the Old One. *Sooner or later, you'll have to go to sleep. And then, when you least expect it, I'll jump on you.*

*

Sunny stopped off to do a little shopping before she headed home. She got a package of wide noodles and a fresh bottle of horseradish. They had a container of stew stored in the freezer, and that reheated with the noodles would make a warm and filling meal for a frosty day.

She parked the Wrangler in the driveway and started for the door with her bags when she spotted Mike looking out the living room window at her. His expression warned Sunny that he'd heard about her latest adventure.

No sooner did she get the door open than a furry gray rocket came careening down the hallway toward her from the kitchen. Shadow got underfoot, determinedly sniffing at her as Sunny tried to make her way to the living room. "Hey, Dad."

Mike appeared in the arched entrance way, looking much as he had after getting reports of some high school misdemeanor. A bit older and whiter, to tell the truth, and more worried than angry. "Saw your office on the noon news," he said, "not to mention the outside of the fish shop."

"I suppose I was gone by then." Sunny took off her coat. "They took me up to Levett to make a statement." She paused for a second. "Did they come up with an identity for the guy we found in the freezer?"

Mike shook his head. "I was wondering if you could tell me."

"Nobody from around here, as far as I could make out." She figured that was the main thing on Mike's mind. "He was wearing a raincoat in this weather."

From the look on Mike's face, she might just as easily have reported that the dead man was a nudist.

"Maybe he was a New Yorker." Mike looked relieved enough to try a weak joke. "Even a Bostonian would have better sense."

"Well, I didn't recognize him." Hefting her shopping bags, she headed for the kitchen with her cat and her father trailing behind. Shadow made a detour over to his bowl while Sunny restocked the refrigerator. She glanced over at Mike who stood in the kitchen doorway.

"You were worried about me, and I didn't call." She shook her head. "You know, I thought I handled the situation well, but it looks as though my brain was only firing on two cylinders. I'm sorry, Dad."

"Well, you're here now. And I got a little more exercise than my usual three miles, pacing around the living room."

They talked about nothing in particular as Sunny brought the water for the noodles to a boil and defrosted the stew in the microwave. Together, they set the table. Then Sunny freshened up Shadow's bowls.

Soon dinner was ready and Sunny portioned out two plates. Mike put a healthy dollop of horseradish on the side, and so did Sunny. After a few mouthfuls, Mike sat back in his chair. "Do you want to talk about it?"

"There's not much to say. I heard Neil pulling up the gate to his store, went over there, and realized something was wrong. We found the back door open and a dead man in the freezer. After that, everything was in the hands of the police—and that included me. Captain Ingersoll had one of the deputies take me up to Levett, Lenore Nesbit asked some questions, and I signed a statement."

"You didn't talk to Will?"

"Not until after I'd given the statement. He drove me back to the MAX office. Did I mention there's a federal marshal in town? She was in the office with Ollie."

Mike laughed. "His past misdeeds finally catching up with him?"

"Actually, I think she was there to flirt."

"With Ollie? That's the problem with the federal government—misplaced priorities." Mike paused for a second. "So what did Will say about the case?"

"Not much," Sunny admitted. "And maybe that's the way it ought to be."

Claire Donally

"But he's your partner. You worked on cases together."

"We worked on cases together mainly because his bosses didn't want to investigate them. You remember how Frank Nesbit was about the crime statistics. He didn't want to admit any serious crime happened in Elmet County." Sunny took a breath. "But now Will is Lenore Nesbit's chief investigator. He's official now."

Mike nodded. "And this is his first big case. How do you think he's doing?"

"It's not easy," Sunny said. "They don't even know who the dead guy is. Will said he had no wallet and no identification on him."

"Could he have been homeless?" Mike suggested. "That might explain the wrong clothes for the weather, and even why he broke in."

"It might explain something else." Sunny took a sip of seltzer. "Zach Judson described the guy who attacked Shadow as wearing a raincoat."

"So—maybe a nut, homeless and looking to get out of the weather." Mike looked worried. Kittery Harbor was a blue-collar town, where a lot of people were only a paycheck away from homelessness.

"But if he wanted to get out of the cold, why go in the freezer?" Sunny asked. "And most importantly, who shot him?"

Mike chewed on a piece of meat for a moment, then said, "Neil Garret?"

"There was frozen blood around the dead guy." Sunny shuddered a little at the memory. "So he had to have been there for a while. When I came into the store, Neil looked shaken—but not 'I shot somebody' shaken." She shook her head. "I have a hard time picturing Neil as the shooter. And why would he open the freezer and show me the dead body?"

"Maybe he wanted it found at that time," Mike suggested. "Or maybe he wanted a witness to see when he supposedly found the body."

Sunny nodded slowly. "Sheriff Nesbit was pretty interested in making sure when Neil arrived at the store."

"You mentioned that she questioned you," Mike said "How is Lenore handling all of this?"

Sunny poked at her stew. "She said she's skipping anything with tomato sauce for the time being, but she asked some good questions." She frowned. "I suppose they have to concentrate on Neil. He's the obvious suspect. It's his store, and the body is in the freezer he specially ordered."

"You say this guy broke in," Mike said. "Wouldn't Neil have been justified in shooting him? Self-defense or something?"

Sunny shook her head. "Not the way this guy was killed. He was shot from the back. And it's not as though Neil just walked into the store and found an intruder. The blood had frozen."

Her frown grew deeper. *So, you've got a dead body in your freezer. It's not impossible to get rid of. Lock up the shop, wait until things get good and quiet, and bring your car round the back where the deliveries get made. Open the back door, bundle the embarrassing body out, and drive away. You've got almost 3,500 miles of coastline to dump it,* she thought, remembering a factoid she'd used in some of her promotional copy.

So if Neil was the shooter, why did he need to show the body to me—or whatever other unlucky first customer he had today? What's the advantage for him? And if the body in the freezer was a surprise to him, how did it wind up there? With all that coastline to choose from, why would someone take the risk and go to the effort of breaking into Neil's place to dump a body there?

She smiled at Mike. "If you smell something burning, it's probably just a few brain cells. I don't envy Will on this case. Not only is it a whodunit, but a whowuzit, and why'd he get killed?"

They talked about other things as they finished the meal. Mike joked about whether having Abby around would cramp Mrs. M.'s style on the local gossip grapevine. "She might have to come to you for the latest info," he said.

Smiling, Sunny shook her head. "She'd probably get more from reading the *Harbor Courier.*"

As she spoke, the phone rang.

"That could be Helena right now," Mike joked.

Close, but no cigar, Sunny thought when she heard the voice on the other end of the line. It was Ken Howell, editor, publisher, most of the reporting staff, and printer of the *Harbor Courier.*

"So, you forget your old friends now?" he asked.

"Oh, I remember you," Sunny replied. "The problem is, I don't have much to say. Maybe you should be having this conversation with Will."

"I think you mean talking to the sheriff department's public information office," Ken corrected her. "I'd have better luck trying to get something out of Lenore Nesbit."

"Maybe you would," Sunny agreed. "All I can tell you is that I walked into the fish store this morning and saw a dead body in the freezer. After that, it was all in the hands of the cops."

"You mean Will Price."

"And other people. I talked with Captain Ingersoll and Sheriff Nesbit. You know, the official people," Sunny told him. "They've been working since the morning. By now, they must have assembled some more information."

"You'd think." Ken didn't bother to keep the sarcasm out of his voice. "But not really. They still don't have any identification on the fellow you found. And if they know anything else, they're being mighty economical with it."

"You're saying Lenore Nesbit is hiding something?"

"I'm trying to decide if this situation merits a special edition," Ken confessed. "We delivered this week's issue around the time you discovered the body. It's an expense, you know. And after the murders we've had in the last year or so, can I justify going up against the local dailies, or publish on my usual schedule?" He sighed. "Ollie is pressuring me to soft-pedal the story."

"Well, he would, considering his investment in the tourism market." *Including my job*, Sunny silently added. "Do you think Lenore is actually stonewalling you?"

"I can't be sure," Ken said. "But if I decide to go to press, what the hell am I going to say? You're a pro, Sunny. What do you think?"

"The victim seems to be an out-of-towner, non-local," Sunny said slowly. "You've got the online edition now. Why not break the story there and hold back on print until more facts come to light?" She had a sudden inspiration. "Dad was wondering if the guy was homeless—wearing the wrong clothes for the local weather. That might be an angle to examine, using the murder to springboard into a more general concern."

"Yeah." Ken's voice sounded a little hollow. "'Cause if I guess wrong, the paper and ink bill might make *me* homeless." He paused for a second. "I know that Will is supposed to be doing the investigating and this is his first case, so I can understand you backing him up." His voice grew pleading. "But you really have nothing for me?"

"Nothing more than I already told you," Sunny assured him.

Ken thanked her and hung up.

And, Sunny was a little surprised to realize, *I have no interest in getting involved.*

*

The *Harbor Courier* restricted its coverage to a box on the home page of its virtual version, reporting the bare facts that had come out. But there was a jump to an editorial page, raising the homeless theory and promising to look into the homelessness situation in Elmet County. That was more than the other local news outlets managed to do with the story. The discovery of an unidentified dead body is hot news at first. But without identification or other developments, that kind of story got pushed into the back pages (or the TV equivalent) pretty quickly.

Sunny had a hectic Friday, catching up with weekend reservations that had come in while she was away the day before. The weekend dragged, though, because Will was working and Mike was being very circumspect around Mrs. M. Sunny spent a lot of time binge-watching some cable shows and playing with Shadow.

She did give in to curiosity on one point. Saturday evening she went online and checked how long it was supposed to take the FBI's fingerprint system to identify someone. According to the websites she hit, it was supposed to take no longer than seventy-two hours.

So, she thought, *Will —and maybe Ken will have something to go on by Monday.*

She also got a heads-up from Ollie Barnstable on Sunday afternoon. "The police are going to let the store reopen on Monday," he told her over the phone. "The crime-scene people have finished."

Sunny had a brief mental image of hazmat-suited CSI geeks dusting the frozen fish in the freezer for fingerprints. "I guess that's good news," she said.

"We'll see if that marshal is right about a spike in business." Ollie seemed to have lost his nervousness about Val Overton. He sounded just like a demanding landlord.

"I'll wait until there's a gap in the line before I remind Neil about his rent," she told him.

When Monday morning came and Sunny arrived at the MAX office, it seemed as though Val's prediction was right on the money. The New Stores had much more foot traffic than usual. Sunny saw a steady stream of people pass her office window, on their way to gawk into Kittery Harbor Fish.

But I don't know how many of them are actually going inside to buy anything, that irreverent voice in the back of Sunny's head spoke up. *Maybe Neil should charge for guided tours of the crime scene.*

Claire Donally

She wasn't altogether surprised when her phone rang and she heard Helena Martinson's voice on the other end. "Thank heavens the weather has moderated a bit today," she said. "Abby and I are thinking of going downtown for lunch. Would you like to join us at the Redbrick? We can pick you up at the office."

Sunny agreed, smiling as she hung up the phone. *Very smooth, Mrs. M.,* she silently complimented her neighbor. *You'll just happen to stop by right next door to the bull's-eye for every gossip maven in town.*

She put in an hour or so getting the office squared away so she could have a leisurely lunch and then sat waiting for Helena and Abby to show up. Abby came in the door frowning and looking around. "What did this use to be?"

"Barnstable's Sweet Shoppe," Sunny replied.

"Right, right." Abby smiled reminiscently and pointed at the right-hand wall—the one opposite from Kittery Harbor Fish. "That's where the soda fountain was."

"We're not going to get any service there nowadays," Mrs. M. said. "I've really had a hankering for one of those Redbrick burgers all day. Shall we go?"

Sunny got her parka and headed for the door. While she locked it, Helena took her daughter by the arm. "This is the place that was on the news," she said, steering Abby over to the window of the fish store. Sunny trailed along, eager to see what kind of crowd Neil Garret was actually attracting. He looked pretty busy, standing behind the counter and dealing with several customers.

Abby froze in mid-step, reeling back as if she'd been struck. If not for Helena's grip, the younger woman might have taken a tumble to the pavement.

"Are you okay?" Sunny hustled to take Abby's other arm.

In spite of looking as if she were about to collapse at any moment, Abby hauled them away from the store window and back to the MAX office. "That man in there." She nodded back toward Kittery Harbor Fish, her voice a harsh whisper, her face looking as if she'd just seen a ghost.

"You mean Neil Garrct?" Sunny said.

Abby shook her head. "That's not his name. I know him— I'd know him anywhere. And he's supposed to be in jail."

7

"In jail?" **Helena** Martinson echoed, looking shocked. "What do you mean?"

The same questions were floating around in Sunny's head, but she had some practical matters to take care of—like getting Abby seated before she fell down. She unlocked the office door and maneuvered Abby and Helena inside, bringing the younger Martinson down for a landing on one of the office chairs. "Coffee?" she asked.

Abby silently nodded. She looked as if she'd just received a serious jolt. Her perfect princess face was pale, her jaw hung loose. She swallowed hard a few times before she was able to thank Sunny when she returned with a cup.

Sunny managed to get Helena into a chair rather than fluttering over her daughter like a mother hen. After Abby

Claire Donally

had taken a couple of sips of coffee and a little color had reappeared in her cheeks, Sunny said, "Now do you want to tell us about it?"

"That man in the store," Abby began.

"The one behind the counter?" Sunny asked. After this buildup, it would be a heck of a thing if one of the customers had gotten such a reaction from Abby.

She nodded. "The one you called Neil Garret. That's not his real name. He's Nick Gatto—and he's a crook."

Now that Abby had begun to calm down, Helena started getting agitated. "How do you know that?"

Abby took a long breath. "Mom, I guess there are some things you have to know. The streets in California aren't paved with gold, you don't get discovered by Hollywood while sitting at a soda fountain . . . and I wasn't living in a convent the past few years."

Just the words to gladden any mother's heart, Sunny thought. "So how did you meet this Nick Gatto?"

"'Nicky Suits,' they used to call him. He was always beautifully dressed." Abby actually smiled at the memory. "And I worked for him. I know it's a cliché, but I was supporting myself between acting jobs by waiting tables. There's a reason—you can set your own hours to accommodate auditions or rehearsals, even open up your schedule for filming something. I was good enough that I got offers to work in the front of the house, as a hostess, and let's face it, my career wasn't exactly setting Hollywood on fire. A lot of the stuff I did, I was just an extra—walking scenery."

"I've seen movies and TV shows where you acted," Helena loyally disagreed.

But Abby shook her head. "Usually about five lines, maximum. Anyway, when I heard about this upscale Italian place opening, I applied for a hostess job, and I got it. That's where I met Nicky. It was his restaurant."

"And this restaurant landed him in jail?" Sunny asked.

"No, the way he got the money for the restaurant put him in jail," Abby said. "He was manipulating stocks."

"A guy named Nicky Suits was messing with Wall Street?" Sunny didn't have much to do with high finance, just an anemic 401(k) from her days at the *Standard*. But the idea of an apparent mobster muscling into the stock exchange made her stare.

"It's not the big corporations that you hear about all the time," Abby explained. "It's what they call the small cap market, small companies trying to raise capital or going public. Nicky figured out how to use investment firms and force dealers to push up the prices of some stocks that he and his boss bought into for pennies and sold for big bucks. It's not all that well-regulated, and he was doing pretty well."

"Well enough to buy a little respectability with a restaurant." Mrs. M. didn't sound happy. "And you worked for this man?"

Abby nodded. "He was a good guy to work for, and the restaurant took off—until his, um, associates started hanging around. Nicky's boss Jimmy just about turned the place into his private clubhouse. Then Jimmy started taking an interest in me."

"Oh, yes?" Helena's approval reading was way down in the negative numbers by now.

Abby looked as if she'd just taken a dose of very

unpleasant medicine. "That's not the point. What's important is that Nicky helped me. When he saw that Jimmy was after me, he got me a job in a completely different business and helped me to move out into the Valley. I'd seen the handwriting on the wall for my acting career for a while. Nick got me working for a law firm, and I've moved on and up from there."

"And he did all this just because you worked for him?" Helena's tone reminded Sunny of her own mom's approach when digging into some messy situation in her teenage life.

Except this is a lot more serious, she thought. *It's not promising when the good guy in the story is a gangster, saving Abby from a worse gangster.*

"We were—involved," Abby admitted. "He was going through a messy divorce, and he really is—was—a nice guy, Mom."

"Mmmmm-hmmmm." Helena was definitely reserving judgment on that score.

"Anyway, he made a clean break when he got me the new job. The next thing I heard about him was when he got arrested. He pushed his luck on a deal and it blew up on him. The feds got involved, charging him with securities fraud, wanting to make an example out of him. The last I knew, he was supposed to be going off to federal prison."

"And instead he ends up in Kittery Harbor, selling fish."

Sunny could have smacked herself in the forehead. She should have seen the signs—Will's interest in the incident with Shadow. He didn't check into it because Shadow was her cat, but because it took place in front of Neil Garret's *or rather,* she corrected herself, *Nick Gatto's store.* That also explained Val Overton's sudden appearance, chatting with her about Shadow's misadventure. Sure, federal marshals delivered writs and chased fugitives. But one of their big jobs was running the witness protection system.

Well, Val's job had just gotten a lot harder, with a murder happening in her witness' place of business. *And Ken Howell was begging me for something juicy . . .*

Sunny quickly shook that thought away. Abby had stumbled across a dangerous secret, something with possibly fatal consequences, and now the three of them knew it.

The situation hadn't quite penetrated for Helena Martinson. She was still preoccupied with her daughter's unwise life choices. But it had started to sink in for Abby. She was going from shocked to sick.

Sunny spoke up in a firm voice. "Now, listen," she said. "This story does not go beyond these four walls. It involves gangsters, and now murder."

She knew how Mrs. M. loved a good secret to spread around the gossip grapevine. The fact that it didn't do her daughter much credit should dampen her usual enthusiasm— or so Sunny hoped. "So we've got to keep this under wraps," she went on. "It may have already gotten someone killed."

That finally got through. "Subject closed," Helena Martinson said. But judging from the look she gave Abby, they would be discussing many other matters soon.

Abby simply looked apprehensive, whether from her discovery or from her mother's reaction, Sunny couldn't say.

After a moment, Helena turned to Sunny. "I'm sorry, dear. With all of this. . . ." She made a vague gesture with her hand to include the whole mess. "Maybe we should take a rain check. Would that be all right with you?"

"Don't worry about it, I understand perfectly," Sunny assured her neighbor. "There's always something I can do around here to fill the time."

Silently, she added, *Maybe I can get Will over for lunch instead. I definitely have a bone to pick with him.*

She got the Martinsons out of the MAX office, watching them set off in the opposite direction from Kittery Harbor Fish. Then Sunny went to the phone on her desk. She got through to Will's cell phone and suggested lunch. "Unless you're busy with Val Overton," she teased.

"No, no," he said. "Where would you like to go? I'm up in headquarters—"

"I was thinking of something simple," she said. *And private*, she silently added. "Why don't you pick up some sandwiches and lemonade? We can have a picnic in my office."

"Well, I guess that beats getting frostbite outside." From Will's tone of voice, the office sounded only marginally better. "What kind of sandwich would you like?"

"Surprise me," Sunny said. *It's only fair. I'm going to surprise you.*

Will arrived about fifteen minutes later with a paper sack. "Hope you don't mind lemonade out of a bottle. I stopped off in Saxon and picked up meatball sandwiches at Avezzani's."

"One of the fanciest restaurants in the area, and you pick up a meatball sub?" Sunny shook her head.

Will grinned. "Before it went all fancy, Gene Avezzani's folks ran a deli—and they made meatball parm sandwiches on garlic bread—best I ever ate. You should just count your-self lucky that I'm pals with Gene, and he still makes these things for me." The smells seeping through the slightly greasy paper reminded Sunny that it had been a while since break-fast. She almost regretted what was going to happen next.

Sitting down across from Sunny, Will spread the wrapped sandwiches on the desk she'd cleared. Soon they were hard at work on their lunch.

"You know, I got my job at the *Standard* because of a meatball sub." Sunny took another appreciative bite and chewed. "I was interviewing with the editor "

"Randall McDermott," Will put in.

"Yes. Randall took me out to lunch. He said he hired me because I had the nerve to eat such a sloppy sandwich at such a crucial meeting."

"You still have plenty of nerve," Will said.

"I sure do," Sunny told him. "That's why I'm asking how come you never told me about Nick Gatto."

Will made some interesting noises. Whether it was meatball getting caught in his throat or lemonade coming out his nose, Sunny wasn't sure. He went through a couple of napkins wiping his face while Sunny glared at him.

"I can see you're trying to come up with something, but at least pay me the courtesy of not saying, 'Nick who?' I'm talking about my next-door neighbor here, Neil Garret, aka Nicky Suits, California man-about-town and supposed securi-ties fraud convict."

Will was pretty quick on the uptake. "California," he said. "Damn. Abby Martinson recognized him?"

"She worked for him, and nearly fainted when she saw him."

Will shook his head. "Of all the lousy luck."

"Your luck's about to get lousier," Sunny warned him. "I'm furious at you. How could you lie to me?"

"I didn't lie," Will said carefully. "I didn't tell you anything, because it wasn't my secret to tell."

"So you just strung me along ever since that shop opened last summer," Sunny accused.

"I didn't know anything myself until after the November election when the sheriff made me her chief investigator," Will said. "Then I got brought in on this whole WITSEC thing."

"WITSEC?" Sunny repeated.

"Witness Security," Will explained. "It's what the marshals call the witness protection program these days."

"Well, you'd better get used to being called mud, because that's what your name is gonna be."

"Right, because the first thing I should do with a witness hiding from the mob is to talk all about him to my girlfriend, the newspaper reporter."

"I'm not a newspaper reporter." The denial burst from Sunny's lips with enough anger to surprise her. *Keep this up,* she thought, *and I may not be a girlfriend much longer, either.*

"You write stories for the *Harbor Courier,*" Will said. "And I can imagine how Ken Howell would react to a story like this."

Sunny was ready to give him an argument about that until she remembered Ken's voice trying to wheedle something out of her for the paper. "Maybe you have a point," she admitted.

"And this is the kind of thing that, if it got out, could

get someone killed." Will paused for a second. "Maybe it did."

"You mean that guy you tried to claim you couldn't identify?" Sunny said.

"We couldn't, until the prints finally came back this morning." Will sighed in defeat. "His name was Phil Treibholz. He was a Los Angeles private detective, a would-be peeper to the stars."

"Sounds pretty high-end."

"Maybe 'extortionate' would be a better word." Will looked grim. "From what I was able to find out about him, he collected big bucks from lawyers to help with their cases. One witness complained that Treibholz tried to intimidate him by hanging a rat from the rear-view mirror of his car."

"So the guy who tried to put the noose around Shadow's neck—"

"Was almost certainly Treibholz," Will finished the thought. "When you consider that 'gatto' means 'cat' in Italian, it's kind of obvious that Treibholz was trying to send a message."

"A message that wouldn't have done Shadow much good." Sunny sat for a moment. "You know, I'm having a really hard time scraping up any outrage over this guy getting shot."

"I can understand that." Will shrugged. "Other folks, though, take a dim view of murders happening in these parts."

"Sounds as though the new Sheriff Nesbit is a lot like the old one in that respect," Sunny admitted. "Well, your job can't be that difficult. Treibholz turns up from California and threatens Neil—we'll call him Neil to keep the secret.

That's motive. Treibholz gets two bullets in the back of the head in Neil's freezer. That's opportunity. You're two-thirds of the way to making a case."

Will hesitated for a moment before he answered. "It's not that simple. There's a big racketeering trial due to open soon against Neil's boss."

"And the federal prosecutor wants Neil's testimony."

"It could put a dangerous criminal away for life," Will said.

"You mean, somebody better known than Nicky Suits," Sunny corrected. "I used to help cover some of the federal trials in New York. The prosecutors knew that nailing big names meant career advancement."

"That doesn't mean that Jimmy DiCioppa doesn't deserve prison time," Will argued.

Sunny gave him a disgusted laugh. "Yeah, having a colorful nickname like 'Jimmy de Chopper' because of what happened to the fingers and toes of people who owed him money—that didn't enter into the equation at all." She paused for a second. "So what's the deal? Is Val Overton trying to save her witness? I thought that if you broke the witness protection rules, you got kicked out of the program."

"There's the question of innocent until proven guilty," Will said. "And Neil keeps swearing that he's innocent."

Sunny took a moment to digest that, contrasting the Nick Gatto she'd heard about with the Neil Garret she knew. On one side was the guy who'd broken the law and gone to prison. On the other was the boss that Abby Martinson had more than liked, the pleasant store owner that Sunny had come to know . . . the rattled guy who'd opened the freezer and let a body out of the bag.

"So what do you make out of what he's saying?" she finally asked.

"He sounds good," Will replied. "But then, he made a lot of money scamming people on the stock market."

"So, has he got some sort of alibi that required the body to be found at nine thirty-seven in the morning in the presence of a witness? If we're thinking he killed this Treibholz guy, why did he drag me into it?"

"The medical examiner has had a lot of fun trying to determine a time of death. Apparently the body hadn't frozen through, so we have a rough window between twelve and fourteen hours before you found the body."

"Sometime after the store closed and well before morning," Sunny said. "So was Neil Garret out of town, or surrounded by witnesses at the time in question?"

Will laughed, with precious little humor. "That's the thing. He hasn't got an alibi at all. Not even a favorite TV show he was watching. If we believe him, he was in his lovely rental home out in Sturgeon Springs, reading a book."

Sunny sat back in her chair. "A literate criminal. That's something we don't see every day. But it kind of clashes with his alibi. That sounds like something he came up with between the fish market and the interrogation room in Levett. You'd expect better workmanship, considering this is a guy who swindles people."

"So far he's stuck with it, and we haven't been able to challenge his story. You know the area. It's pretty countrified, the houses are spread out, nobody really notices anything."

"He had to know that he couldn't just talk his way out of having a body turn up in his freezer." Sunny squinted her eyes, as if that would help her focus on her memories of

Claire Donally

Thursday morning. Neil trying to tell her the store wasn't open yet. The chill in the air. Finding the door open. Did he look surprised or scared? What was his expression when he checked the cash register? When he opened the freezer door? It hadn't seemed rehearsed, and Neil hadn't been checking her reactions. Unless . . .

"What if he had an accomplice, someone he expected to clean up the crime scene, and they didn't—or couldn't do it?" Sunny bit her lip as the idea came out of her mouth. Who would be the most likely accomplice, someone who knew all about Neil Garret's former life? Someone who had just turned up from California?

Abby Martinson.

Sunny shook her head. "No, that's a ridiculous idea. What was I thinking?"

It doesn't make sense, she realized with a feeling of relief. Abby as an accomplice would only work if nobody knew of her connection with Nicky Suits. So why would she blab that to Sunny? But that question still paled beside the biggie. Why would Neil Garret reveal Treibholz's dead body? And of all the people he could have had in front of that door when he threw it open, why choose Sunny?

"So Neil is the obvious choice, but you're not sure he's the right one," she said slowly.

"Maybe someone here knew about Garret's California connection and didn't want it coming out. A business associate, or competitor." Will leaned across the desk with their half-eaten sandwiches. "It strikes me that your father has a lot of friends in the local fishing community. Now that you know what's going on, maybe you could work some of those contacts."

"I should still be furious with you," Sunny told him.

"I'll say I'm sorry, if that helps," Will said. "The sheriff really wanted to keep this under wraps. When Lenore revealed the truth about Garret, she said that Frank hadn't even told her."

"So now that I know, the old team is back together again?" Sunny gave him a rueful grin.

And that snarky voice in the back of her head chimed in, *Just when you thought you were out . . . they pull you back in.*

8

The rattle of the key in the lock quickly brought Shadow to the door. He did his usual circuit around Sunny's ankles, checking for odd smells and marking her with his personal scent. She reached down and gave him a quick pat on the head, then walked into the living room, calling to the Old One. But he wasn't in.

Often when Sunny was alone with Shadow, she'd get down on the floor and play with him. He rolled on his back, hoping that would happen now. Instead, Sunny went to a chair and flopped down with a sigh.

Shadow immediately got to his feet. Was Sunny sad? He'd caught some traces of Sunny's He when he checked her ankles, so Sunny must have seen him today. Shadow knew that when male and female humans got together, sometimes they were very happy—and sometimes not.

He scaled the chair, not going for Sunny's lap but instead climbing up onto the arm, stretching so that he could press his forehead to hers and let her know that he thought she was special, even if that stupid He didn't.

But as he brought his face close to hers, he caught a scent that made his nose twist and his eyes blink. Shadow drew back in disgust. This was another of those crazy two-leggity things he'd never understand. With all the foods humans enjoyed, why would Sunny eat something that smelled like that?

Sometimes, in his wandering days, hunger forced Shadow to eat food that was old or tasted odd. Even so, he wouldn't put something that smelled so bad into his mouth. Shouldn't Sunny know enough not to do that?

Annoyed, he jumped back to the floor, stalking away with his tail lashing the air. *She always yells at me when something I eat comes back up,* he thought. *I'm going to stay away from her. She's a lot bigger than I am, and I don't want to be around if she gets sick. That will be a real mess.*

He headed for the room of food and a quick bite from his bowl. The box that kept things cold loomed over him. That would be a good place to go, somewhere that would let him look down on everything.

It's even taller than Sunny, he thought. *So if that bad-smelling food comes back up, I'll be well out of reach. Safe.*

*

Mike came into the living room, rubbing his hands together after being outside in the cold. "I'm surprised to see you sitting," he told Sunny. "Usually when you're here alone, you're romping around on the floor with the furball."

She smiled. "Yeah, well, he went to do that Vulcan mind-meld thing he likes to do, bopping his forehead against mine. It's called bunting. But I'm afraid the ghost of the garlic bread I had for lunch put him off. What's the matter?" she asked as an inquisitive gray-furred face poked around the entrance to the room. "Are you a vampire?"

"Well, he's got the fangs for the job," Mike said as Shadow yawned, revealing an impressive set of chompers.

Sunny glanced at the wall clock and got up. "Guess it's time to start supper—which I'll do after I brush away the offensive garlic breath." She headed upstairs, brushed, and then went to the kitchen. Dinner was simple—and bland. Boiled potatoes, frozen veggies, and baked pork chops. She put a pot on to boil, preheated the oven, and got out the jar of unsweetened applesauce. Spooning out a few ounces into a bowl, she sprinkled some powdered ginger on top and set to mixing. *That should give it a little taste without setting off Shadow's finicky nose.*

He sat by his bowls, watching Sunny but still not coming close.

Arranging the chops in a pan, she topped them with the spiced applesauce and put them in the oven, setting the timer. Then came the potatoes. After a half hour, she checked the meat and stepped into the living room, where Mike was watching the news. "About five minutes," she reported. She went back in to microwave the vegetables.

Mike came into the kitchen and helped set the table. Sunny stepped over to the pot and stuck a knife in one of the potatoes, testing for doneness. "Should be ready any time now."

The timer bleeped, and a moment later the microwave

joined in, not exactly in harmony. Sunny took one more look at the chops and then began moving things onto plates.

Mike immediately attacked his chop with knife and fork, putting a bite into his mouth. "Nice," he declared after he'd chewed and swallowed. "Do you think His Nibs over there will approve of your breath after this?"

Sunny shrugged, mashing some potato under her fork. "Jane Rigsdale tells me some folks use ginger when a cat or dog has an upset stomach."

"Well, she ought to know, being a vet." He glanced over at Shadow, who still sat regarding them. "Should we have given him that when he tried to eat that frog?"

Sunny shuddered at the memory of that epic disaster. "Only if he ate the ginger *instead* of the frog," she said. Slicing off a bit of pork, she asked, "How was your day?"

Mike shrugged. "Pretty quiet. Went up to outlet-land and got in my walk, ran a few errands, and stopped in to say hello to Helena. That was a pretty weird visit. She and Abby seemed so distracted, I wondered if they'd had a few drinks with lunch."

Probably no lunch, Sunny thought, *although they had a lot to chew over mentally.*

But that was nothing to talk about. She'd promised both of the Martinsons she'd keep quiet about Abby's little secret and asked them to do the same. Remembering her own lunchtime conversation with Will, she decided to try and steer the conversation in a new direction. "You know a lot of the fishermen around here, Dad. Did any of them get particularly friendly with Neil Garret?"

"Friendly?" Mike frowned in thought. "I wouldn't go that

far. A lot of guys were glad he opened that shop, though. Neil offered a better price than they'd been getting, and if a guy had a small catch, he could sell it all here and not have to hump it over to Portsmouth or one of the other big wholesale markets. Guys who managed to get a prime item would do deals with Neil before taking the rest of their catch elsewhere."

"You make Neil sound like a big deal."

"He was, to the guys still shipping out from here." Mike's frown deepened as he tried to explain. "Remember that movie, *The Perfect Storm*?"

"Sure," Sunny replied. "George Clooney going down with his ship."

Mike nodded, his face grim. "The only thing worse for our local fishermen is that they *didn't* drown. The story they based the movie on happened in 1997, and catches were falling even then. Foreign trawlers were coming into our fishing grounds, huge factory ships, and a lot of locals jumped in, upgrading their ships to compete. A lot of areas got overfished. And when there are no fish, that kills jobs for a lot of fishermen."

He sat for a moment. "You know, years ago, before your mother and I talked about getting married, I thought I might go out on the fishing boats. It seemed a pretty manly way to make a living. Shows how much I knew." Mike laughed, but there was a lot of bitterness in his voice.

"Instead, I went to work hauling salt—which turned out to be the better call. Every winter, it snows somewhere, and the folks need road salt."

They both sat in silence for a moment. That might be true, but it meant that Mike was out of town when the ice storm of the century hit Kittery Harbor . . . and a fatal car accident took Sunny's mom.

Mike cleared his throat. "Funny thing. The company started out providing salt to preserve all the fish coming out of the waters around here."

"I know a lot of your buddies only do sportfishing now, or they find other ways to make money, like Ike Elkins and his floating tours," Sunny said.

"A lot of fellas pay for their boats by acting as fishing guides," Mike told her. "That's okay during the tourist season, but nobody in their right mind pays to go out in the Gulf of Maine during wintertime. So the boat owners head down where the water is warm—Carolina, Florida—and take people fishing for bass. Pretty much everybody does that now."

He frowned for a moment, going over a mental list. "The only guy who goes out regularly from these parts is Charlie Vane."

"I don't think you ever mentioned him among your fishing buddies," Sunny said.

"He's not a buddy. And for him, fishing is business, not pleasure. He's the only fisherman who works the winter months around here. Of course, he's a bit of a nut." Mike shook his head. "Charlie claims to be a direct descendant of another Charles Vane, a pirate who got hanged about three hundred years ago. Maybe there is something to his claim, if stubbornness is something that sticks in people's DNA." Mike leaned forward, in storyteller's mode. "Here's something they don't usually mention in those pirate movies. There was a point when the British government offered pardons for past bad behavior to the pirates operating out of their colonies, provided they knocked it off. The 1700s Charles Vane rejected the deal—and ended up at the end of a rope. Our Charlie Vane refuses to stop fishing, although from what I hear, he's at the end of his rope, too—financially speaking."

Sunny looked at her dad. "You don't sound as though you've got much sympathy for him."

"Oh, I have a little sympathy," Mike protested. "Charlie's family has fished these waters for generations. It's not his fault, what's happened to the business. But I don't like what Charlie does to keep his head above water."

"You're not telling me he's a pirate—are you?" Sunny asked in disbelief.

"No, that would be more honest. Charlie cuts any corners he can. Some areas have been declared off-limits to fishermen to let the fish population grow back again. But Charlie will sneak in to get a catch. Or he'll finagle when he's caught more than the allowable quota." Mike scowled. "You're supposed to dump any overcatch back into the water. But it's not as though those fish are going to go swimming off, thinking, 'Whew, that was a lucky break.' They're dead, and dumping them back isn't going to make them alive again. It's the law, though, and that's what fishermen are supposed to do."

"Sounds like a stupid kind of law, with so many people around here struggling to put something on the table," Sunny argued.

Mike nodded. "I'm not saying you're wrong. But that doesn't make it right for someone to slide around the law because he's supposed to be protecting his birthright as a fisherman."

"So is that why you never mentioned Charlie Vane to me?" Sunny asked. "Because he's a crook?"

"Not a crook." Mike hesitated. "But he is crooked."

"What's the difference?" Sunny wanted to know.

Mike gave her a shrug and a grin. "I guess he hasn't been caught yet." He got a little more serious. "I have heard, though, that Charlie's been thick as thieves with your friend Neil Garret."

Sunny sat a little straighter. "You make it sound as if they've been up to something together."

"Well, they've gotten in trouble together," Mike said. "When Garret began cherry-picking local catches, he disrupted the usual way of doing business."

"What was that?"

"Boats brought their catches to the wholesale fish market in Portsmouth, which is just a long-winded way of saying they dealt with Deke Sweeney."

Sunny frowned. "So this Sweeney guy owns the operation?"

"No, but he might as well. Anyone who buys or sells fish in Portsmouth knows Sweeney. They call him the Shark of the Fish Market."

Sunny laughed. "Nice nickname." Then she got thoughtful. "You think this shark might have tried to take a bite out of Neil Garret?"

"No need," Mike replied. "Sweeney already cut him—as in cut him off. I hear he put out the word. Several of the guys who did deals with Garret couldn't sell their fish in the Portsmouth market. And Garret can't even buy a sardine there."

Maybe that explains the lack of variety in Neil's store

lately, Sunny thought. *It sure didn't help the drop-off in business.* "Do you think that really hurt the fishermen?"

"It's more than half an hour, driving to Kennebunkport, and an hour, hour and a half getting to Boston or Gloucester," Mike said. "Going by boat makes the trip even longer. When you're racing the clock to bring in your catch as fresh as possible, that can become a factor. And if you land in a market where no one will buy from you, the wasted time may make for a spoiled catch."

Sunny frowned. "So that's it—all those fishermen are ruined?"

"Oh, when they come back around the beginning of tourist season, Sweeney will probably let them off the hook. He's a businessman."

And the way things are going, by then Neil's store should be bankrupt and safely out of Sweeney's way, Sunny added silently. "But what about Charlie Vane?" she asked. "You told me that he's still up here fishing, out in the cold—in more ways than one."

Mike only shrugged. "He's played it cute with Sweeney and the other guys in the fish market for years, hornswoggling them whenever he can. Sooner or later, that was going to catch up with him. If it hadn't been his side deals with Garret, it would have been something else."

"You think maybe he's angry with Neil Garret for dumping him in it?" Sunny didn't quite bring off the nonchalant tone, because Mike shot her a sharp look.

"If you're going to ask him that, I'll have to come along," he told her. "Frankly, I'd prefer if Will went with you, but I don't think Charlie will say anything if there's a cop around."

"I don't—" Sunny began, but Mike cut her off.

"Of course you're pumping me about the local fishing scene—probably because Will asked you to do it."

"He may have suggested that I talk to you, but I thought of that in terms of getting background, not expecting you to come up with a possible suspect." She gave her dad a look.

"Charlie may be crooked, but I don't believe he's a killer," Mike said. "Just in case, though, I do intend to be there when you talk to him. Let me make a couple of calls and see if I can find out where Charlie is supposed to be."

"Tell him I'm trying to sell a piece to the paper." The moment Sunny said it, she realized it might be more than just a cover story. If she got some interesting quotes, Ken Howell might actually buy it.

They did the dishes together, and then Sunny left her father in the kitchen to use the phone. The doorbell rang as she came down the hall, and she answered it to find Will Price.

"Figured I'd check in and see what your dad had to say," he explained.

Sunny passed along what she'd learned from Mike about Charlie Vane. "Dad's working the phone to see if he's in town and whether we can talk to him."

The phone rang, and Mike came into the living room, trailed by Shadow.

"Was that someone calling with info about where to find Charlie Vane?" Sunny asked.

"No, that's already set up," Mike replied. "Charlie's coming in to port tomorrow morning and he'll see us—but no cops," he added with an apologetic glance at Will. "The call was from Helena Martinson, inviting us over—and she'd be happy to see you, Will." Mike smiled. "I believe cake is involved."

"Sounds good to me," Will said, ignoring the look Sunny sent his way. It had been hard enough drawing the whole story about Neil Garret/Nick Gatto out of Abby, and harder still deciding to tell Will after promising to keep Abby's secret. It wouldn't be easy, socializing with the Martinson women—more like walking on eggshells. But now Will wanted to go waltzing into the Martinson place, face-to-face with Abby and Helena . . .

Will leaned toward Sunny, lowering his voice. "Do you know how much of my job involves playing dumb?"

"I guess I'll find out," Sunny muttered, following Mike to get her coat.

A brisk walk through the cold air brought them to the Martinson house. Sunny braced herself for a big welcome from Toby, but the overgrown pup was nowhere to be seen. Mrs. M. caught it immediately. "Toby is downstairs in his dog crate. Abby's working with me to train him better."

Muted woofs and whines came from beneath their feet.

"You can't let him out because he's crying, Mom," Abby scolded. "That's just rewarding bad behavior. He's got a nice blanket and toys, and soon enough he'll realize it's his safe place—his den."

She gave the guests an apologetic smile. "I may not be a dog whisperer, but I was a dog walker, and I saw how people got their puppies to grow up into good dogs."

"Well, if I can't give Toby a treat, how about you folks? Who's up for coffee cake?" Helena gave Will an admiring glance. "You must have come straight from work. That's a very nice tie you're wearing."

Yeah, interesting design—except for the spot, Sunny added to herself. Will was wearing her Christmas present again. He obviously didn't have many ties in the rotation, and he hadn't gotten it cleaned yet.

This wasn't some polyester cheapo tie. It was embroidered silk, handmade and expensive, even though she'd managed to snag it in outlet-land. Sunny had started shopping as soon as she learned Will was getting out of uniform. It had been a long and difficult hunt, and she'd been proud to present him with something appropriate and nice for Christmas.

Less than a month later, the spot had appeared, and it had just seemed to grow every time she looked at it, although Sunny had pretended not to notice.

Abby was a lot more blunt. "Yeah, it's a shame you got something on it."

Will winced. "I'm afraid I'm still getting used to the whole jacket-and-tie thing, although I have learned now that ties and pens don't mix well."

"Could have been worse. I had an audition for a part but had to get through half a shift first. So I wore my good silk blouse in to work. Somehow, some ink transferred from a pad—" She moved her hand chestwards. "To my left boob."

Abby shrugged. "Lucky thing I knew how to deal with that." She turned to her mom. "Do we have any rubbing alcohol?"

Mrs. M. was still getting over the location of Abby's ink stain. "I—I think so." She headed to the bathroom as Abby stepped into the kitchen, returning with a wad of paper towels. "You'll have to take off the tie." She grinned. "Not as embarrassing for you as it was for me. I spent the lunch rush in a suit jacket pinned together up top so I didn't show off too much while my blouse dried."

Helena Martinson reappeared with a plastic bottle of clear liquid and some cotton balls. "I thought these might be useful."

"Just what we needed. Thanks, Mom." As Will took off his tie, Abby put the paper towels down on a table. She put the tie facedown and soaked a cotton ball in alcohol. Then, checking the position of the ink stain, she pressed the wet cotton to the rear of the tie.

After a moment, she lifted the tie and pointed to the toweling—and a big splotch of ink that had appeared. "See? The alcohol soaks through, taking some of the ink with it."

She moved the tie to fresh sections of the toweling, applying new alcohol-soaked cotton balls until the stain had all but disappeared.

"Thanks," Will said when she handed the tie back. "That's pretty amazing. How did you know that?"

"Welcome to the wonderful world of acting," Abby told him with a laugh, "where the people have to look perfect while scraping by on a waiter's salary. Trust me, you learn to take care of your clothes."

"But you're not doing that anymore," Mike said.

"It still comes in handy." Abby's smile turned impish. "I had to use that trick for a partner who had a disaster right before heading to court. That twenty minutes probably did more for me with the firm than the year of paralegal stuff I'd been doing."

They enjoyed coffee and cake, with Abby telling some stories about her adventures on the Left Coast. Will just sat back and relaxed, barely asking any questions at all, and

Sunny tried to do the same, although curiosity led her to dig a little deeper when Abby mentioned a catering job where she met George Clooney.

Finally, Mike looked at his watch. "I hate to be a party pooper, but we have an early morning tomorrow."

"I usually hear that when the weather's warmer and you want to catch fish," Mrs. M. told him.

Mike shrugged. "Close. Tomorrow we're trying to catch some fishermen. Sunny's thinking of interviewing a few of them over a cup of coffee and selling Ken Howell on a story for the *Courier*."

"Good luck with that," Helena said. "From what I remember of my Vince's fishing buddies, having coffee with them won't be like cocktails with George Clooney."

They got their coats and walked back home. Mike zipped ahead to the door. "I'll say good night here, Will. Darned coffee."

That left Sunny and Will together for a proper good-bye kiss. She was still smiling as she came through the door, to find Shadow on guard in the hallway. He wound his way around her ankles, his tail flicking about in displeasure.

Is he catching a whiff of Toby? she wondered. *Or is this just general annoyance?*

Shadow was very much a creature of habit. He didn't like the human members of the household gallivanting off after dark, and he took a dim view of Sunny and Mike preparing for bed hours before their usual time.

Still, he shouldered his way around the door and into Sunny's room as she turned down the sheet, blanket, and quilt. A quick leap brought him into bed with her, but he didn't settle down in her arms as he usually did.

Instead, Shadow brought his face close to hers.

"Checking for garlic again?" Sunny teased. "I brushed my teeth just now—promise."

Shadow slowly closed his eyes, then opened them again. Sunny had read somewhere in her cat research that this behavior was a sort of air kiss, a sign of trust and affection.

"So all is forgiven, huh?" Sunny brought her own eyelids down in a slow blink. Shadow gave her his double-barreled wink again and then snuggled against her.

Yeah, yeah, very affectionate, Sunny thought. *But we both know that as soon as I'm really asleep, you'll be off patrolling the house.*

9

Shadow crouched in the upstairs hall, his tail lashing the air. The house was still deep in darkness, but Sunny and the Old One were both up and talking, hours before their usual time. Shadow wasn't quite ready to call this a bad thing, but it was certainly out of the ordinary. He didn't like when two-legs started fooling around outside their schedules. It often meant trouble. For instance with all this running around, suppose one of them forgot to feed him?

He followed them into the kitchen, keeping a suspicious eye on them as he watched them eat. At least Sunny got up and put food and water in his bowls. When they finished and ran water over their bowls and eating things, Shadow ambled over by the door. The Old One surprised him by venturing outside and getting into both of the go-fast things, making them rumble. He came back with his mouth wide open, putting a hand in front of it as he opened the door. Shadow saw humans do that sometimes when they were tired and took advantage of it, darting past unseen.

It was cold and dark, but he could see well enough. Now he had a choice to make. He wanted to go along with Sunny on this strange dark-time adventure, but her go-fast thing was very hard to get into. Still worse, she'd been on her guard these last few days, either keeping him from getting out or catching him and putting him back inside when he tried to ride along.

The Old One's go-fast thing, on the other paw, had a big, open space in the back, very easy to jump into.

I'll just have to hope they're going to the same place, Shadow decided. He came to that conclusion just in time, hearing two-leg voices coming closer to the door. Shadow gathered himself and sprang up, high, over the wall of the go-fast thing and landed in the open space. The metal floor vibrated slightly under his paws. He was never sure if go-fast things were alive or not. They moved, and they made a noise sort of like purring, but they only did that when a human climbed inside them. Otherwise, they seemed to sleep a lot, even more than a cat. And they never seemed to wake up when Shadow crept up and pounced on them.

But that was something to think about for another time. The go-fast thing rocked as the Old One climbed inside, and soon they were moving. Shadow's plan had worked out perfectly.

Except for one thing.

I should have eaten more when Sunny put out my food, he thought. *They may not be going to the place where the Generous One gives out fish.*

*

Kittery Harbor didn't have a rush hour like New York, although there were times when the roads got busy with people off to early jobs in the navy shipyards in Portsmouth. But Sunny and her dad were heading into town even before that modest surge in traffic. This was more like the times when she worked the graveyard shift on the newspaper, driving off in search of a story in the dead of night. Usually, that meant something unpleasant: a car accident, a fire, a crime committed or a criminal caught.

Better not think that way, she scolded herself. *You want to look like the eager young reporter hoping to sell a story on local fishing.*

For the fourth time since she got in the car, she stifled a yawn. *Right. Yeah. Eager.* She took a deep breath, trying to get some more oxygen to her sleep-deprived brain. *Maybe not as young as I'd like to think anymore.*

This looked to be a long day. Sunny sincerely hoped she wouldn't get one of Ollie Barnstable's random supervisory visits while she was stumbling around trying to keep awake.

She followed her father's pickup down toward the Piscataqua River, passing the touristy piers with their convenient benches for lunching, past a more upscale marina, and finally came into what was left of the working port. Once there, it was hard to miss the neon glow of the Dockside Diner's sign, although an occasional sputter in the letters turned that into the DOCKSIDE DI E every once in a while.

The diner was a twenty-four hour operation, but cars were pretty scarce at this time of day. The only activity

Sunny could see was a crew of men tying up a small boat on a nearby pier. Was that Charlie Vane and his crew?

Sunny parked beside her dad and got out of her Wrangler. Mike was already out, pounding his arms against his sides. "Oh, yeah, cold water and an onshore breeze. Now I remember why I decided not to take that fishing job."

They headed for the diner entrance. Sunny laughed when she spotted a hand-lettered sign in the window. COME OVER TO THE DOCKSIDE . . . WE HAVE COFFEE.

Somebody in there must be a Star Wars *fan,* she thought.

They entered to steamy air filled with cooking smells and got a booth by the window. Mike ordered coffee and Sunny followed suit, quickly regretting the decision as a thick, chipped mug full of viscous black liquid was deposited in front of her. Mike stirred in a little sugar. "At least the spoon doesn't stand straight up. Reminds me of what we got out of the crankcase of my friend's Chevy when he put off changing the oil filter for too long."

He added some milk, took a sip, and blew out his cheeks. "Guess that's what you need to bring you back to life if you've been out at sea in weather like this."

Sunny followed his example, took a sip, and shuddered. "On my worst day in the office, leaving the pot on the coffeemaker heater too long, I never got it to taste like this." She called the waitress over and ordered an English muffin.

"Sounds like a good idea," Mike chimed in. "I'll have one, too." He leaned forward as the waitress headed to the kitchen. "Although I don't think that will manage to cut the taste."

There speaks the experience of forty years in drive-ins and greasy spoons, Sunny thought mournfully. She didn't have much time to complain, though, because the door banged open and a guy in an orange dayglow outfit came strutting in. His parka was open to reveal a heavy sweater and bib-style pants, making him look bulkier than he really was.

Mike rose to his feet. "Hey, Charlie."

Charlie Vane swaggered over to shake hands. He had to be about four inches shy of Mike's six-foot height, but he acted as though he were the bigger man. "How's it goin', Mike?"

"This is my daughter, Sunny." Mike made the introduction, and Sunny found her hand encased in a rough, calloused paw. Charlie Vane had a gaunt face with thin lips and eyes as colorless as ice cubes—about as warm as them, too. All of his visible skin looked as if it had been lightly sanded by the elements, with the exception of the pale white scar that traveled up his right cheek, continuing again above his eyebrow.

Charlie quirked that brow when he realized Sunny was staring at it. "Binding wire snapped and whipped right in my face. Another inch, and I'd be wearing a patch."

Sunny managed to find her voice. "I guess that would make you like your famous ancestor—although it would probably make navigating a boat a lot more exciting."

Vane grinned, exposing strong, yellowish teeth. "Good, so you aren't going to faint." He slipped into the booth on the opposite side from Sunny and Mike. The waitress was already there with a big, battered cup of sludge for him. Charlie took a long swallow and sighed.

"The taste takes some getting used to, but at least it warms your insides." He turned those ice-cube eyes on Sunny. "So what does your boyfriend the cop want to know?"

"I'm trying to develop a story about local fishing," Sunny began, but Vane cut her off, waving his hand.

Claire Donally

"Yeah, yeah, Mike told me all that. I know you write for the *Courier*. But I know you also team up with that Price guy to tackle cases." He grinned. "I actually read the *Courier*, besides using it to wrap fish. And while you've got a nice line there, Ken Howell will never run a story about me. I was supposed to give him an exclusive about a screwup by the government's supposed fishery experts. But I had a chance to get it on TV, and I went with it."

Considering that Ken's paper only comes out once a week, I can see why he'd take that personally, Sunny thought.

"So ask me some questions." Vane settled back in his seat. "I don't guarantee you'll get answers, but at least I'm here."

Sunny couldn't see any advantage to sticking with her cover story. So she decided not to circle around. "I'd like to know about your business dealings with Neil Garret."

"Whoa, very fancy. 'Business dealings,'" Vane said. "I did what any businessman tries to do—get more money for my product. Garret was willing to fork over above the fish market price for the better quality fish right out of the ocean. I took his money, and all I can say is too bad he couldn't buy my whole catch. But he didn't have the storage capacity for everything I brought in, and I couldn't supply all the different kinds of fish he needed. Not that he didn't try. He began making the rounds of the restaurants around here, checking into what kind of seafood they wanted. He figured on setting himself up as the local middleman, offering us fishermen better payment, charging his customers a below-market price, and still making money. Pretty ambitious."

Ambitious—I guess that would be Nick Gatto's middle name, Sunny thought.

Vane continued, "Of course sooner or later Deke Sweeney—you know about him?" When Sunny nodded, he went on. "Sweeney did his best to punish the guys who'd done deals with Garret."

"Including you," Sunny put in. "That must have been annoying."

"Yeah, but I was more annoyed with Sweeney." Vane glanced at her. "You think I was involved in what happened at the store? I still got two eyes, honey. No way would I mistake some out-of-towner for Neil. Mind you, I don't blame him. If some bozo tried to climb aboard my boat, he'd get exactly what was coming to him."

"Neil denies seeing the man before discovering him in the freezer," Sunny said. "Where were you—"

"On the night of the murder?" Vane finished for her. He leaned back in his seat, enjoying her attention. "I was in the Gulf of Maine after a quick turnover to refuel and resupply, hoping to make a decent catch of plaice. We had almost nothing to show for our last trip, so we thought we'd try our luck off Cape Elizabeth."

"That's more than fifty miles up the coast," Mike said.

Vane nodded. "A bit far to try sneaking back in a rowboat. And I had two crew with me—my boy Jack, and my son-in-law, Rennie Yates."

Both family, and dependent on him for jobs, Sunny thought. *That makes for a convenient alibi.*

But even if Charlie Vane had been much closer and had managed to sneak back to Kittery Harbor, that still didn't explain how he'd somehow mistaken Phil Treibholz for Neil Garret.

Unless we take the fifty-mile alibi at face value, and

figure that Vane hired himself a killer. It was just bad luck that the killer found Treibholz on the premises and did the job on the wrong person.

The problem with that theory was that contract killings, even cheap ones, cost money. And Charlie Vane didn't look as though he could rub two nickels together.

"Look, I really don't know much about what happened with Neil. I was out fishing, all I heard was a little gossip over the radio. From what I heard, I figured maybe Deke Sweeney sent somebody over to lean on Neil 'cause he wasn't rolling over and playing dead, and things got out of hand. Some leg-breaker getting what he had coming. But if Neil says he never saw the guy before, that he just turned up in the store's freezer . . ." His voice trailed off as he frowned. "I wonder what kind of game Neil is playing."

"What kind of game are you playing, Charlie?" Mike asked. "I hear Sweeney has you cut off in Portsmouth."

"There are other places to sell fish besides Portsmouth," Vane replied. "My family has been fishing these waters from the days when you baited hooks, threw lines over the side, and prayed you got lucky. No way am I going to let some pen pusher who's never stuck his nose out of an office force me out of business—or some guy who calls himself a shark because he can scare a bunch of fish merchants."

His voice sounded as if he had this already memorized, like a politician's stump speech.

Except I think he'd have a mug of beer in his hand, rather than a coffee cup, Sunny thought. She glanced out the window at the lightening sky and then at her watch. "I appreciate your giving us this time, Mr. Vane. But I'm afraid I'll have to be getting on with my day job soon. You may have to talk with Will Price, or even Sheriff Nesbit."

Charlie Vane looked as if the coffee had turned to motor oil in his mouth. He forced a swallow, and then said, "If I have to," with an ungracious look. "We already offloaded our catch, so we'll probably take a few days. But when we try again, we'll be gone for a while. I'll be heading off the Jordan Basin."

Mike stared. "That's almost to Nova Scotia," he said.

Vane shrugged. "You go where the fish are." He turned to Sunny. "So if your boyfriend wants to talk to me, he may have to do it by radio."

Sunny almost began her response with "He's not—" but managed to hold that in. Instead, she shrugged, said, "Fine," and gestured to the waitress for the check. She looked at her untouched muffin and nearly full cup. Somehow during their conversation, Mike had reduced his English muffin to crumbs and had to wave off the waitress when she tried to bring him a coffee refill.

His heart may not be what it used to be, Sunny thought, *but he still has a cast iron stomach.*

She settled the bill, left a tip, and headed back out into the cold.

*

Shadow stood on the front of a go-fast thing, peering in the smeary windows of the place Sunny and the Old One had gone into. From the smell, it had to be one of those places where they always made food. Shadow thought that was a good idea. He'd seen many two-legs just walk in and eat. But he knew that a furred person could get into trouble looking for food. He couldn't count how many places like that he'd entered—and been chased from.

I don't know why Sunny would go into one of those places now, he thought. *She just ate.*

He watched her take a drink and make a face. Maybe it was one of those situations like when the Old One put out food for him, and just to be polite, Shadow would have a taste.

Thinking of that reminded Shadow of the food Sunny had set out back home. Now he wished he'd had some of that before he went out. Shadow continued to watch Sunny and finally saw the reason why she was hanging around. A strange two-legs came into the place and sat down with her.

When the stranger had walked by, Shadow had noticed him because he smelled of fish—some of it not very fresh. A bare glance at the way this one moved, though, and Shadow knew he couldn't expect to see any tidbits falling to the ground. This one was angry.

But there were no loud voices and fighting when the Angry One spoke with Sunny. That was good, although Shadow wasn't happy to see Sunny with this two-legs. Sunny was good, but she chose some very odd humans to hang around with sometimes. Why couldn't she visit with nice two-legs like the Generous One?

The thought of that one made Shadow's empty stomach growl. He stretched and noticed that the sky above was growing brighter. More two-legs were moving around now.

Shadow wondered if the Generous One was already in the house where he chopped up fish. A quick surge of his muscles, and he dropped to the pavement. He set off down the street, ignoring the cold wind coming off the big water. It would be warm where he was going.

*

Sunny arrived at the MAX office early enough that she was able to stop at Judson's Market for supplies. She wanted to get the taste of the Dockside Diner's coffee out of her mouth, and she didn't trust the office brew to help. So she got a cup of Judson's plain (but flavorful) American coffee and a toasted bagel to make up for the muffin she'd missed out on.

She'd just cleared the office decks and finished her second breakfast when she heard the metal gate rattle up next door. Sighing, Sunny dropped her disposable cup in the trash. She'd let the subject of rent slide after Abby's surprise revelation, but she knew she couldn't allow it to drag on forever. Sooner or later, she'd get a call from Ollie on the subject. And knowing Ollie, it would be sooner—like when he realized he still hadn't gotten cash or a check.

Sunny rose from behind her desk, walked to the door, and then scampered through the cold to Kittery Harbor Fish. Neil Garret had just installed himself behind the counter. "Oh, hi, Sunny," he said. "What can I do for you?"

"It's not so much what you can do for me as for Ollie," she told him. "He wanted me to remind you about the rent. It's—"

"Overdue, I know," he finished for her. "Things have been—well, you know how things have been." Neil rubbed his hands together, like a man getting down to a big job. "The good news is that I had a decent day yesterday. A lot of nosy people had healthy dinners last night. Can you let me slide until I see how today goes? You can tell Ollie that I'll have something for him by the end of business."

"I'll pass that on to Ollie when he calls in and let you know." Sunny made no promises when it came to her boss' reactions. Although Ollie wasn't the wild man he had been when Sunny had first started working for him, he still had his good and bad days—good and bad moods.

"Thanks, Sunny." Neil arranged a tray full of fish filets on a fresh bed of ice and added a sign with the price. He raised his head above the counter and asked, "Is there something else?"

Sunny realized she'd been staring at him, comparing this small businessman starting off his day with the big-shot stock market mobster that Abby had described. Other than his willingness to rock the boat on the local fish business, Sunny still didn't see any trace of that guy.

"I, uh . . ." She stumbled over her words as she realized that Neil was now staring at her in a way she recognized, the look of a man with a secret who wonders if it's somehow gotten out.

For a second, she almost blurted out that she'd been up early to catch Charlie Vane, but she managed to head that off before the words left her mouth. *Not helpful to talk about his wholesale fish coconspirator—and potential murder suspect,* Sunny thought.

Her final response was less than original but had the merit of being true, as far as it went. "Sorry. I didn't get much sleep last night."

No need to mention why, she added inside her head.

Neil nodded in sympathy. "I know what you mean. This hasn't been easy. I never expected—" He broke off, staring at her intently, as if looking for some sign of shared knowledge, a green light for him to speak up.

And then he was looking past her. "Don't look now," Neil said, "but you're being shadowed."

Sunny whirled around to discover a familiar furry figure resting its forepaws on Neil's store window.

"Shadow! What are you doing out there?" She opened the door, and Shadow trotted in, tail high, its tip bent forward, cat body language for *Hi! Nice to see ya!*

It seemed as though he'd completely forgotten the unpleasant circumstances from the last time he'd been in front of Kittery Harbor Fish. Nor was he the least bit embarrassed that Sunny was watching his overtures to Neil.

Maybe a little bit of Nick Gatto peeked out as Neil's attitude suddenly shifted. He laughed, coming around the counter to reach down, letting Shadow sniff his hand before gently rubbing his fingers through the fur between the cat's ears. "This little guy must have some premium stones, coming down here to see what's doing."

Actually, he's been fixed. But Sunny didn't see any use in mentioning that.

After a brief head rub, Neil went back behind the counter. He produced a sharp knife and carefully removed a sliver from one of the filets in his counter display. Standing up again, he prepared to toss the morsel to Shadow but then paused, looking over at Sunny. "Is it all right for him to eat something like this in the morning?"

Sunny glanced over at Shadow who sat back on his haunches, his body erect, eyes locked on the bit of fish in Neil's hand. "He can have a little bit," she responded, shaking her head. "Just not too much."

That smart-aleck voice in the back of her head laughed. *We don't want a rerun of the frog incident.*

10

So this is what it feels like to be a prison warden, Sunny thought, looking up from her desk to see what Shadow had gotten into now. She'd chatted with Neil Garret while he tossed bits of fish to Shadow, who started catching them on the fly. When she thought her cat had eaten enough, she picked him up and brought him to her office, figuring he'd curl up someplace warm and take a nap.

He hadn't.

Instead, Shadow prowled around the office, looking at Sunny and then the door, constantly going to rest his fore paws against the window as if to make sure it was still solid, craning his head as if he were trying to get a look at the fish shop next door. The prisoner didn't just check possible routes of escape, however. He also did his best to sabotage the administration of the prison. Sunny had to keep a sharp eye peeled as Shadow nosed around papers, pawed at the wastebasket, and stared all too fixedly at Sunny's cup of coffee until she finally drained it and tossed the empty container in the trash.

She breathed a sigh of relief when Shadow climbed onto her lap to watch her work. But that relief was short-lived as he eeled his way up onto the desk and across Sunny's keyboard.

And when the computer goes down, they're going to find cat fur in there and void the warranty, she sourly thought while trying to remove a suddenly boneless cat from her work space.

Someone appeared at the entrance to the office, and Shadow suddenly streaked from the desk to the door, with Sunny in hot pursuit. The only glitch in a near perfect escape came when the door didn't open. Will Price stood outside, looking down at Shadow, who faltered, staring up at him.

Sunny managed to swoop down and gather the cat in her arms as Will entered. "Didn't know it was Take Your Cat to Work Day," he said.

"I think Shadow decided it was Take Your Cat to Town Day and stowed away on Dad's pickup." Sunny wanted to tuck back an errant curl that had fallen on her face, but her hands were too taken up with a squirming cat to do the job. Will took care of it, smiling down at her. "That's right. Your dad went along for your meeting with Charlie Vane. So how was your interview with the pirate?"

"Not as many 'Ahhhhrrrs' as I expected, although it looks as though he almost wound up with an eyepatch."

Sunny frowned. "I don't think I'd go so far as to call him a pirate. He says he's a businessman, but he's got a whole set speech to justify anything he does to screw over people he deals with. Somehow, I don't see him getting good citizenship awards anytime soon."

Will nodded. "Think I should bring him in and tighten the screws?"

"I think he'd just batten down his hatches, if you'll excuse the term, at the sight of a cop. The only reason he talked to me is that he didn't take me seriously. A lot of what he had to say started out with 'tell your boyfriend.'"

"He don't know you very well . . . do he?" Will said in his best Bugs Bunny impersonation.

"He knows enough to trot out an alibi," Sunny told him. "According to Vane he was out to sea, fishing with two witnesses."

Will lost some of his good humor. "Anyway, if he had a problem with Garret, why would he kill Treibholz by mistake?"

"Unless someone else was doing the job," Sunny suggested. "Somebody who didn't know Garret by sight." She frowned. "But it would have to be someone he really trusted. His son and son-in-law were on the boat as his alibi witnesses. And from the way he complains about money, I don't think that Vane could afford to hire a pro."

"We'll look into Vane's associates and finances," Will said. "But I still think the root of this whole situation can be found next door—or rather, that it comes from California, like Treibholz."

"I was just next door, and Neil Garret was fooling

around with Shadow, tossing scraps of fish for him to catch. Can you kill a person one day and do that the next?"

Will shrugged. "Distraction, maybe."

"And everything that happened, discovering the body, what was that? An act? Was Neil ready to throw that little production for whoever walked in first thing that morning? He knows you and I are going out, so was it aimed at me?"

"Well, you are next door, a perfect witness, and he is behind on what he owes for the month. Maybe he kinda expected you to come by—or rather, that Ollie would send you over to dun him for the rent." Will shrugged. "Or maybe he just panicked when you walked in."

"Right," Sunny scoffed. "The guy's a mobster, and he just panics."

"Nick Gatto was just a money-shuffler for the mob, not a made man." Will frowned impatiently. "Or maybe he killed Treibholz and staged that whole rigmarole to confuse the issue. Amateur killers—first-timers—have been known to do that."

Sunny remembered the way Neil Garret had frozen in the doorway to the freezer, staring at the dead body on the floor. "Well, if he's an amateur killer, he's a professional actor. I'd swear that he didn't expect to find Treibholz when he opened the freezer door."

"Back in California, the guy was little better than a swindler," Will said. "That involves some acting ability."

"Yeah, but there's a difference between convincing a grandmother to invest her life savings and reacting to a dead body," Sunny argued. "I know how I felt and acted when I stumbled over poor Ada Spruance. I remember it. Sometimes

I dream about it. Neil didn't look as though he was faking when he saw that body."

"Didn't *look*." Will emphasized the word. "When I look at this case, I see motive sticking out a mile high. Phil Treib- holz was a mortal danger to Neil Garret. He recognized him as Nick Gatto and could have hit men turning up here to cash in on the contract Jimmy the Chopper decided to put out on him. As for opportunity, Garret still says he was home read- ing when Treibholz got whacked."

Sunny stared. "You mean he doesn't have an alibi at all? He didn't say anything more?"

"Poor planning on his part," Will said. "Or maybe no planning at all. Maybe he didn't expect to need an alibi. It might have started off as a meeting that took a sudden, dan- gerous turn. Val Overton has been working some federal sources to get the story on Treibholz. He didn't just dig up information, he used it. Word is that he had a thriving side business in blackmail. Maybe he made a demand and things went downhill fast."

"And Neil just happened to shoot him?" Sunny didn't hesi- tate to put a pin in that notion. "I thought Neil came here after serving a term in prison. How would he get hold of a gun?"

Will laughed—sourly. "In the home of the brave and the land of the second amendment? Maine isn't the strictest state when it comes to gun laws. You can get a piece, espe- cially if you're not a law-abiding type."

"So Neil rates high on the MOM chart—motive, oppor- tunity, and means," Sunny had to admit. "But—"

"But you've got a feeling about our strongest suspect," Will finished.

"He's not the only one," Sunny argued.

"The only one who doesn't need to be seriously near-sighted, taking Phil Treibholz for Neil Garret," Will replied.

"We haven't really mentioned that Deke Sweeney guy yet." Sunny frowned. "Charlie Vane threw out a theory that Sweeney might have sent someone to lean on Neil."

"Another case of mistaken identity getting Treibholz shot?" Will sat in silence for a moment. "I talked to some old buddies from the Portsmouth PD. Sweeney doesn't have a criminal record—exactly. Years ago, though, one of the guys in the fish market accused him of pulling a gun and threatening him."

"And that didn't turn into a criminal record?"

Will shrugged. "Charges never got pressed, and the fish merchant left town."

"No part of that story makes Sweeney look very good," Sunny pointed out.

"We'll have to talk to him. And by 'we,' I mean the sheriff's department." Will didn't look happy. "There'll probably be all sorts of jurisdictional hoops to jump through."

"It may be worth it, though," Sunny said. "I'm convinced whoever killed Treibholz wasn't familiar with this area. Otherwise, why leave the body?"

"As a warning—or a message?" Will suggested. "Like the way Treibholz tried to string up your little buddy here." He gestured toward Shadow, who regarded him with unblinking eyes.

"If there's a killer still around here, then why isn't Neil dead?" Sunny wanted to know.

"Maybe he—or she—had orders to make Garret worry. Or suffer."

Sunny didn't like the sound of that. If the killer knew about Abby Martinson, she could wind up at the top of the hit parade. *Another reason to keep her secret safely buried,* she thought. "Well, I think we've talked ourselves into circles long enough." Will glanced at the wall clock. "How do you feel about lunch?"

"I'd love to grab a bite. But"—Sunny pointed toward Shadow—"I'm afraid my lunch hour is going to be spent getting this little guy home. Dad should be done with his walk and his errands. I'm going to give him a call and get Shadow back where he belongs."

As if anticipating that the humans were finishing their business and that Will would leave, Shadow had already started edging toward the door.

"Oh, no." Sunny sprang from her chair and managed to grab Shadow before he could dodge. She caught hold of him by the fur at the scruff of his neck and brought him up. That was the handle that mama cats used to move their kittens around. Sunny had read that holding a cat that way could trigger old kitten instincts.

It seemed to work. Shadow calmed down and drew in his paws for easier carrying. Sunny took some of his weight in her other hand and said, "Wouldn't you like to go home where it's warm and you have your own food? You didn't like it last night when we went out at a strange time. You're doing the same thing now. Let's go home."

Will gave her a skeptical look. "How much of that do you think he understands?

"More than we probably think." Still holding Shadow, she dug out her keys and gave them to Will. "I'll have to depend on you to lock the door and open the car," she told him. "Holding onto Shadow may be a two-handed job."

Claire Donally

Sunny put him gently down on the desk and got her coat. Shadow sat watching her. When she came toward him again, he didn't run away but submitted to being picked up by his scruff. Sunny wrapped her free arm around and under him, supporting his weight while still maintaining her scruff hold.

"Hang on," Will said, moving ahead and opening the door. Sunny exited and walked to her truck while Will locked the office door. Then he hurried on ahead to unlock the Wrangler. Sunny took her seat, bringing Shadow down onto her lap as Will inserted the key into the ignition.

"I'm surprised you made it this far," he said as he closed the door. He leaned close to the window, his voice muffled as he said, "Good luck getting him out."

Sunny gently petted the cat in her lap before getting out her cell phone. After a quick phone chat with her father, she started the engine. "One thing at a time," she said. "One thing at a time."

*

Shadow rested his head on his paws as he lay across Sunny's lap. It was cold, even inside the go-fast thing, and she was warm. Sunny's other place could be interesting. It certainly had some odd smells. But he looked forward to the familiar scents of home. It would be good to come back to his bowl of water and food. He stirred a little. And his litter box. He was going to need that soon enough, after the fish the Generous One had given him.

He settled down again as Sunny's hand gently stroked his fur. They were going home. He didn't have to look out the windows to see that.

*

Midday traffic was fairly thin. Sunny managed the drive out to Wild Goose Lane without any trouble. After parking in the driveway, she gathered Shadow up in her arms and headed for the front door.

Mike must have been watching for her, because the door swung open. "No blood spilled. And I didn't see you engaged in a spirited game of Catch the Cat after you parked. What's the matter, furball?" he asked Shadow. "You feeling tired?"

Sunny carried Shadow into the kitchen and set him down. The cat walked over to his bowls and lapped up a quick slurp of water. Then with a quick glance over his shoulder, he headed away—toward his litter box, Sunny realized.

"Well, Dad, I think we avoided a cat-tastrophe," she told Mike. "I guess I should be glad Will stopped by the office. I don't know how I'd have gotten Shadow outside and into the Wrangler without him."

"It's a shame you're wasting your lunch delivering the furball instead of spending time with Will," Mike said. "I know which I'd prefer you to be doing."

"Oh?" Sunny asked. "And were you going to come to town and collect the dreaded cat?"

Mike's startlingly blue eyes twinkled. "Do you want the fatherly answer or the honest answer?"

"The honest one," Sunny told him, laughing.

"I wouldn't touch that job without a cat carrier, a dart gun, and reinforcements," Mike said. "I've seen what that animal can be like when he decides to be uncooperative."

Claire Donally

Shadow returned, took a slow spin around their ankles, and turned to his food bowl.

"There's a good idea," Mike said. "I could make you a sandwich before you head back. We're well stocked with all that healthy stuff you insist on feeding me."

He quickly whipped up a low-sodium turkey and low-fat cheese sandwich on grainy bread with a shot of honey dijon mustard. It went down pretty well with a glass of seltzer. Mike joined her at the kitchen table with the same lunch. "I still think you'd have a better time with Will," Mike insisted after chewing a bite.

"He came by for work," Sunny told him. "Wanted to hear what Charlie Vane had to tell me."

"He was pretty forthcoming, I thought." Mike took a sip of seltzer and grinned. "Didn't have to bring out the rubber hose or anything."

"Yeah, but most of it was covering his you-know-what." Sunny frowned in thought. "He did take a swipe at Deke Sweeney, though. What do you know about the guy?"

Mike prided himself on his near encyclopedic knowledge of people and things around Kittery Harbor. Portsmouth, though, was a little out of his orbit, as he himself admitted.

"That is across the river," Mike said. "Most of what I know about Sweeney I get from my fishing buddies. He's the boogeyman of the Portsmouth fish market. Buying or selling, his word is pretty much the law."

"Who died and left him boss?" Sunny wanted to know. "Was he a fisherman or a fish merchant?"

"He was—muscle, I guess," Mike replied. "Back in the day, the Portsmouth market was a pretty rough place. Different factions of merchants were competing to run the place, getting in one another's way, and fighting. That was bad for business. Several of the bigger merchants brought Sweeney in to impose some order. But by the time the dust settled, they weren't giving the orders, he was."

"Will told me a story about him pulling a gun on someone."

Mike nodded. "I heard that story, too. It happened shortly after he came into the market. One of the merchants ran his mouth and made the mistake of picking up a fileting knife. I guess in that case, gun trumped knife. Usually, though, Sweeney was more indirect. Troublemakers had accidents, or suffered business disasters."

"Like the one he arranged for Charlie Vane and Neil Garret," Sunny said.

"Nobody got their kneecaps broken."

"But somebody ended up dead in a fish freezer." When Sunny saw Shadow stop eating to stare at her, she lowered her voice. "Could Garret have been such a threat to Sweeney's business—to his control over the market—that he had to be taken out?"

Mike was silent for a moment. "I don't think so," he said slowly. "But I don't know the market, or the man, well enough to be sure."

They finished their sandwiches in silence. Then Sunny rose, knelt to give Shadow a head scratch, and told him to be good.

"Right," Mike said as he got up from his seat.

Sunny had a moment of worry as she opened the door, but at that moment a gust of wind blew in like a spike of freezing-cold air. Shadow actually retreated. Sunny closed the door with the cat on the right side, got in her Wrangler, and headed back to work.

Traffic wasn't a problem, but parking was. Sunny actually had to walk a couple of blocks to get to the office. She passed Neil Garret's fish market and noticed several customers.

That looks like a good sign, she thought.

No sooner did she come through the door than she noticed the blinking light on the answering machine. "It's Ollie," the familiar voice of her boss came from the speaker. "Just checking in on the rent situation with Neil Garret."

Sighing, Sunny pulled her parka back on and went next door. "Got a call from Ollie," she said to Neil as he turned to her after helping a customer.

He nodded. "Tell him I'll definitely be in tonight," he promised.

Sunny returned to the office to call Ollie's cell phone and pass along the good news.

"Fine," Ollie replied. "I'll be there."

Sunny worked through the rest of the day wondering which was worse—Ollie turning up unannounced, or waiting it out until Ollie arrived? She discovered that Shadow had left a memento from his visit. Somehow he'd managed to sneak into the bathroom and unspool half the roll of toilet paper. In the end, she tossed the evidence and replaced the roll, hoping that Ollie wasn't monitoring TP use as an office expense.

She was dealing with a flurry of late-in-the-day e-mail traffic when Ollie finally turned up. He nodded to her as she talked on the phone with a B and B provider, collected a file from the locked cabinets in the rear of the office, and spread papers on a desk to peruse.

It was dead dark outside when Neil Garret appeared at the office door. Ollie looked up from his reading as Neil came in and shamefacedly approached his desk. He carried a plastic bag printed with the logo of his store which he placed in front of Ollie. "Figured you might as well have it in cash," Neil said.

"Better than trying to pay me in fish." Ollie reached into the bag, removed a sheaf of bills, and began counting them out. "You know, I could charge you a late fee."

Neil winced as if he'd taken a body blow.

"But I'll let it slide—this month." He finished counting, nodded, and said, "All there. Sunny, can you make out a receipt?"

It took longer than she liked, checking through desk drawers to find the printed pad. With so much of the business online, she rarely had to deal with cash anymore. Sunny filled in the appropriate spaces and handed the receipt to Neil, comparing the smiling guy who'd fooled with Shadow earlier in the day with the tense, silent man who took the slip of paper.

"Always a pleasure doing business with you, Neil." Ollie's eyes went back to his papers. "Let's hope we don't have these kinds of problems next month."

"Yes." Neil unbent a little as he headed for the door. "Good evening, Sunny."

As he went out, a swirl of wind came in the open door. Ollie darted out a hand to hold down the pile of bills on his desk.

"Should I get the cash box for those?" Sunny asked.

Ollie shook his head. "I think I'll make a bank run—" He broke off, grabbing for the money as the door opened again. This time Will and Val Overton entered.

"Damn, we are definitely in the wrong business, Will," the federal marshal said, pointing to the cash under Ollie's fingers.

"Neil Garret's rent." Ollie fumbled the money back into the bag Neil had left. "I'm going to deposit it in the bank."

"We'll come with," Val offered. "You'll feel safer with two armed officers on either side. Although with a windfall like that, maybe you ought to take us out and treat us."

Will glanced at his boisterous companion. "I was wondering if you'd like to go out." He leaned a little closer, lowering his voice. "To make up for that lunch. Val offered to come along."

"Ollie, you should come, too," Val said with her gleaming smile. "We'll make it a double date."

Ollie tried to back out, but Val wouldn't hear of it. "Come on. You can go to the bank, and then we'll head over to the Brickhouse."

"That's the Redbrick," Will said.

"Why not?" Ollie said, trying to accept defeat gracefully. Sunny shut down the computer, she and Ollie got their coats, and they left the office.

Sunny shivered as a blast of wind caught her in the face. "Damn. It's gotten even colder."

Ollie just hunched down, clutching the bag of cash. They caught the bank just before it closed, Ollie hurriedly filling out the deposit slip.

Guess they'll be a little later getting out tonight,

counting all of that, Sunny thought. *A problem I don't encounter these days.* She took the opportunity to take out her cell phone and call her dad. "Will asked me out for the evening," she reported. "Will you be okay for supper?"

"So you'll get to see him after all. That's good," Mike said. "Don't worry about me. I've got soup and lots of that healthy glop to make a sandwich. And your friend won't miss you. At last report, he was asleep on the couch."

Sunny laughed. "Okay, Dad. I won't be too late. It's a school night, after all."

"Not to be a party pooper, but early would be better," Mike told her. "I've been watching the news, and they're talking about a storm blowing in later."

"The wind's getting stronger even now." Outside the bank, Sunny watched a woman vainly clutch for the hood of her parka as a stiff breeze flipped it back. Sunny said good-bye to her father and then turned to Will and Val. "Dad says the weather is going to take a turn for the worse. So if we do this, we should keep it short."

Val Overton watched Ollie come back from the teller's counter. "Just have to make the most of our time." She grabbed his arm and wrapped it in hers. "Lead on, you gorgeous man."

Her outrageous flirting kept Ollie flustered all the way to the Redbrick and through the first round of beers. By the second round, his face was pinker, but he'd loosened up. Val asked him about local business conditions, and he gave his opinions freely while she seemed to hang on to his every word.

Sunny glanced at Will, who gave her a crooked smile and a shrug. *Well, this is turning into a real hot date for a cold night,* she thought. *I could have had a better time if I'd stayed in the office and worked.*

Then Val steered the conversation to the fishing business, and Sunny realized that Will and the Fed actually were working.

"Sportfishing, as a tourist attraction, still holds up," Ollie said. "But the thing there is the excursion, the experience, rather than the catch."

"My dad says a lot of people go on those jaunts for the beer rather than the fish," Sunny remarked. "If they catch anything, they leave it to spoil."

"Just as I was saying." Ollie nodded. "Commercial fishing, people who have to depend on what they catch, that's something I'd never touch." He went on to give a pretty detailed and thoughtful history of local fishing and its problems—especially with government control.

"With the government cutting down the fishing season for some types and reducing maximum catches, I don't see any way the local fishermen are going to get back to the good old days they're always talking about," he said. "Seems to me like a very expensive way to go out of business."

"How about business when the fish finally get to land?" Val asked.

Ollie looked as if someone had mixed vinegar in his beer. "Frankly, it's not as good as I had thought. As you know, I rented a property to a fellow opening a fish store, and I got taken in by statistics showing that American households were trying to get more fish in their diets."

"That's what everybody says," Will said.

"Yeah, but around here, how do you expect that to happen

when a pound of fish can cost as much or more than a pound of prime steak?" Ollie gave his beer a rueful look. "That pile of cash you were kidding me about was late rent on that store. I'm not at all sure Neil will be able to come up with next month's payment."

"So is it a retail problem, or a wholesale problem?" Val asked.

"Both," Ollie replied. "The local wholesale fish market is in Portsmouth. It doesn't do the business of big markets like New York or Boston, or even Gloucester, where there are still some processing plants. They're caught between a declining number of fishing boats servicing them, subpar catches, and rising prices. Like I said, not a business I'd want to put money into."

Sunny exchanged a glance with Will. *If business is getting bad at the market, maybe Deke Sweeney isn't sitting as pretty as Charlie Vane thinks he is.*

Their burgers arrived, and the conversation went into other channels. Sunny kept an eye on the time, and even though Val Orton pouted, the party broke up pretty early. The marshal did plant a big smooch on Ollie, which turned him bright red and left Sunny wondering how far Val was taking this joke.

The weather had gotten even worse when they emerged from the Redbrick, continuous blustery winds and a very fine sleet that left exposed skin feeling as if it had been sandblasted. Val was staying at a national chain motel. "It's on a main road, so it shouldn't be a problem," she said.

Will turned to Ollie. "Can you follow her in your Land Rover? This has all the signs of turning into an ice storm."

"I can handle it," Val insisted.

Will shook his head. "That's what people think until the weather really turns on them. I'd do it myself, but I've got to get Sunny home."

For a second, Sunny was tempted to argue, but the memory of her mother's accident shut her up. *Let's not tempt fate,* she thought.

From the look Ollie was giving her, he must have remembered what had happened to her mom, too. "I'll be your wing man up to the motel," he told Val in a gruff voice. "Bad weather in these parts is nothing to fool around with." His Land Rover was actually parked the nearest to the tavern, so he gave them lifts to their various vehicles. Sunny stayed in her Wrangler, warming it up, until Will's pickup truck pulled up beside her.

The ride to Wild Goose Drive wasn't all that bad. They kept a careful speed, and except for a couple of times when the wind did its best to rock the boxy SUV, nothing exciting really happened. Sunny parked her Wrangler and then climbed into the cab of Will's truck to say good night. "So did Ollie have anything to add to your case?" she asked as Will put an arm around her.

"Just more reason to have a chat with Deke Sweeney—as soon as the weather permits." He turned to look at Sunny. "I'm sorry that this turned into a fact-finding mission instead of a date date. But Val was kind of insistent."

"On information, or going out with Ollie?" Sunny asked. "She played it for laughs before, but now she's got me wondering if she's got a thing for older guys."

"Is that a problem?" Will asked, looking puzzled.

"In case you didn't notice, Neil Garret is a good-looking older guy," Sunny pointed out.

And Val Orton is a lonely gal who doesn't have much of a social life—and incidentally carries a gun, she silently added. *Could she have more going on with Neil Garret than a witness and protector relationship? And could she have used that gun if Phil Treibholz threatened Neil?*

11

The air outside the car seemed even colder after the warm good night kiss. And the sleet had turned sloppy, more like icy mush flying into Sunny's face as she hung onto her hood. She turned back and knocked on the window. Will brought it down. "Forget something?" he asked.

"Just that I want you to call when you get home," Sunny told him. "It's getting worse even quicker than we thought, and I want to be sure that you get back safely."

Will rolled his eyes. "Okay, Mom." Then, belatedly remembering what had happened to Sunny's mother, he said, "Sorry. I'll call. Promise."

Sunny leaned in through the window for another kiss, then stepped back, waving, as Will drove off. She turned and made her way up a driveway that seemed to get slicker with every step until she reached the front door. Fumbling with the key, Sunny got the door open and stepped inside, stamping heavily to remove the slush sticking to her boots.

Shadow arrived in the middle of her ice removal dance. Sunny noticed that he didn't do his usual circle and sniff routine, avoiding the melting glop sinking into the bristly fabric of the foul-weather rug they kept near the door. He waited until he had her boots off, intercepting Sunny as she headed for the arched entrance to the living room. Even then, he kept his inspection brief, wrinkling his nose at the cold that clung to Sunny's legs after her short trip through the storm.

Sunny poked her head into the room to find her father dozing in front of a reality TV show he wouldn't have tolerated if he'd been fully awake.

"Hey, Dad," Sunny called.

Mike woke up, smiled at her, frowned at the TV, and then used the remote to turn the program off. "A boring night," he announced. "I hope you had a better time."

"I wouldn't score it high for romance," Sunny told him. "Val Overton came with, and she dragged Ollie along as her date."

"That could have been entertaining." Mike sat up straighter and stretched. "Did she chase him very hard? Did Ollie let himself get caught?"

"Mainly Will and Val picked Ollie's brains about the local fish business and the situation in the market over in Portsmouth."

Mike laughed. "Oh, boy. Lots of love stuff." He paused as the wind suddenly picked up, flinging semisolid sleet against the window. "Sounds as though you got home just in time."

Sunny nodded, dropping into a chair. "I asked Will to call when he gets in. Maybe I'm being too much on the nannyish side—"

Mike shook his head. "No. Not with this kind of weather."

She rose and went to give her dad a hug. His arms went around her, and they stood together for a moment, not speaking.

The moment was broken as Shadow jumped up onto the couch, leaning into the hug as well.

Mike cleared his throat, and Sunny laughed, leaning down to pet the cat. "You didn't want to be left out, did you?"

Reaching out carefully, Mike stroked Shadow's fur, too. "I think your mom would have liked the little guy."

"Right," Sunny said. "Until he tried to walk along the keyboard of her piano."

"Hey," Mike spoke up in defense, "she barely let *me* touch that thing."

They smiled at the happier memory. Then the phone rang.

"Safely arrived," Will reported. "Although I don't know how long I'll be here. The weather forecast is getting rougher, and there's a good chance the sheriff will call everybody in while they can still get to headquarters." He paused for a second. "But I didn't want you to worry."

"No problems," Sunny told him. "And look on the bright side. Overtime."

"Yeah. When I get a day off again, we'll have a nice evening out somewhere—without any tagalongs." Will sighed. "Till then . . ."

"I know." Sunny was silent for a moment. "Be careful out there, and good luck."

They said good-bye, and she hung up the phone. When she turned to Mike, he was struggling to contain a mighty yawn. "Overtime?" he said. "Is he going out in this weather?"

"Not yet," Sunny said. "But he expects to be called." She put a hand over her mouth as she yawned, too. "Nothing much we can do about it. I vote for B-E-D."

"Sounds like a plan." Mike got up from the couch and stretched. Then they headed up the stairs, with Shadow trailing behind them.

*

Patrolling the house in the dark, Shadow pricked his ears. He knew it was just the wind outside, but it howled like some huge, angry beast. And the stuff from the skies rattled against the walls as if that beast were scratching at them, trying to get in.

He trotted over to the stairway and began leaping up the steps two at a time, trying to work off his unease. Upstairs, he made his way down the hall to Sunny's room.

Might as well check things out, he thought, easing his way through the slightly open door.

Sunny lay on her side, unconsciously hunched up against the noises from outside. Shadow lightly jumped up onto the bed and daintily made his way over the hills and valleys of the covers to where Sunny's head rested on the pillow. Her eyes were closed, and she breathed evenly. Fast asleep. Outside, the howl rose in intensity. Shadow shot a worried glance at the window. But it was closed, and it wasn't too cold in here.

He could feel the warmth rising from Sunny's body, and carefully edged his way under the covers to share it.

Shadow crept into her arms. Even in her sleep, Sunny made a pleased noise and ran her fingers over his fur.

Shadow snuggled closer. *Well, if it makes her feel better . . .*

The howling outside seemed to fade a bit as he closed his eyes.

*

Sunny opened her eyes, surprised to hear a faint mew as Shadow stirred beside her. "What are you doing here?" she asked him as he pushed his head against her, looking for a scratch between the ears. Sunny obliged, but she frowned. On a good day, she could manage to get her eyes open just before the alarm went off. She'd gotten to bed early last night, so maybe she was up a little earlier than usual. But dim as her room was, it was brighter than her normal wake-up hour. She looked at the clock-radio—no digital display.

Rising from bed, she shivered as she got her cell phone from the bedside table. An hour past her usual time. She tried the lamp—nothing. Sunny walked to the window, finding the air even colder the closer she came. And there really wasn't a view. Flying ice had frozen in place, creating a sort of pebbled glass effect.

She went to the closet, got out her heaviest robe, and headed downstairs. The house was definitely chillier than usual, but as she reached the front hall, she heard voices in the kitchen. Sunny paused for a second, getting a brief head-butt in the back of her right calf. Shadow was sticking pretty close to her this morning.

After a moment, Sunny realized it was the news radio station and walked in just as the kettle began to wail. Mike rose from his seat at the table, took the kettle, and poured the boiling water into a teapot. "No coffee maker this morning," he said. "The power's out."

He pointed to the old transistor radio on the table. "Lucky we still have that around, and plenty of batteries. Matches, too, otherwise I wouldn't have been able to light the burner."

Sunny stepped over to the kitchen door. This side of the house must have been sheltered from the wind, because she could see through the glass storm door. The backyard had been transformed into a winter wonderland, gleaming even in the dull light thanks to a coating of ice on everything: bushes, tree trunks, the patio fence—even a couple of holdout leaves glittered in the glaze.

It was as if everything in the world had been carefully preserved under glass . . . except for the tree limb that had broken off and landed on the ground.

That, and probably hundreds more, Sunny thought, turning back to the table and taking a seat. A moment later, she had a steaming cup of tea in front of her and had woken up enough to make sense of the reports coming from the radio. Foreign wars, politics, and pestilence were all shoved to the back of the line this morning, as the news anchors talked about car accidents and local power outages.

"You don't have to worry about work," Mike told her. "The sheriff's told everybody to stay in because basically there's nowhere to go. They're still trying to clear the bridges to Portsmouth and the interstate. Any of the other local roads are either skating ponds or have downed trees across them." He glanced over at her. "Looks like we're in for a siege."

He rose and went back to the stove. Sunny realized he'd

replaced the kettle with a pot of water. "Looks like oatmeal instead of toast today—unless you figure on grilling the bread outside on the barbecue."

Sunny shuddered, looking at the frozen landscape. "Oatmeal sounds fine to me. Nice, warm oatmeal."

They spent the day hunkered down, reading as the clouds cleared away and the light got better. Shadow was in his glory, enjoying an unexpected play day with Sunny. Apparently his nighttime nap left him bursting with energy, which he used to race around the house, flying into Sunny's lap and in numerous vigorous games of Pounce on the String.

The landline telephones worked, and Mike insisted on calling Helena Martinson.

Sure, Sunny thought, *it's the Kittery Harbor Way. And she is his girlfriend or whatever.*

After a low-toned conversation with Helena, Mike turned to Sunny. "Abby would like to speak to you."

Helena's daughter seemed in a pretty good mood. "Now I really remember why I moved to California," she joked. "We were on the phone with the power company. Mom spotted a downed line from our upstairs window. And thank heavens you guys called. Mom was about to dispatch me over there to make sure you were all right. It wouldn't have been too bad getting down our driveway—Mom had me salting that last night. But the rest of the way, I'd have to see if I still fit into my high school ice skates."

Sunny felt a pang of guilt, remembering how Mike had urged her to go out and enjoy herself the night before.

At least he wasn't lugging around bags of ice melt, she thought.

"How are you guys fixed for supplies?" she asked.

"We also did an end-of-the-world shopping expedition before the weather got too bad—and the stores got too crazy," Abby said. "So if you need anything, we probably have a couple weeks' supply of it. Afterward we crashed. Talk about an exciting night." She paused for a moment. "Mom mentioned you were going out." Abby sounded a little wistful. "How was it?"

"Fine, if you don't mind having your boss tag along." Sunny cut herself off there. Yes, she was annoyed that her father had gossiped about her evening with Will. *On the other hand, Abby had a boss she definitely didn't mind going out with.* "I guess it was all right, but getting home was sloppy and it was beginning to get dangerous." She sighed. "And speaking of salting, I guess I have to go out and play catch-up now."

She gave the phone back to Mike, bundled up, and headed for the kitchen door. Shadow accompanied her that far. He put a curious paw down on the ice-covered ground, slid a little, and pulled himself back inside. As Sunny stepped out, she was aware of him giving her that odd look he usually reserved for watching humans do something he apparently regarded as foolish.

Maybe he's right, Sunny thought as she skidded her way to the garage. She was really glad Mike hadn't tried this. *If I fall, there's a chance I might bounce,* she thought. *I'm afraid Dad might break something.*

It was a surprising amount of work, making progress with baby steps, and her thighs began to hurt by the time she reached the garage. Sunny got the door open and rooted around for the sacks of ice melt Mike always kept on hand. After all, he used to deliver the stuff all over the Northeast. He'd consider it a professional embarrassment if he didn't have a generous supply ready to go.

She found an open sack and began spreading the granules in front of the garage door. Then she went to dig out the metal scraper with the long handle. It was tedious, tiresome work, especially out in the cold. Mike made her take several breaks to come in and have a cup of hot chocolate. He might not be able to do the job himself anymore, but he wanted to make sure Sunny was well fueled.

The light was beginning the fade by the time she finished, but Sunny managed to clear a path from the door to both trucks in the driveway, and then a wider passage to let the vehicles get to the road.

Not that we'll be driving soon, she thought. *Wild Goose Drive is a sheet of ice.*

They made supper by the light of two LED lanterns that Mike had picked up. "We'll save the candles until we really need them," he said.

The meal was simple: canned soup heated up on the top burner and thick sandwiches. They couldn't cook anything on the stove, and Sunny was afraid that without power, the refrigerator wouldn't keep the cold cuts fresh.

Shadow had his usual canned food and fresh water, but he kept turning from his bowls to regard the two lanterns up on the kitchen table.

"Don't even think about it," Sunny warned him.

She and Mike each took a light into the living room, where they also took the radio to hear how the recovery process was going. CMP had managed to restore power to a lot of folks nearby, so Mike rose and switched on one of the living room lamps. It stayed dark.

"But if it goes on, we'll know we're back in business," he said.

They sat for a while, talking in the dim light. Sunny played a few more games with Shadow and kept him from trying to play with the lanterns glowing on the coffee table.

She was just about to suggest that they turn in when the lamp that Mike had turned on suddenly popped to life. Sunny blinked—the lamp's bulb was a heck of a lot brighter than the LEDs.

Mike went to the window, looking out at the street. Light began to appear in the windows of the houses across the way. "Yep, they noticed," he said. Then he frowned. "And here comes a damned fool."

A vehicle made its way slowly along the dark, deserted street. At first, Sunny couldn't even make it out. All she saw were headlights. It was a dark car, no, a pickup truck that skidded to a halt at the bottom of the driveway. When the driver opened his door, the dome light revealed Will Price's features.

"Well, maybe not such a fool," Mike said.

"What would bring him up here?" Sunny went back to the kitchen to open the door.

Will came slowly up the drive, checking carefully to make sure there was no black ice to slip on. He'd changed his clothes since their date the night before, but he had a day's growth of beard, and his eyes looked tired.

"Are you okay?" Sunny asked.

"Had about enough time to change into some fouler

weather gear before Lenore Nesbit called me in," Will said. "Then a lot of slow-motion driving to accident scenes and enforcing no-drive restrictions. I was heading off people from using the road to Sturgeon Springs. A whole tree went down, cutting the route completely. Then, after we completed the emergency stuff, we went on a lot of well-being checks. One caught my attention. Charlie Vane's wife—or almost ex-wife, considering she moved out on him a couple of months ago—called that he wasn't answering his phone. We checked with the son, he hadn't heard from his father, and his car was out of commission since before the storm. The Vane place is on the edge of town, so I said I'd stop by on my way back in."

He reported all this in his usual cop voice, but Sunny caught an undertone that she didn't like. "Something happened to Charlie Vane?"

Will nodded. "Three gunshots. Recently dead. And, as if that wasn't enough, the place was like an arsenal, enough rifles and pistols around to outfit an army—or at least a platoon. Let's just say, a lot more than for personal use, unless personal use involved starting a war. And he had all new locks—the place was like a fortress."

He tried to joke, but his expression remained grim. "Looks as though he went from playing Pirates of the Caribbean to the Alamo."

12

After taking a moment to digest what Will had said, Sunny asked, "Can we tell my dad?"

Will shrugged. "It will be on the news soon enough. After they get through with this 'storm of the century' stuff."

Sunny led the way into the living room. "Charlie Vane is dead," she announced. "Will found him tonight."

Mike paused in the middle of turning on a few more lamps. "From the look on your faces, I don't expect it was some run-of-the-mill thing like a car crash or hypothermia."

"Shot," Will said. "With all this weather stuff going on, it will take a while for the crime-scene guys to arrive and get to work." He paused for a second. "Have you ever been in Vane's place?"

"A long time ago, when he was more prosperous. It was a nice little place, away from the built-up part of town but close enough to the docks. Charlie's father built it, and Charlie's wife kept it spotless." Mike shook his head. "Too bad about that."

"You knew that Vane's wife had left him?" Will asked.

"More like she got tired of trying to hold on," Mike said. "I didn't see much good coming from airing that piece of dirty linen. Whatever Charlie got up to, Eileen would never be a part of it."

He frowned, looking at the floor for a moment. "But with a murder involved, I will tell you something odd I heard. Not about Charlie, but his son, Jack. He's trying to keep a wife and son on what he makes on Charlie's boat, and lately it's been a real struggle. Kid has to drive around in an old wreck—the kind of car mechanics call a moneymaker. The owner can't afford to replace it, so he limps along from one repair to another to keep it running. A mechanic who's not bothered with a conscience can string along that kind of situation pretty profitably. But Sal DiGillio told me—"

"I wouldn't think Sal DiGillio was that kind of mechanic," Sunny objected.

"He's not," Mike replied, "and that's the thing. He wouldn't work on Jack's car because the kid couldn't scrape up what it would take to fix the wreck properly. But about a month ago, Jack came to Sal's shop with the money to do the work. Sal fixed the car, but when I went to his station for gas the other day, he was aggravated because something new had died on Jack's car. All his work for nothing, and the kid is still behind the eight ball."

"Was Charlie Vane into guns?" Will asked.

Mike peered at him in bafflement. "Unless it was about

shooting fish in a barrel. No, I take even that back. Charlie was a fisherman. He didn't hunt, he didn't trap, he didn't even go after lobsters. I'd be really surprised that he even owned a gun." His frown deepened. "You're not saying he could have used a gun on himself?"

"No, but he had a house full of the things," Will said. "Cheap revolvers, more high-end deals, long guns too. Some hunting rifles with big magazines, shotguns, a regular arsenal."

"And now he ends up shot." Mike shook his head. "I don't know what I can tell you."

"But it's out of character for Charlie Vane." Will jumped in.

"That's not the Charlie I knew," Mike said.

"Maybe it's a case of dead men tell no tales," Sunny suggested.

Will gave her a skeptical look. "Back to the pirates again, huh? But who made the man dead? Not so long ago, you were suggesting that Vane hired someone to kill Neil Garret, but they got Phil Treibholz instead." He thought for a moment. "Of course if Garret knew about that, he could have returned the favor."

"Wait a minute," Sunny said as something struck her. "Neil lives up in Sturgeon Springs. And you said the road out there was blocked by a fallen tree."

Will nodded. "So if he was in town killing Charlie Vane, he'd be trapped there, or crawling along an alternate route home." He turned to Mike. "Could I borrow your phone for a moment?"

On getting the okay, Will quickly dialed. "I need a check on a Neil Garret in Sturgeon Springs—you have the address on file. Is the south road still blocked? Yeah. So you'll have to send a car from Elmet."

He hung up and smiled. "So, if he's not home, we'll have him."

"Excellent police work," Sunny told him, "but that's not what I was thinking. We've got two dead bodies: a crooked California private eye, and a fisherman who's willing to do anything to keep his business going. What if they found out or knew something that had to be kept secret?"

Will glanced at Mike then turned to Sunny, his expression reminding her that they had secrets of their own. "My money is still on Garret."

"But there could be someone else," she argued. "Someone with a motive we don't even know about."

"We've got a perfectly good suspect as it is." Will must have heard the tone of complaint in his voice, because he started over again. "Why do we need a hypothetical killer when we have one already? What could this unknown motive be?"

"Blackmail," Sunny suggested. "The fewer people who know a secret, the more lucrative it could be."

She decided not to push it, because the scenarios spinning around in her mind weren't things she could talk about in front of Mike—or even discuss with Will, until she had something more solid than a theory.

Or maybe the motive was protecting Neil Garret, she thought. *I already wondered about Val Overton. But what about Abby Martinson? She says that she and Helena had an early night. Abby could have gone out to deal with Charlie Vane and been back before all traffic was restricted.* Sunny turned away, frowning. *Maybe this whole trip back to Kittery Harbor is because of Neil. Oh, Abby put on a pretty good act after seeing him in the window. But she's supposed to be an actress.*

She sighed. This was something she'd never have considered in the simpler if somewhat lonelier days when she first came back to her old hometown, before murders and killers seemed to swirl around the streets like bad weather. *I'll start suspecting Dad next,* she scolded herself. *Or Shadow.*

Maybe Shadow heard her thinking his name, because he appeared from under the coffee table, his paw hooking around in an attempt to snag one of the lanterns.

"Oh, no you don't." Sunny swooped in to rescue the lantern and turn it off. "No need to waste the batteries."

Mike nodded, getting the other lantern. Will dropped to one knee, holding out his hand in a "stop" gesture. "Hey, little guy, maybe you don't want—"

He stopped in surprise as Shadow suddenly reared back and raised a paw to land in Will's palm, like a cat version of a high-five.

Will stared at Sunny. "Did you teach him that?"

"Oh, yeah," she replied. "I train cats to do tricks in my copious spare time. Like Shadow would cooperate with something like that."

They all laughed at that thought. Then Will said, "Look, I'm still on the clock. I have to get back up to Levett."

"Be careful on the roads," Mike said.

"Definitely," Will replied. "I've seen enough bad examples in the last day. Anyway, I'm glad you got your power back."

Will and Sunny walked to the kitchen door and shared a quick good-bye kiss. "Still can't get over that cat," Will said. Then the storm door closed behind him and he headed down the driveway.

Sunny became aware of a furry presence down around her ankles and bent to pick up Shadow. His warmth was welcome after the blast of cold air she'd just gotten.

"I see you didn't show up until the door was closed and winter was safely kept outside," she told the cat.

Shadow just shifted in her arms and purred, looking out into the night.

*

Perched in Sunny's arms, Shadow let his eyes follow Sunny's He as he went to his go-fast thing. It had been so long since he'd played the paw game, he'd almost forgotten it. One of the two-legs he'd lived with used to play it, patiently kneeling with his big paw out until Shadow raised his paw to tap it. Then Shadow got a treat.

Which reminds me . . .

Shadow twisted to look up at Sunny, who still stood peering after the go-fast thing's lights disappearing down the road.

I guess Sunny doesn't know about the treat part of the game, he thought. *I'll have to teach her about that.*

He really couldn't complain, though. It had been a good day, and they'd had a lot of fun together. His jaw suddenly opened in a big yawn. He'd spent a lot more time awake than usual today, even with his dark-time nap.

Shadow settled back into Sunny's embrace. *I hope they decide to go to bed soon,* he thought, remembering how they'd snuggled together under the covers. *That would be a good thing.*

*

Sunny opened her eyes to predawn grayness. She leaned over to check the clock radio and relaxed when the display showed she still had half an hour before her official wake-up time. Then she reached over to get her cell phone and double-check the time.

She stretched and sat up in bed. Maybe it would be just as well to get up now. If the roads had been cleared, she'd have a jump on the day. If not, she could always head back for a little more sleep.

Stepping out into the hallway, Sunny saw Shadow appear at the top of the stairs. The cat came forward to wind his way around her legs before preceding her down the steps.

The kitchen was empty, and Sunny switched on the lights to banish the gloom. *Looks as though I even beat Dad down,* she thought, heading for the coffeemaker. Once that was charged up and ready to go, she turned on the radio. The weather and traffic report promised no more ice from the skies and a steadily improving travel situation.

Sunny shrugged. *Looks like no hookey today.* She busied herself refilling Shadow's bowls and getting a pot of water for oatmeal set up on the stove as Mike padded in, drawn by the scent of brewing coffee.

"I figure this means the winter wonderland out there has been cleaned up enough for you to get in to work." He squinted up at the wall clock. "Guess it wouldn't hurt to start a little earlier."

"They've cleared the major roads, and it's possible to get around if you're careful—or so the guy on the radio says." She sighed. "I do need to get some stuff done at the office, so I'm heading in. I don't know what's going on up in outlet-land—"

"I'll tell you one thing that won't go on—my walk," Mike said. "I figure the less traffic out and around today, the better. Besides, missing two days won't be such a big deal."

Sunny just nodded, grateful she didn't face an argument over Mike's usual schedule. They prepared breakfast and ate it, listening to the news reports. "Doesn't sound too bad," Mike had to admit. "Go on upstairs. I'll take care of the dishes."

He didn't need to repeat the offer. Sunny mounted the stairs, took a shower, and got dressed. She went to the front hall to get her coat and then went back to the kitchen. Dad had returned to the table, listening to the radio. Shadow sat on his haunches, watching her.

Sunny leaned down and gave her father a peck on the cheek. "Okay, I'm off. Wish me luck."

"Good luck," Mike said. "And if it's worse out there than the newsmen are making it out to be, just turn around and come home."

"Sounds like a plan." Sunny went to open the storm door, surprised to see Shadow accompanying her. Usually when he was comfortable inside, he avoided the cold air. The cat stood in the doorway and put a single experimental paw on the ground outside.

He remembers the ice from yesterday, Sunny thought. "It's all gone now," she told Shadow. In a lower voice, she continued, "And I've got the aching back to prove it."

Shadow gave one of her shins a head-butt and retreated back to the warmth. Sunny stepped out and closed the door.

She moved carefully in case any part of her clearing job had refrozen but had no problem getting to her Wrangler. Then the fun started. There was a lot of ice on the streets, and Sunny kept her Jeep in two-wheel drive. Most people had the idea that SUVs were built to conquer all weather conditions, but the Wrangler's four-wheel drive could cause more problems, especially on curves.

Sunny drove slowly, giving other drivers a lot of room. That was the other misconception some folks had about SUVs. They could go anywhere, but on ice, the problem wasn't going—it was stopping. Luckily, the long incline down to town was clear, and the sun had begun to shine, causing a little more melt. Sunny drove down to the New Stores, found a parking space, and had more skids on the sidewalk than she'd had on the street. The guys from Judson's Market had cleared a single lane all the way down the block, with a lot more work done in front of their store. Sunny unlocked her office door and headed to the back of the office to the sack of ice melt. Using an extra coffee cup, she scooped and sprinkled along the front of the store until she had an island of damp but non-slippery pavement.

She couldn't help noticing that Kittery Harbor Fish remained shuttered with just the little lane that the Judson's guys had deiced. Was Neil Garret still stuck out in Sturgeon Springs, or was he in custody somewhere?

"Would be nice if Will could have let me know," Sunny muttered as she came inside. But she forgot about that as she got the daily routine started. She'd been working a couple of hours on e-mail inquiries when the phone rang. It was Will.

"I was thinking of you," Sunny began, but Will cut her

off. "I've got a kind of weird favor to ask, and I need a quick answer," he said. "I've got Deke Sweeney on the other line. He says he knows I want to talk with him, but he doesn't want to do it at the sheriff's office. If I can come up with someplace private, he can come in right now. I thought of your office, if Ollie isn't camped out there."

"He's not, and . . . sure," Sunny replied, thinking, *This way I get a front-row seat.*

Will had managed to change and shave since the previous night, but he looked hollow-eyed and tired when he arrived at the MAX office. He was in businesslike mode, so no kiss as he came in the door. "Thanks for this," he said, taking off his coat and sinking into a chair. "Apparently Sweeney thinks that hanging around with the police is bad for his image or something. He wouldn't even go for meeting in a restaurant. Too public."

"And this isn't?" Sunny nodded toward the plate glass window fronting most of the space.

"I think it will be a pretty slow business day," Will said. "Not many people coming by to gawk in the windows."

"You mean people won't be beating a path to the fish store?" Sunny asked. "I see it's still closed."

"Yeah, I guess they haven't finished chopping their way through the felled trees to clear the road to Sturgeon Springs." Will didn't look happy. "Garret was stuck in his house and apparently didn't make any kind of a move. Even the wheels of his car were iced in place."

"That's a pretty impressive alibi," Sunny said.

"Yeah, unless we can find a cab record that says different, or if Scotty beamed him into town and back, it's pretty hard to imagine Garret killing Charlie Vane." Will glanced at his watch. "When Sweeney called, he said he was in downtown Portsmouth. So, depending on how things are moving on the bridge, he should be here fairly soon."

Traffic must have been moving pretty well, because shortly afterward a tall man in a parka and a knit cap came down the block, glancing at a scrap of paper in his hand. He opened the office door, stepped in, and said, "I'm Sweeney. I think you're expecting me?"

Will stepped forward. "I'm Will Price, and this is Sunny Coolidge."

"Oh, yeah. I've read some of your stuff," Sweeney said, removing his cap.

So he probably knows Will and I are a team, Sunny thought.

Sweeney shrugged out of the parka, revealing a rumpled brown suit and a wool knit tie. To Sunny's eyes, the shark of the fish market looked more like a snapping turtle. Sweeney was a raw boned kind of man, with knobby cheeks, a hard, determined chin, and a bald head. His remaining hair was cropped so short, it looked like grayish stubble above his ears. His eyebrows, however, were wild and bushy with stray white hairs sticking out. His lips curved in a sort of default smile, giving Sunny the impression that he was a rough but cheerful type until she looked him in the eyes. They were the most shark-like things about him, having as much color and feeling as a pair of brook pebbles.

"A couple of friends on the Portsmouth force said you were asking after me," Sweeney said, taking a seat in front of Sunny's desk. "Of course, with this storm, any formal request you might have made has gotten shifted to the bottom of the pile." The corners of his mouth moved upward maybe another millimeter. "So I decided to take the bull by the horns. For a person in my position, getting visits from policemen just looks bad. And visiting police stations looks even worse. People might get the wrong idea."

"And what exactly is your position, Mr. Sweeney?" Sunny asked.

Sweeney's smile went up another millimeter. "Why, I'm the manager of the Portsmouth Fish Market, Ms. Coolidge. I'm responsible for everything running smoothly and honestly."

"And publicly dealing with the police would cause a problem with that?" Will inquired skeptically.

"The market is a rough-and-tumble kind of place," Sweeney explained. "Certain elements might interpret the presence of the police as a sign of weakness."

"That you might be arrested, you mean?" Will asked.

The smile disappeared from Sweeney's lips. "That I can't keep order in my own house," he said. "I can . . . and I do."

"I've heard stories that the fish market was kind of a wild and wooly place, until you came in and . . . imposed order," Will said easily. "Though for a while, that looked like a difficult job. I understand one of the fish merchants made a complaint about you threatening him with a gun."

"Is it ancient history you're interested in?" Sweeney asked. "That happened years ago, and it was never followed up."

Will nodded. "Yes, the complainant left town in something of a hurry."

"I certainly can't speak to that," Sweeney said primly. "But if that old complaint is the only thing you can find on me, then I think my reputation speaks for itself. Besides, waving guns is a young man's game." He gestured to himself. "I'm not a young man anymore."

"No, nowadays I suppose you'd have to delegate that to, as you say, a younger fellow," Will said. "Still, I have to ask, where were you a week ago Wednesday?"

"You're trying to connect me to what happened next door?" Sweeney's smile was back. "I have to admit, it was a bit of a shock when I passed the place. I'd never been to Kittery Harbor Fish before. Fact is, I've never even set eyes on Neil Garret."

"You know," Sunny broke in, "a suspicious mind might pick up on that statement as actual truth. That someone who'd never seen Garret mistakenly killed Phil Treibholz in Garret's store."

"Well, I've never seen either of them, and I was more than a hundred miles from here the night of that murder," Sweeney replied. "I was over in Hanover, at a Dartmouth hockey game. My son's on the team, and I try to root for him."

"Were you alone?" Will asked.

"I was with a couple of thousand other fans." Sweeney's smile rose a bit more. "But I went by myself. My wife is afraid of all this propaganda about concussions and such. She can't stand to watch. But this is the sport my boy likes, and Lord knows, I did stupider things when I was his age. Still, the game ran a hair short of two-and-a-half hours, which is about what it would take to drive from Hanover here to Kittery Harbor. I was in the team locker room after the game to see my son, and from what I've heard, my schedule doesn't exactly jibe with yours."

Will nodded. "Could you tell me your whereabouts last night?"

Claire Donally

Sweeney's emotionless eyes gave Will a long look. "Why I was iced in at home, like most of the people in this area," he said. "My wife and I were lucky enough not to lose our electricity, so we watched some television. Why do you ask?"

"I guess your friends haven't mentioned that Charlie Vane was found dead last night." Will paused for a second. "He was shot three times."

For the first time, a genuine expression surfaced on Sweeney's face—surprise. "Who would bother with a small fish like Vane?"

"Excuse me?" Sunny asked.

"Oh, to hear Vane talk about it, there was a great feud between him and me." A look of distaste crept onto Sweeney's face. "But to me he was more of a hangnail than the thorn in my side he made himself out to be."

"You blackballed him from the fish market," Sunny pointed out.

"More as a warning to others who might get ideas than anything else," Sweeney replied.

"So it wasn't an attempt to drive him out of business?" Will asked.

"You needn't go blaming me for that. The way Charlie Vane conducted his business, something would catch up with him and sink him. Same as with Garret." He jerked a thumb in the direction of the store next door. "Too clever for their own good. Those are the sort who, sooner or later, find themselves in bankruptcy court." He shook his head. "But I never expected it might end up in murder."

13

Sunny and Will spent some more time fencing with Deke Sweeney, but in the end they had to admit defeat. This obviously wasn't Sweeney's first rodeo when it came to interrogations. He just kept that masklike smile and stuck to his alibi while they tried their best to trip him up — and failed.

"Well, I don't know how much help I was, but I was glad to give it," the shark of the Portsmouth Fish Market said blandly as he headed to the door. "Good luck on your case."

Will glared at Sweeney's retreating back. "We'll damn well need it, if he's the guy we're after."

"Doesn't look like it, though." Sunny sighed. "He seemed like such a good suspect from a distance, somebody who leans on people for a living. But that's the problem—distance.

I used to go up to Dartmouth for games and stuff during my school days. It's at least a two-hour ride."

Will gave her a moody nod. "Not to mention that our estimated time of death would fall just about in the middle of that hockey game. That cuts the margin even thinner. No way could Sweeney get from here to Hanover in time to see his son in the locker room." He considered that for a moment, then smiled. "Of course, maybe this is a carefully constructed alibi, placing Sweeney a hundred and twenty miles away while somebody else did the deed."

"That sounds like the theory I suggested about Charlie Vane," Sunny said.

"Of course, that theory has a little drawback now that Vane is dead." Will grimaced. "Two murders a week apart. We have to figure they're connected."

Sunny nodded. "But the only connection seems to be Deke Sweeney and the fish market."

Will rose from his chair to work off a little frustration by walking around the office. "This stupid storm delay with the crime-scene people is driving me crazy. If we got a ballistics match, at least we'd have something solid tying in the two killings."

"But are you sure the bullets came from the same gun?" Sunny asked. "You told me Charlie Vane had a house full of them."

Will halted in his tracks and gave her a look. "Thanks for cheering me up."

"Just pointing out that Vane's murder could be a crime of opportunity," Sunny said. "With all those weapons around, someone with a totally unrelated grudge against Vane could have killed him." She paused for a second. "He doesn't strike me as the kind of guy who left business partners with warm fuzzy feelings toward him."

"Are you seriously suggesting that?"

Sunny shrugged. "Well, of our three strongest suspects in the Treibholz killing, two of them are excluded from this one by the ice storm—and the third is the victim."

"We really don't have a time of death for Vane," Will argued, but Sunny suspected he was clutching at straws. "The murder could have happened before the weather got too bad."

"I guess that will depend on when those trees fell on the road to Sturgeon Springs . . . and when the bridges from Portsmouth got too icy for traffic—that usually happens a lot more quickly than on the roads." She glanced at Will. "Figuring that he would hire a killer from his side of the river."

From the look on Will's face, he wasn't sure whether to laugh or start hollering. "So you think we're back to square one?"

"I think that at least for this murder, we need some new suspects who are closer to the scene of the crime."

Will frowned. "You're saying someone in town."

Like Val Overton, in her motel on the main road, Sunny thought. Aloud she said, "I don't think we can go farther out than my neighborhood." *Which would let in Abby Martinson, depending on how early she and her mom hit the hay.*

Will looked as if he'd just bitten into a big, fat bug burger.

Well, it can't get much worse, Sunny decided. "How well do you know Val?" she asked.

"What?" Will seemed thrown by the shift in the conversation. "Why do you ask?"

"She came on pretty strong with Ollie," Sunny pointed out. "I'm still wondering if she has a thing for older guys. Because Neil Garret is an older guy, and he's a lot better-looking than Ollie the Barnacle."

"Garret is her witness, and it's her responsibility to keep him from getting killed," Will immediately objected. "She would never—"

"It never happens?" Sunny asked. "An attractive witness, a marshal who's on the road so much, there's no room for a private life?"

"I don't—it's not—" Will floundered around for a moment, then said, "You're making a big jump from bad judgment to murder."

"Well, this hypothetical person with bad judgment carries a gun," Sunny pointed out.

"And what's the motive for killing Treibholz?" Will challenged.

"The crooked detective from California who was playing mind games with Neil?" Sunny shrugged. "Treibholz could put him in the crosshairs for a bunch of contract killers."

"But that's not a reason to kill the guy," Will said. "If Neil's new identity was in danger of being exposed, the WitSec people would move him again."

"And would Neil still be Val's witness? Or would he just disappear out of her life into still another new identity and never see her again?"

Will's expression turned grim. "You're throwing a lot of stuff on Val."

"I'm just asking some questions," Sunny replied. "We've had to ask them about friends of mine in the past."

That got a stiff nod from Will. "Okay. So how do you tie in Charlie Vane?"

Sunny spread her arms. "Suppose he found out about Neil's past. Maybe Treibholz came around asking questions that got Vane suspicious. Old Charlie was a guy who cut a lot of corners and needed a lot of money. I wouldn't put it past him to try a little blackmail on Neil."

"And then it would be the same situation as Treibholz." Will really wasn't liking this line of thinking.

Sunny took a deep breath. "It's not just your friends I'm wondering about," she said. "How about Abby Martinson? She had a prior relationship with Neil when he was Nick Gatto, and it seems a hell of a coincidence, her turning up here after being away for so long. What if she was in contact with Neil?"

"That's a big WitSec no-no." Will still looked serious, but some of the grimness leaked away as he considered Sunny's suggestion. "Although the program has been a hundred percent effective when people follow the rules, that's the one that gets broken most—and gets people killed."

Sunny nodded. "What if Abby found that Treibholz was sniffing around and came to warn Neil?" Now she frowned. "The guy died the day after she got off the plane."

"So, motive and possible opportunity," Will said. "What about means?"

"Abby's dad was an outdoorsman," Sunny replied. "A real huntin' and fishin' guy. He had guns."

Will strode around a little more, silently stewing. "You've

got the start of a case—for both of them," he abruptly admitted. "But there's no evidence."

"Maybe the crime-scene people will get lucky," Sunny suggested. "They managed to recover the bullets that killed Treibholz, didn't they?"

He nodded. "One got pretty messed up after exiting his head—a lot of metal in that freezer. But the other is in decent shape. The slug came from a nine millimeter pistol—which, yes, is kind of government issue these days." His hand made an absentminded gesture toward the Glock holstered under his coat. "But I need something stronger before I'd ask for ballistics on Val's piece. Think you can find out anything about the late Mr. Martinson's gun collection?"

"I can try." Sunny was pretty sure her face wasn't a picture of joy. "Can you let me out of my promise to keep playing dumb about Nick Gatto? That would let me talk to him about that part of his life."

Will stared at her. "Why would you want to do that? We just about cleared him as a suspect."

"Yeah, we cleared Neil Garret, but Nick Gatto got involved with both of our new suspects. I'd like to see how Nick talks about each of them."

Will laughed. "You think your feminine instincts can turn something up?"

Sunny shrugged. "Something is better than the nothing we've got now."

Will grudgingly gave his okay. Then he leaned in to give Sunny a quick peck on the cheek before heading up to Levett to report on his meeting with Deke Sweeney.

Better than when he came in, Sunny thought. *But still distracted with work.*

She sighed and returned to her keyboard. *Speaking of work, I suppose I'd better get some done.*

But as she went through the day's activities, Sunny kept an ear out for the sound of the gate next door opening. It finally rattled up sometime after lunch. Sunny actually found herself jumping to her feet but then forced herself to sit down again. *Let him get settled first. I'll want to work my way into this.*

Sometime later, she decided it was time to put her plan into action. She slipped into her parka and headed next door, just another shopper looking for something out of the ordinary to make for supper.

Immediately, her plan hit a snag. Someone else was at the counter, shopping ahead of her. Sunny noticed that the display cases were pretty bare. Between the ice storm and Deke Sweeney's embargo, Neil must really be hurting for merchandise.

He brought out a tray with triangular pieces of pink, grooved flesh resting on the crushed ice. "Have you ever tried skate wings?" Neil asked the older woman on the other side of the counter. "I've already prepared it, so you have no skin or bones to remove. Actually, it's not a bone, but a piece of cartilage. Anyway, you can see it's nice and thin, you can sauté it quickly. I can give you some recipes—"

"Does it smell fishy?" the customer, obviously a meat-and-potatoes type, interrupted.

"It shouldn't, because this is fresh." Neil held out the tray and waved a hand over it. "If you're worried, though, I'd suggest soaking the fish in water and lemon juice. Skates are related to sharks, and like them, they urinate through their skin. The soak will neutralize the slight trace of ammonia that sometimes turns up in even fresh skate—"

The woman shook her head.

I suspect you lost her at "urinate," Sunny thought.

Neil's other offerings didn't pass muster either, and the shopper left, heading in the direction of Judson's Market. The shopkeeper stared after her. Sunny wondered whether the fury on his face was aimed at her or at himself.

It turned out to be aimed at the fish. Neil jammed the tray of skate into the display, muttering, "This is what I get for going into this business. Trying to sell people on something we used to cut up for bait."

"Maybe you cut it up for bait on the west coast," Sunny said, "but we New Englanders have been eating it—probably since we arrived here."

"Yeah, but you New Englanders are cheap." Neil had the grace to look embarrassed for letting that slip out. Then he did a double take. "Wait a minute. How do you know I'm from California?"

Sunny smiled. "How do you think, Nicky?"

Garret deflated behind the counter. "I guess your friend Price told you."

"Well, I was looking into things, after that California detective tried to kill my cat." She leaned across the counter. "That made a lot more sense when I learned your real name—Gatto."

Neil gave an embarrassed shrug. "Guess there was a cat involved somewhere in the family tree. My grandfather's people were fishermen in the Mediterranean, and he'd take me and my dad on fishing expeditions. That's where I learned the business." He gestured around the shop.

"But you wound up in the stock market."

"My dad was a blue-collar kind of guy, like a lot of the folks around here," Neil said. "I wanted the things a white-collar job could bring."

Like a stint in prison for white-collar crime, Sunny thought.

"Dad couldn't pay my freight through school, so I tried a little entrepreneurship—pharmaceutical sales." He smiled at the reminiscence, but then his expression went sour. "Until somebody got caught with a bag of pot. Then those fine legacy students got a stern talking-to, while the blue-collar kid got a couple of years as a guest of the California penal system."

Neil carefully rearranged the trays of fish on display. "By the time I got out, my old school buddies were starting careers as brokers and wouldn't have anything to do with me. But I made a couple of connections in the joint."

"Jimmy DiCioppa?" Sunny asked.

"Nah, someone way down on the totem pole. But he got me in the door. When I met Jimmy, he was still in the dark ages. He thought robbing banks was a big deal. But he saw where the other crews were going, and he didn't want to be left behind. I came along at just the right time."

"To do what?"

Neil actually laughed. "That's the funny thing. What I did for Jimmy was what a lot of my honest, upstanding class-mates were doing. Pump and dump—singing the praises of a particular stock to investors so they'd buy and push the price up, then selling out at the top of the market and making a killing. They had B-list small customers they could play that with, while we had to do boiler rooms, selling over the phone, like that Leonardo DiCaprio movie. Nowadays, I suppose they do it over the Internet. Cold calls. It got easier when we had our own stock-trading firm. We could get the ball rolling on a hot IPO then get out fast when the price inflated enough. Or a few guys could control the market for a stock by trading it among themselves—"

"I thought the stock market was a little more sophisticated than that," Sunny said.

"Back in the day, small-capital shares moved around more like a flea market than the stuff you see in the movies. Guys would offer a price that they'd hope to get for a stock—the ask. Guys representing buyers come in with a bid, the price they want to pay. A broker is supposed to go around to every stall in the flea market and find the best ask they can. But here's the thing. The difference between the ask and the bid in big financial represents the brokers' profit. So if you run the sales between you and your friends, you can keep the spread wide and make some nice change."

"That's what you did?" Sunny asked.

"That's what a lot of guys in the market did," Neil said. "But when I brought Jimmy into the market, we didn't threaten to blackball people at the country club like the so-called legit brokers did. We smacked heads."

Sunny stared. "As simple as that?"

Neil smiled. "You ever hear the saying, 'The market is driven by fear and greed?' Well, we used fear. After getting roughed up, a lot of those big, bold masters of the universe peed themselves and fell in line. As for greed, a lot of them wanted to know what their cut would be."

"That's all you needed to make a lot of money."

"Oh, there are more wrinkles. We could use offshore accounts to buy stocks at special low prices for foreign investors. Then we'd sell it to make big profits." Neil went silent for a moment. "At least Jimmy the Chopper made big profits. The rest of us got crumbs. At first I figured he brought the money into the deals."

And the leg-breakers, Sunny silently added.

"But as time went on, I realized I was never going to see much out of this. Maybe you've heard another saying about the market, how there are bulls, bears, and pigs. Jimmy really turned into a pig. He wanted tribute, he wanted kick-backs, and he thought the market was like his turf. We had a situation where another crew was trying to sell short on a stock we were playing with, driving down the price when we wanted it to go up. They leaned on one of the brokers we had, um, persuaded to help us, and Jimmy went crazy. I saw him lose it completely and order a hit on the guy."

"That's how you wound up in witness protection?" Sunny asked.

"That, and the fact that I knew where a lot of Jimmy's money was parked," Neil said. "Jimmy should have had a sit-down with the other crew rather than start shooting. But instead he had to be a pig about it."

And some broker got killed, Sunny thought. *A crooked broker, but he got killed.*

"Still, I'd have probably kept my mouth shut, but he took the one legitimate thing I had and ruined it," Neil went on. "I used my little cut from all these various deals to open a restaurant. It was a nice little place. I know a lot about fish, I had some recipes, got a good chef, and we were doing pretty well. But Jimmy wouldn't leave us alone. He started hanging out there, with all his friends. They drove off the other customers. And Jimmy, well, you just couldn't hand him a bill."

Neil's expression went dark. "Then Jimmy got interested in one of the hostesses, a nice kid trying to make it in Hollywood. That got really dangerous. You don't say no to Jimmy the Chopper. I managed to get her out of town, out to the Valley, but Jimmy wasn't happy. After that, he screwed me on some deals I set up for him."

"Sounds as though you kind of liked this girl," Sunny said.

Neil's face softened. "She was a good kid—bright, talented. But she wasn't getting anywhere. I managed to find her a job in a different field. At the time, I was going through a nasty divorce. Then some federal prosecutor thought it was time to do something about the various crews getting involved in the market and decided to make an example out of me."

His shoulders rose and fell. "I could see the handwriting on the wall, so I let my ex-wife Terry have everything, the house, the restaurant. Then the feds floated the idea of testifying against Jimmy. Hell, what did I have to lose?"

"Everything you were," Sunny said. "Your name, your family . . ."

Neil shook his head. "My father wanted nothing to do with me after I threw in with Jimmy. My wife just wanted my blood after she got everything else. The only one who might miss me was Abby—the girl I helped. But let's face it, she was better off without me, and in her new line of work, being involved with a mobbed-up guy wouldn't help her career. I did my best to keep my other business away from the restaurant, and a lot came out in the trial that, well, it wouldn't impress a girl."

"And you came from sunny California to here." Sunny glanced through the store's plate glass window to the leaden skies outside. Nothing more had fallen after the ice storm, but the clouds remained.

"Yeah, it's a shock for a guy with thin blood, but I managed. The feds helped out with some money, and I opened the shop here. They keep an eye on me."

Sunny smiled. "You mean, Val Overton does."

Neil laughed. "Yeah, she's a real pistol. Makes me wonder what she'd be like if she ever let her hair down. But she's all business with me. They've got her stretched pretty thin, managing a bunch of us witnesses. Got to hand it to her, she works hard—and you wouldn't believe how little money she makes. And what are the guys in Washington doing? Cutting the budget."

Sunny watched Neil's face. *He seems a lot fonder of Abby than he does of Val,* she thought. *Unless this is all a line of BS.*

"Still, you got in trouble," Sunny prodded.

"Hey, I tried to push the market a little after I got settled in. It should have been good for the local fishermen and for me. I knew the restaurant business. If I could supply some of the big buyers around here, everybody would have benefited."

"Except Deke Sweeney," Sunny said. "Will had a talk with him."

"That guy's a piece of work, from what I hear." Neil shook his head. "If he had a problem he should have sat down and talked with me. Instead, he tries to kill me—businesswise, I mean," he quickly clarified.

"And what about Charlie Vane?"

"I don't know what happened with that guy." Neil shook his head vigorously. "He was a local contact, a guy who was eager to sell a little off the top of his catch for a better price. I treated him square, but after Sweeney lowered the boom, he kept his distance."

Sunny took a shot in the dark. "You said you had breakfast with some fishermen the day before Phil Treibholz was murdered. Didn't that include Charlie Vane?"

"He was willing to eat on my dime," Neil said bitterly. Then he broke off, staring at her. "Hey, he pretty much blew me off, telling me I was on my own. You're not trying to tie him in with Treibholz, are you?"

"They've both ended up dead, and the only thing that seems to connect them is you."

"That's crazy. Vane always talked about his pirate ancestor, and I figured he chiseled around the edges of some shady stuff. Maybe he got in over his head on some deal, but it wasn't with me."

"And how about Treibholz?" Sunny pressed. "Will tells me you've been playing dumb about him, but he suspects there's stuff you're not telling him. And now, with Vane getting killed . . ." She let the sentence trail off.

"You can't lump the two of them in together," Neil protested. "Charlie Vane was small-time all the way. Treibholz was dangerous, dirty as hell."

"Who was he working for?" Sunny asked the question Will couldn't get answered. "Was it Jimmy the Chopper?"

Neil surprised her by laughing. "No, Phil was afraid of

Jimmy. If he'd been working for him, Phil would have never tried to pull what he did."

"So who was he working for?" Sunny pressed.

"George Foster, esquire," Neil replied. "My ex-wife Terry's lawyer. A real lightweight. That's why Treibholz figured he could play the two of us off each other. He tried to put the bite on me. Hell of a time to do it. I was pretty much broke."

14

Sunny struggled to keep her expression neutral even as her heart began to race. This was something Neil hadn't told Will. *Maybe a little needling will get some more out of him,* she decided.

Curving her lips in a smile, she said, "I wouldn't go telling everyone a story like that. You could wind up with a big, red check mark in the box marked 'Motive' next to your name."

Neil made a disbelieving sound. "Come on, you know I'm not that kind of a guy. My big-time criminal career was basically doing market research on small-cap stocks, just like the guys I'd gone to school with. I think my research was better, and we were in a stronger position to push the market—"

By breaking the occasional head, Sunny thought.

"But in all the years I worked for Jimmy, I never even

touched a gun, much less owned one," Neil finished. Reluctantly, Sunny had to believe him. Her reporter's antennae were scanning like mad, but Neil came across as rock-solidly telling the truth. He smiled. "When I had to solve a problem, I used money."

"Fine," Sunny said, "but you just told me you were broke. That makes it hard to pay blackmail."

"I just had to come up with some earnest money, to keep playing along until I could get Treibholz's investigation shut down."

"So you were going to use Val Overton to do it?" Sunny watched Neil carefully and was surprised to see him shaking his head. "Only as a last resort. Yeah, Phil was probably breaking a bunch of federal laws tracking me down. But if Val thought my identity was compromised, she'd be yanking me out of here."

"And you've come to love Kittery Harbor so much, you couldn't bear to do that?" Sunny figured she managed to dust that with just the right tone of skepticism.

But Neil was surprisingly serious. "I couldn't let this business just go down the pipes. I had too much invested in it."

"Don't you mean the Feds had too much invested in it?"

Neil laughed, not a happy sound. "You're years out of date on that, Sunny. This isn't the seventies, where a guy like Jimmy Fratianno could dig a million dollars out of witness protection. They've got it down to a science nowadays. Each week you get a modest stipend to keep you going while you find a job and get settled. And then they tell you to bank the Feds' money and live off your paycheck."

He shrugged. "I've used the payments to live on while

trying to make a real profit here and earn *my* money back. The money I came here with."

"You just told me you gave everything to your wife," Sunny pointed out.

"Okay, not everything," Neil admitted. "The restaurant, the savings and checking accounts, the portfolio. But I always tried to squirrel a little away, for a—I don't know if it's okay to talk about saving for a rainy day when L.A. has been living through a drought for years."

His smile faded a little. "It would be nice to say I headed east with a suitcase full of bearer bonds. But it was more like a coffee can half-full of hundreds and fifties. Still, it sounds like a lot, until you start shelling out to get a business off the ground." Neil jerked a thumb over his shoulder. "Do you have any idea what that freezer system set me back?" Then he waved his hand. "Better not to ask. The problem is, these expenses soaked up all my 'buzz off' money."

Sunny's face must have shown her surprise at hearing such an old-fashioned term, because Neil laughed again. "I'm trying to be polite, Sunny. People usually refer to this kind of fund with two other one-syllable words, and not very nice ones. Besides, I thought that name worked—I didn't know if I would be the one telling people to buzz off, or if I'd be buzzing off myself."

Well, that's the way it turned out, Sunny thought.

Neil tried to keep his tone light, but his face was dead serious as he spoke. "If I buzz off now, I'll have nothing behind me. I can't do that, Sunny. My whole life, I've been my own boss."

"What about Jimmy DiCioppa?" Sunny asked.

"He was just a client, not a boss," Neil replied.

Sunny nodded. "Things didn't work out so well for you when Jimmy the Chopper started throwing his weight around."

"You mean, when he decided he was my boss." Neil frowned for a second. "I rest my case. But look at me, Sunny. Could you see me greeting folks at Big Box, Inc. or wearing an orange apron at Tools R Us? I need my own business, and to do that, I need money."

"I hear there are these places called banks where you can get a business loan," Sunny said.

"You try to get a loan recently?" Neil asked.

She shook her head. "Not with my credit rating."

"It's not just a credit rating. They want your life story, references, financials, everything but your DNA—and that might be coming. Val and her people did a good job of creating a backstory for me, but there's only so far they can go." He sighed. "And banks want to go a lot farther. Believe me, I've tried."

Sunny stood silent for a moment. "I appreciate that you're trying to be honest with me, but you're just making your motive for killing Phil Treibholz stronger and stronger. Claiming you've never touched a gun isn't going to cut much ice when it comes to means. And you've got a big fat blank space on your schedule during the probable time when Treibholz got it. That's opportunity. The storm gives you an alibi for Charlie Vane's time of death, but you're a strong suspect in the Treibholz case. Folks around here are going to demand some action, and the sheriff's department may decide that half a loaf is better than none. They could make a case against you."

Neil scowled, staring sightlessly down at the few fish displayed in his large, no doubt expensive case.

"Suppose I wasn't in town that night," he finally said.

Bingo! Sunny silently cheered, but she kept all trace of celebration out of her voice. "And whatever you were doing out of town was worse than being accused of murder?"

"If Val heard about it, I might get yanked—or maybe dumped out of the program," Neil confessed. "You can't tell her."

"How do I know until you tell me?" Sunny said.

"Technically, I'm still on parole," Neil said. "Which means I can't hang around with criminal types. But I had to."

"Had to?" Sunny repeated.

"If you can't get money from banks, and nobody in the area knows you, the only place you can get money is from criminal types," Neil explained. "Also known as loan sharks."

"I know a little bit about them. Not from personal experience," she hastily added. "But from working with Will."

"I had to go across the river into Portsmouth to find somebody who could handle the amount I needed." Neil shook his head. "I spun my case as best I could, but in the end they turned me down. Between the talking and the traveling, I was there a good part of the evening—the evening that Phil Treibholz was murdered."

"So you do have an alibi, but the alibi will get you in trouble with the marshals and WitSec." Sunny shrugged. "Will is looking at a murder, and he wants to eliminate you as a suspect. Maybe we can have a private chat with these loan sharks."

Neil looked a little nervous. "I don't think they'd like having any police looking into their business. And I don't want this to blow back on me. One of them was as big as a house. The strong, silent type who could twist me into a pretzel."

That sparked a memory for Sunny. "A foreign gentleman?" she asked.

"Ukrainian," Neil said. "They have a reputation for playing rough. But the one who did the talking was fairly decent with me."

"Dani." It was a good year ago now, but it was hard to forget the Ukrainian loan sharks she'd met while trying to save a friend from getting arrested for murdering her former husband. "And Olek. Danilo Shostak and Olek Lipko."

Neil stared at her with new respect. "I heard that you helped Will Price investigating crimes, and wrote about them for the paper. But you *know* these guys?"

Sunny shrugged. "You do that kind of stuff, you get around. Where did you meet them?" The last time she'd seen Dani and Olek, they were getting out of town because things had gotten a little too warm for them. Supposedly, they'd gone back to Montreal. Now it looked as though they'd returned to reestablish themselves in this territory.

"Shostak had me meet him in a little hole in the wall down in the artsy-fartsy part of town," Neil said. "A place called the Cafe Ekaterina."

Then that's where I've got to go, Sunny thought. *And the sooner the better. Problem is, how do I get out of here gracefully?*

Neil must have seen the change in her expression, because he asked, "Now that you've wrung everything you can out of me, can I interest you in some skate wings?"

"Only if they'll keep till tomorrow," Sunny told him. "I'll be in to get them then. This evening—well, I'll be busy."

She escaped from the fish store, got back to her office, and dealt with a few small-scale emergencies while also getting the address for the Cafe Ekaterina. Sunny closed down the office as early as possible, got aboard her Wrangler, and joined the slow stream of traffic to one of the bridges over the Piscataqua River. She crawled along through greater downtown Portsmouth to an area of old factories repurposed as artists' studios.

Driving around through the neighborhood, she finally found the Cafe Ekaterina. It was in a dingy-looking brick building that had probably gone up in seventeen-something, with dim lighting that made it difficult to see through newer but still pretty old plate glass windows. Sunny pulled up by a fire hydrant across the street to check the place out. Obviously, the landlord hadn't done much to maintain the place, saving his money for when the rush of gentrification drove the artists out and put tenants willing to pay big rents into the property. By then the Cafe Ekaterina would probably be pushed out by a Starbucks or some similar chain operation. For the present, it offered a whimsical sign with its name in mismatched letters.

Like a ransom demand. Sunny pushed that thought out of her head. She was spending way too much time with Will and his investigations.

The door to the cafe opened, and a figure stood silhouetted, blocking most of the doorway. Olek, the muscle end of the loan-sharking operation, had apparently shrunk in Sunny's memory. Looking at him now, the big man seemed even more enormous. He stepped to the side, reaching into the pocket of a coat that looked like a tweed circus tent, and pulled out a pack of cigarettes and a lighter. The brief burst of flame illuminated a face like a kid's drawing, all squares and angles.

So, Olek keeps up his bad habits, Sunny thought. She'd originally managed to track down the Ukrainians because Olek smoked a brand of cigarettes from the old homeland, available only in one store in the area.

He took a deep drag on his cigarette, blew out a cloud of smoke, then abruptly dropped the butt, stubbing it out with his toe. Olek returned inside the cafe. A moment later, a smaller, slimmer figure appeared in the doorway, making a beckoning gesture. Dani. And from the way he was looking at her car, he knew she was there.

Looks as though I have to brush up on my surveillance techniques. Sunny lowered the passenger side window and waved an acknowledgment. Then she pulled out to find a legal parking spot.

Arriving shortly afterward in the cafe, she scanned a sparse crowd and spotted the Ukrainians sitting at a corner table where Olek had a clear view both of the front door and the entrance from the kitchen. Dani Shostak politely gestured toward a seat. Polite, but judging from the look on his face in the dim lighting, not delighted to see her.

Sunny sat. Like the letters on the sign outside, none of the chairs in the cafe matched one another, and this one wobbled alarmingly when she rested on it. The walls were exposed brick, and a designer might call the tables "distressed." To Sunny's eyes, they looked just plain worn.

"Miss Sunny Coolidge," Dani said when she was seated. "Why you come to visit us? I don't think it's because you need money. I think it's because you give something to Olek and me." His face got cold. "Trouble."

Sunny shook her head. "Actually, I'm trying to keep trouble away. Unless you want police coming around to ask you questions."

Dani sat for a second, then said, "Then you are less trouble, Miss Sunny. What questions do you want to ask?"

"I want to ask about a customer." She raised a hand as Dani began to shake his head. "A person you turned down."

"The fish man," Dani said. "I read about the body in his shop the day after he comes here. 'Oho,' I think, 'he finds another way out of his trouble—by making worse for himself.'"

Sunny nodded "The thing is, we do have a time of death. And Neil Garret told me he was here with you when the murder happened."

Dani scowled down at his cup of cappuccino. "You get people to tell you the craziest things."

"Believe me, he didn't want to talk about it," Sunny said. "But being charged with murder was worse trouble."

Dani exhaled heavily. "All right, then. He comes to me Wednesday evening. Not last night, but a week ago. He asks for twenty thousand. I say no. He says how about ten. Again, I say no."

"I thought you were in the business of lending money," Sunny said.

"Lending, not losing," Dani corrected. "If I lend money, I got to get it back—with interest. This fish man, he tells me he needs a bridge loan. He can pay me back when Lent comes. Business will pick up."

He took a sip of coffee and made a face. "Do I look like idiot? How he is supposed to make back twenty or even ten in six, seven weeks? He goes out of business and leaves me holding the sack."

"You could have taken over the business," Sunny suggested. "I've seen you do that."

Dani shook his head. "Best business to take over, dentist who makes too many bad sports bets. Lots of customers, lots of them pay cash. Lets us move other money through to clean it. But what do I know about fish?"

Olek rumbled something, and Dani shot him a look. "Yes, smoked fish is nice. Everything with you is smoke, smoke, smoke. I'm talking about store not even open for a year. If all of a sudden it makes a lot of money, people might notice. Then, trouble. Trouble I don't need. I tell Mr. Fish Man just let his store close. 'Cause if someone like Olek come and he got no money to pay, big, big trouble."

"So when did Neil come?" Sunny asked.

Dani frowned. "Eight o'clock, maybe a little later. He spent a lot of time trying to convince me he was good businessman, just having bad luck. Me, I have nothing important to do that night, so I let him talk. He try very hard, tells me he needs some cash in his hand, but I say no. It was dinner time, so we eat. Food is pretty good here, coffee, not so much. He finish, I guess nine thirty, some later, and goes home."

With the traffic, less than half an hour to get back to Kittery Harbor, Sunny thought. *But that still covers the window for the time of death the medical examiner estimated.*

"Okay," she said. "Thanks, Dani."

Dani leaned across the little table. "I tell you this because I trust you. Don't expect I go tell this in court." He shook his head. "They might ask other questions I don't want to answer."

"I don't think you have to worry about that," Sunny said, silently adding, *I'm the one who'll have to answer unpleasant questions when Will finds out what I've been doing.*

Dani must have been thinking the same thing, too, because when Sunny got up to leave, he sent Olek to accompany her to her car. "This is nice enough neighborhood," he said, "but sometimes things happen. I don't want your cop friend blaming me."

Sunny nodded. "I know. No trouble."

They walked the block to where Sunny had left her Wrangler. She thanked Olek, and the big man rumbled something in reply. Sunny noticed he stood there until she had the engine started and actually pulled into the street. Then he turned around, that enormous coat of his flapping in the breeze, and headed for the cafe.

Sunny's cell phone rang, and she pulled over to answer. It was Mike.

"I tried the office and got the voice mail," he said. "Wanted to catch you before you set off on a big shopping expedition. Helena just invited us to dinner—you, me, and Will, if he can make it. All she asks is that we don't read the latest issue of the *Courier* before we come." He paused for a second, trying to keep the curiosity out of his voice. "Did you?"

The delivery of the local weekly had been a bit late today, probably thanks to the ice storm, and Sunny had been too busy with other stuff to sit back and read it. "Nope, I missed it today," she said. "I guess there must be something in there Mrs. M. wants to celebrate."

Either that, or she wants to use up all the supplies she accumulated for the ice storm, that irrepressible voice in the back of Sunny's head suggested.

Out loud, she asked, "Is there a time set for this dinner? I had an errand to run in Portsmouth."

"I think you can make it all right," Mike said. "You've got about an hour."

Traffic was light enough that Sunny was able to get back, wash up, and put on some nicer clothes than her usual office wear. As she was putting on a little face paint, she heard the doorbell below.

That must be Will, she thought. She'd already decided not to discuss her conversation with Neil or her excursion to Portsmouth until after their visit with the Martinsons. *If he decides to blow his top over Dani and Olek, at least the condemned will enjoy a hearty meal,* Sunny thought.

She came downstairs to find Will hanging up his coat, chatting with Mike. Will turned to her and gave her a kiss on the cheek. "You look nice. I came from work, so what you saw this morning is what you get."

Sunny nodded. "You're wearing the same tie you had on the last time we saw the Martinsons," she said. "They're going to think it's the only one you own."

He fingered the embroidered silk. "It's the only one I like."

Shadow made the usual wary approach he reserved for times when his humans departed from their normal schedule. Still, he came over to give Will's ankles a good sniff.

Laughing, Will bent down, let Shadow sniff his hand,

and then gently ran fingers through the fur on top of the cat's head. "Don't worry, little guy. We'll be back soon."

"Speaking of soon, I suppose we should get a move on," Mike said. "What's the condition of the sidewalks?"

"Looks to me like most people put some kind of ice melt down," Will reported. "Worse comes to worst, we can detour into the street."

They strolled the couple of blocks to the Martinson house without any slippery incidents, and Mike rang the doorbell. Mrs. M. must have been watching for them, because she opened the door almost immediately. Excited woofing rose in volume as Toby came nearer. Then they heard Abby say firmly, "Toby! Heel!"

Even the barking diminished as Helena Martinson led them inside. Toby stood beside Abby, looking up at her and wagging his tail, obviously eager to rush over and play with the newcomers. Abby reached down to take hold of the dog's collar. "Toby, come." She led the overgrown pup over to Mike, Sunny, and Will. Sunny could see Toby's muscles bunching for a jump up to her waist, but Abby saw that, too. "Down, Toby."

Astonishingly, Toby relaxed, just coming forward for a greeting sniff.

"Wow," Sunny said. "You really are a dog whisperer."

"I'm not." Abby shook her head, but she was grinning at her success. "This is what I learned from being a dog *walker* when I first got out to the coast. It's not something you put on your resume, but it left me with some useful skills. Then again, maybe I should have put it on my resume and tried for directing jobs. If I could get animals to behave, maybe

I could do the same with actors." She bent down to Toby. "What do you think, pooch? Aren't you a happier dog now that you have some rules to live with?"

Mike took off his coat. "So, what's in the new newspaper that we weren't allowed to see?"

Abby turned to Helena, looking for a moment like a mortified teenager. "Mom, you didn't invite them over for that?"

"I most certainly did." Mrs. M.'s voice was full of pride as she held up a copy of the *Harbor Courier* and opened it up. There on the third page was a big photo of Abby with the headline,

FROM HOLLYWOOD BACK TO THE HARBOR.

15

Helena Martinson stood beaming, while Abby looked embarrassed. "Mr. Howell was kind of a fan, back when I was doing shows all around the area," she said. "He even reviewed a couple of them and said I could go places. So when I bumped into him on the street the other day, he asked a lot of questions."

"He must have been disappointed to hear that you'd kind of given up on the acting," Mike said.

Abby laughed. "He said Hollywood's loss was the legal profession's gain—even put it in the story. Then he brought me around to his office and shot some pictures."

"I'm surprised he didn't go for a glamour shot and have you perched on a trunk, showing a little leg," Sunny teased.

"If he had the trunk, I wouldn't be surprised." Abby

grinned at Helena. "To tell the truth, I think Mom's more excited about it than I am."

"It's a nice picture," Mrs. M. defended herself. "A nice, *big* picture."

Will took a long look and shook his head. "I guess it makes a change from the number of people hurt in the storm and the Vane murder."

Sunny gave him a worried look. Was he going to bring up the investigation over dinner?

Mike was still looking at the photo. "You know, Sunny's gotten her picture in the paper a few times." He wasn't about to be one-upped in the family pride stakes.

Now Sunny had to laugh. "Dad, when I turn up in the papers, I've usually been conked on the head or just escaped some ridiculous situation by the skin of my teeth. It's not quite the same as this." She looked at Abby's photo. "I just wish I had a chance to look nice in one of those shots. Hey, I'd even pose on top of a trunk if that was the only way."

That got a laugh out of everybody. A moment later, the oven timer pinged and Helena and Abby headed back to the kitchen and started preparing to serve.

It was a nice, stick-to-the-ribs sort of meal: roast beef and gravy, potatoes, and peas and carrots. Abby asked Mike if he wanted to carve. "Mom bought this big hunk of cow when she heard about the storm on the way, figuring we could cook it and live for a week on the leftovers." She looked around the table. "I think it's nicer to use it up this way."

"Better eating than I expected this evening," Will had to admit. "I just hope a satisfied stomach won't put me to sleep."

"You're going back to work after this?" Sunny asked.

Will nodded. "Got a couple of things to look into." He hummed in appreciation as he took another mouthful.

Sunny chewed over that comment—along with the piece of beef she'd just taken from her fork. She hadn't had a chance yet to talk with Will about her conversation with Neil Garret—or with Dani Shostak. So this had to be something new. She glanced at Will, and noticed him quietly watching Abby.

Oh, come on, she silently complained. *Just when I start liking Abby, she winds up as a possible suspect. I hope she's not the reason he expects to work late this evening.*

Will started telling a story about a mishap he'd encountered as a rookie with the state police. "I thought they'd taught me how to handle myself, but a lot of that went out the window when that biker got mad at me. To tell the truth, I was lucky to get the cuffs on him. Folks don't know it, but the biker gangs are the organized crime up by the border. They smuggle over anything the market will bear—drugs, booze, guns, even girls."

Just like Dani's Ukrainian friends, Sunny thought. *And he launders the money for them.*

Abby looked surprised. "You mean organized crime—like the Mafia?"

"Them we have on both sides of the border," Will replied. "In fact, the operations in Montreal are traditionally considered a branch of one of the Five Families in New York. They've had setbacks up there in recent years, and I understand they've turned to some of the biker gangs for muscle."

He laughed. "Anyway, I guess your days starting out in

Hollywood didn't involve messing with three-hundred-and-fifty-pound hairy guys."

Abby waggled her eyebrows, grinning. "Well, if you added up the weights of all those dogs I walked . . ."

Will coaxed tales of work misadventures from the rest of them, along with several war stories from Abby's film career. When she apologized for taking over so much of the conversation, Will said, "Hey, you've got better material than the rest of us."

It sounded like dinner table chitchat, but Sunny noticed that Will managed to draw Abby out not only on her acting, but her restaurant work, even getting her to tell a story about Nicky Gatto.

He's quietly interrogating her in front of everyone, Sunny thought. *Man, I really hope he hasn't figured a way to connect her to either of these murders.*

Sunny helped to clear the dinner dishes away, and Mrs. Martinson came out with one of her famous coffee cakes. "I'm going to say something silly," she said, "but I mean it seriously. The talking and laughing around the table tonight, you made this feel the most like a family dinner since—well, since my Vince passed on."

"Mom—" Abby started, but she didn't know what to say.

"No, honey, I think your dad would approve of us having a good time. He'd just wish he could be here, too." She raised her cup of coffee in a toast. "To memories and good times."

Mike raised his cup, too. "And to Vince, who was so much a part of you both."

They all followed suit and sat around the table finishing their coffee and cake, but it was as if that toast had signaled the end of the meal. All too soon, the visitors were putting on their coats.

Abby leaned in toward Sunny. "I can see why Mom enjoys your visits," she said in a low voice, not wanting Helena to hear. "Maybe we'll be able to get together again before I leave on Sunday."

"I'd like that," Sunny said, silently worrying, *Provided it doesn't involve Will arresting you.*

They stepped out into the chilly air, waving cheerful good-byes before the brisk walk home.

*

Shadow prowled the top floor, his tail lashing around in annoyance. Yes he did this every night, but in the dark time. This was too early, the house was empty, it was all wrong, wrong, wrong. He sank into a crouch at the top of the stairs, glaring down at the door and thinking dark thoughts.

I should get Sunny for leaving me all alone, he thought. *Make her sorry for doing that.* But what should he do? A disagreement between cats was a lot easier. You showed your teeth, sometimes the claws came out, and most times that was enough. One side usually backed down, solving things. If not, the claws really came out and sometimes there was blood. Shadow had been in enough fights. He'd won a lot, but lost a few, especially when he was very young. Mostly he remembered the pain.

The problem with two-legs was that these tactics usually didn't work on them. They were just too big, and often too stupid to realize what a cat was trying to do. He'd have to find a better way to vent his annoyance.

That gave Shadow an idea. *Maybe I can let out a little*

bad air when I'm under the covers with her tonight, he thought. *Sunny really hates when I do that.*

He started down the stairs, aiming for the kitchen where he could bolt down some food and maybe fill his belly, when he heard voices outside the door. Sunny!

For a wild second, he considered leaping down the rest of the stairs to pounce on her feet when she came in. But Shadow pushed that idea down. *No. You're mad at her. No playing.*

Although a good sneak attack might scare her . . .

He forced himself to a sedate trot as the keys rattled in the lock, getting halfway to the kitchen before the door opened.

Shadow turned to look over his shoulder, and his heart lurched for a moment just at the sight of his Sunny, her face pink from the cold outside, stepping in and taking off her coat. He ruthlessly crushed the desire to run to her, to wind round her ankles, sniff out where she'd gone, and mark her as his.

No being nice, he reminded himself. *She went and left me.*

It turned out that getting off the stairs was a good thing, because the Old One mumbled something and began climbing up to the hall above. Sunny and her He went into the room with the picture box. They didn't turn it on, though, sitting on the big chair together and talking. Sunny was doing most of the speaking. Shadow couldn't understand it; but her tone sounded nervous.

Maybe you're blaming the wrong one, the cat thought. *What if Sunny's He came here and made them go away?*

He seemed to turn up more and more lately, taking Sunny away at all sorts of odd times.

The problem was, how could Shadow show his displeasure? Sunny's He was even bigger than she was, and dumber about a lot of cat things. *If I just ignore him, he'd probably like that,* Shadow thought. *He'd get to be with Sunny instead of me.*

This was very bad, and Shadow couldn't solve it by charging in with a war cry and his claws out.

Maybe I can sneak up and bite him on the ankle when he tries to rub faces with Sunny. Shadow started skulking forward.

I just hope he's not wearing those high foot-covers he sometimes uses, Shadow thought. *Don't think I could bite through those.*

*

Sunny gave Will an uncertain look as they settled on the couch. Mike, as he often did, had made his excuses and headed upstairs, leaving the living room to them.

But I don't think there'll be much smooching involved, Sunny thought. She sat on the edge of the couch. "Well, you dug just about as deeply as you could into Abby Martinson without announcing it," she said.

Will blinked at her tone. "You're not jealous, are you?"

"No, I could see what you were doing. That doesn't mean I won't be glad when she takes off back to California this weekend." Sunny paused for a second. "Did you get what you wanted?"

"Not sure." Will backed that up with a shrug. "Mainly I

was just trying to get a read on her when she wasn't biting my head off or cleaning my tie. I had hoped to gauge her reaction to a couple of things, but it wasn't easy. Abby's a trained actress. She can hide things." He glanced at her. "It's like your pal Neil Garret. Do you know the marshals actually train people in WitSec on how to evade giving answers?"

"He's not my friend." Sunny took a deep breath. "And he did talk to me after I called him Nicky. The problem is sorting out anything useful from the stream of good old BS."

"Did he say anything about Val Overton?" Will asked.

"Neil seems to like and respect her," Sunny replied. "Although I don't think he's above trying to use her if he had to. He might have asked her to squash Phil Treibholz, but he was holding that as a last resort." She explained about Neil's "buzz off" money. "He'd lose all that if Val decided it was too dangerous to let him stay around here."

Will scowled. "So now we've got Garret protecting his life and his money—a strong, double-header motive. And his pal Vane had a house full of guns. That could cover means. And he has no alibi—"

"Actually, Neil does," Sunny responded. "He just didn't want Val to hear it, because he'd get in trouble."

Will stared. "Worse trouble than a murder charge hanging over his head?"

"Trouble that might get him bounced out of witness protection—or hauled out of town without his money." She explained Neil's quest for alternate funding to pay off Treibholz. "He wound up trying to deal with a couple of guys we know, over in Portsmouth," she continued, but Will cut her off.

"Shostak and Lipko," he said, peering at her. "And you went and talked to them, didn't you?"

"They confirmed that Neil Garret was trying to hit them up for a bridge loan to keep his store going. Dani wasn't interested in his business. He figured it was going to fail, anyway. The thing is, though, that Neil was trying to convince them he was a good prospect through the estimated time of death. So, unless the medical examiner was way off, Neil has an alibi for both murders."

"Yeah, nice work, Sunny, but what were you thinking, talking to those guys alone? Maybe they seem like a charming foreign comedy act, but they're dangerous. Lipko especially."

"He saw me back to my car," Sunny told him.

That didn't make Will feel any better. "Sunny, you can't make a joke out of this." His voice grew sharp and he leaned toward her.

With a sound more like a throaty growl than a hiss, Shadow suddenly came leaping out from behind one of the chairs, attacking Will's ankle. Unfortunately, Will was wearing heavy boots, and the cat couldn't get his teeth set. He spat in disgust, then rocketed up, trying to attack the tie dangling from Will's neck. Shadow's hiss of triumph turned into a cry of dismay when one of his claws got caught in the heavy embroidered silk.

He dangled for a moment, then Sunny knelt to take his weight in her hands. "Now you've done it," she said.

"Are you talking to the cat, or to me?" Will asked.

"Both," Sunny answered, trying to work the claw free without leaving a big pull in the middle of the tie. "You for making him think he had to protect me, and him for almost destroying your Christmas present."

Having gotten Shadow loose, she got back onto the couch, keeping the cat in her lap. Sunny gently ran her fingers over Shadow's fur. "No problem here, Shadow. You take it easy, now."

She looked at Will. "I'm not going to make a joke or argue about it. You know how skittish Dani gets when he sees a badge. But he talked to me, and he confirmed Neil's alibi."

"I doubt if that would hold up in court," Will grumped.

Sunny laid a restraining hand on Shadow's shoulder. "I'm not talking about the DA. I'm talking about you."

"Yeah, I believe him. Dani wouldn't want the trouble." Will thought for a moment. "Did you get any kind of a feeling about things between Val and Neil?"

"I got the impression Neil is keeping a lot more secrets from her than about her," Sunny said. "He respects her—and the power she has over him. And while he's playing her to an extent—going to loan sharks, for instance—I don't think there's anything romantic involved. Neil showed more feeling over Abby Martinson." Remembering Will's quiet interrogation earlier, she asked, "Have you turned up something to make you suspicious of her?"

"Frankly, I wanted to see how she'd react when I mentioned guns." Will frowned. "I spent most of the day going over Charlie Vane's financials, which were, to put it mildly, a mess. But I stumbled across an ATM receipt that was pretty interesting. It was for the maximum amount, and it was drawn in a town called Vincentville, almost an hour's drive north of Augusta."

"What makes it so interesting?" Sunny asked.

"The date," Will replied. "According to Vane, on the day in question he was supposed to be out in the Gulf of Maine."

"Could it be a case of identity theft?" Sunny suggested.

"It's long enough ago that Vane would have gotten a statement—and should have noticed that there was a hole where that money should be. Just to be sure, I checked to see if the bank has anything on its security cameras. I also checked to see what was going on in Vincentville that would drag Vane so far inland. Went over the local newspapers and such and did find one item."

Will smiled. "On that date, Vincentville had a gun show."

16

Sunny stopped petting Shadow. "You think that's where the guns in Charlie Vane's house came from?"

"Well, some of them, I figure," Will said. "I expect he might have made himself a little conspicuous, buying an arsenal like that at a single gun show. Although there is some evidence he may have been using straw buyers up in Vincentville."

"Straw buyers?" Sunny frowned.

"That's a nice way of saying phoney-baloney buyers—people who step in to make a purchase for somebody who may have bad credit, or maybe a criminal record—or maybe just to hide the identity of the real buyer."

"I know that," Sunny told him. "What I was wondering about is how you dug up any evidence."

Will shrugged. "A friend of a friend. Or maybe I should say someone who owes a favor to an old state police buddy of mine. The guy owing the favor had a table at the Vincentville gun show. He went through his papers and found that he had a customer from Kittery Harbor."

"Somebody who wasn't Charlie Vane," Sunny said. "Kind of a coincidence, two people from our little town both being so far away in those parts."

"It will be a bit more trouble, trying to look at the records of other sellers—"

"Guys who don't owe favors," Sunny put in.

"But my bet is we'll find several other names from this part of the woods buying up guns there," Will finished. "At last we got one of them."

"And who is this fine, upstanding citizen?" Sunny asked.

"One Delbert Scabetti, according to the paperwork for the gun he bought. Local police records show he's got the colorful nickname of 'Scab.' While he's done a lot of borderline illegal stuff, he hasn't been convicted of a felony, which means he's still legal to own or buy guns."

Will grinned. "Best of all, we have a good chance of catching up with him right now. He may not be a pillar of the community, but he spends a lot of time propping up the bar at O'Dowd's."

O'Dowd's was the diviest dive bar in Kittery Harbor, the center of a little patch of urban blight at the edge of the old downtown district.

"We figured on going down there tonight and asking a few questions," Will went on.

"We who?" Sunny wanted to know.

"Val and myself," he replied. "I think she's more than capable of handling that joint."

"And I'm not?" Sunny said. "I've been in there a couple of times since I came back to town, for business and pleasure."

"You don't have to," Will began, but Sunny cut him off.

"What, I'm only good for sweet-talking information out of suspects like Charlie Vane and Neil? If this Scab guy can throw some light on whatever Vane was doing that got him killed, I want to hear it."

She got up and went to get her coat, Will reluctantly following—especially since Shadow jumped to the floor and took a fighting stance, making unpleasant noises at Will.

"This is unfair," Will muttered. "He's blaming me for your pigheaded behavior."

"Hey, I'm sorry, little guy." Sunny picked up the cat and brought him to the kitchen. She placed him beside his bowls and knelt to stroke his fur. "I won't be gone long—promise. I'll come home soon, and then we'll have some time together."

Shadow made a little sound of protest, but he didn't follow Sunny as she went to rejoin Will standing at the kitchen door. Still, his tail wig-wagged a mournful message as he watched her go.

Outside, she turned expectantly to Will. "What's the plan?"

"We go to pick up Val, and then off to O'Dowd's."

They had a quiet drive into town. Will apparently wasn't in the mood for conversation after what Sunny had told him—and how she'd insisted on tagging along. Val Overton stood by the front door of the motel, hurrying out when they arrived. It was a close fit as she squeezed in beside Sunny on the pickup's front seat.

"Hi, Sunny. Didn't expect to see you." Val reached into

her shoulder bag and brought out a can of beer. "There should be more than enough for the three of us."

Sunny stared. "For what?"

"Let's call it, oh, verisimilitude." Val popped the top on the can and offered it to Sunny. "Take a mouthful and swish it around. Having beer on our breath will make it look as though we've been bouncing around to different joints in town."

Will nodded as Sunny took a sip. Then he reached over for the can, raised it to his lips, and took a healthy swig, his cheeks working like the guy in the mouthwash ad.

Only this is sort of the opposite, Sunny thought as she worked the beer around in her mouth. Will swallowed, and so did Sunny. Val grinned and emptied the can. "Now we're set," she said.

Will started the truck, and they headed downtown.

"Has Will been keeping you in the loop on the investigation?" Val asked, her beery breath fogging the window.

"As much as he can, I guess," Sunny replied. "Looks as if you've run out of suspects."

"I know Neil doesn't have the most rock-solid alibi, but he's my witness, damn it," Val scowled. "I don't want him to be guilty. Maybe this gun show angle will turn up something new."

She didn't look very upbeat about it, though. "I'm thinking I may just have to pull Neil out of town. We've been over the crime scene and Treibholz's hotel over in Portsmouth. His briefcase hasn't turned up. Treibholz wasn't a high-tech kind of guy. He worked off paper and a cell phone, and he never went anywhere without his briefcase.

That's disappeared, along with the file on his search for Nick Gatto."

"So you're afraid someone has that information." Sunny frowned. "If that were the case, you'd think they'd have used it by now."

"Maybe they're still haggling over a sale," Will suggested as he smoothly negotiated a turn. "I'm sure Jimmy the Chopper would pay big for it."

"That's a consideration." Val's face was grim as the truck's heater finally kicked in, spreading the smell of beer through the cabin. "What I want to find is the leak that got Treibholz out here in the first place. We keep our cards pretty close to the vest in WitSec. Only three other people besides myself are supposed to know where Neil is."

"Well, I know where we are." Will pulled into a half-full parking lot fronting a wooden building that had once been painted white and had faded to a sort of moldy gray. "Welcome to beautiful O'Dowd's."

The long, low, squarish building looked like some sort of equipment shed that had grown beyond its useful size. It reminded Sunny of a block of cheese that had been nibbled by time instead of mice. The only sign that it was a business was a neon beer ad in one of the windows, and even that blinked on and off erratically, as if it were on its last legs.

"Let's get the show on the road." Will opened the door, slid from his seat, and then did the honors on the passenger-side door. Standing outside, Val sized up the place dubiously. "Can't be worse than some of the places I've visited in the line of duty," she said. "But you guys will owe me another meal in the Redbrick before I get out of town."

She sauntered up to the front door, a featureless ply-wood panel with a handle bolted on, pulled, and swore under her breath. "Stupid thing's stuck."

"Yeah, the wood swells." Will began reaching for the handle. But Val gave a sudden heave and the door swung open, letting out a blare of music and top-of-the-voice conversation, as well as a cloud of cigarette smoke flavored with beer fug.

Val sniffed appreciatively. "I think there's a little weed in there, too."

She swaggered in with Will and Sunny right behind. The interior décor was pretty much as it had been when Sunny and her college friends used to come in for a little underage drinking. Back then, O'Dowd's had been seedy, with a long bar against the back wall and scattered tables made from splintery plywood. Posters from long-forgotten rock bands dotted the walls, fumed into sepia tones from the cigarette smoke that hung in the air. State law made bars smoke free more than ten years ago, but the clientele wasn't the most law-abiding sort.

Jasmine the barmaid glanced in their direction, recognized Will as a cop, and hurried to the far end of the bar. *That's kind of snooty, denying us service,* Sunny thought until she saw Jasmine grab a guy by the arm and whisper— or was that shout quietly—in his ear, nodding toward the newcomers. Her friend stared at Will, and the sloppy-looking cigarette dangling from his lips suddenly disappeared into his mouth. He squeezed his eyes in pain as he gave a convulsive swallow.

Val obviously caught that byplay, because she grinned. "Nice bunch. And a really jumping place."

She stepped up to the bar, and now Sunny had to grin at the reaction from the regulars. On the one hand, Val moved like a cop. On the other, she was a good-looking, unfamiliar female. A sort of push-pull effect ran its way through the scruffy-looking guys lining the bar.

Will stood beside Val and pulled Sunny onto a stool on his other side. *Guess he wants to be surrounded by bait,* she decided.

Jasmine the barmaid continued pretending to ignore them. For Sunny's male classmates, Jasmine had probably been a greater draw than cheap beer. An English major had described her as an exotic flower rising in the middle of a squalid swamp. *More like an exotic dancer,* Sunny thought. Jasmine specialized in outfits that combined brevity and astonishing engineering to give the impression of ripe fruit about to—but never quite—spill out.

These days, Jasmine was more on the overripe side. Fifteen years of beer and cigarette smoke had not done wonders for her figure or her skin. A strip of gray always showed at the part of her unnaturally black hair. And somewhere along the way she'd lost a tooth. But she still kept up her femme fatale act . . .

Sunny blinked. Something had been nagging her subconscious, and now she realized what it was. Jasmine was wearing one of her signature seriously-strained tops, but she was wearing it over what looked like a leotard. Sunny leaned over to Will. "Is Jasmine suddenly worrying about the cold?" she yelled.

The answer came from a guy lounging against the bar on the opposite side. "Her old man don't like her showing off so much."

Sunny gave him a once-over. The stranger had a hatchet face with too much nose and chin, a wisp of mustache between them, and a pair of beady, greedy eyes. "Came along and ruined the one good thing about this bar." He glared at Jasmine. "It sure wasn't her beer or her personality."

Somehow, Jasmine must have caught the conversation, because she came charging over. "Don't make a bigger jackass of yourself than you need to, Scab. She's with the cop." Jasmine jerked her head in Will's direction.

Bingo, Sunny thought.

"It's a free country. I can say whatever I want," Scab blustered.

"And Bear can kick your scrawny butt from here to Augusta, even if he is all banged up," Jasmine told him. "You want me to ask him and find out?"

Scab stepped away from the barmaid and headed down the bar, gravitating in Val's direction this time.

Jasmine grimaced. "What can I get you?"

"Beer." Will brought up a good, yeasty burp. He nodded toward Val. "I've got a friend in town, and we've been hitting all the bars."

"Yeah, and on a cop's salary, I guess you want to keep it cheap." Jasmine got busy below the bar. In a moment she came up with three plastic mugs of beer, about half of it rapidly disintegrating head.

Val took her mug, drained it, and handed it back. "Thanks."

That surprised Jasmine, who refilled it and then took the charge out of the twenty Will put on the bar.

"I miss all the exciting news," Sunny said. "How long has this Bear guy been around?"

Jasmine's expression softened a little. "Just a while."

"He's got Scab jealous."

Jasmine responded with a scornful laugh. "Scab. All he does is look down my tops."

I thought that's what they were designed for, Sunny thought, but she didn't say that out loud.

"Bear is . . . different." Jasmine leaned forward, as if she were happy to find a female she could confide in. "Oh, he's got his rough edges—he wasn't an angel. But he respects me—and wants me to respect myself more." She gestured to the cover-up she was wearing under her tawdry-looking top.

Sunny grinned. "Yeah, but I bet it cuts down on your tips."

Jasmine winced a little. "To tell you the truth, the tips haven't been rolling in lately. Bear is—was—a biker. He's got a really cool Harley, but he came down here from the other end of the state to leave that life behind. He's a great mechanic, fixed up my old wreck. Once he finds a job around here . . . well, I think I'll be saying good-bye to O'Dowd's."

"The place won't be the same without you," Sunny said, surprising herself to discover she meant it. "I hope it all turns out right."

"Thanks." Jasmine smiled, then turned to head down the bar to where another patron was holding out his mug.

Sunny turned her attention to the conversation proceeding on the other side of Will. Scab Scabetti was puffed up like a toad, telling Val what he would do if Bear so much as looked at him cross-eyed. "Aaah, he's big but slow," Scab said. "I'd be in and out, before—"

"Before he still kicked your butt from here to Augusta," Will interrupted.

Scab gave him a dirty look. "Look, buddy, you already got a girl. Why do you have to get all up in my face?"

"Hey, it's just business," Will replied. "You were up that way recently, weren't you?"

"Ummmm—maybe." Scab's beady eyes got wary.

"A little buying trip, I hear."

Scab began to get alarmed, but Val draped an arm over his shoulders. "Oh, wow, this sounds interesting. What were you buying? Something dangerous?"

Scab's male hormones kicked in again. "Guns," he said, swelling up once more. "There was a gun show up north, and a friend took a bunch of us."

Val's eyes went wide. "You bought guns? Do you have one on you? Can I see it?"

That's all we need, guys bringing guns into booze joints like O'Dowd's. Sunny glanced around. *Then again, we don't have the sharpest tools in the shed on display here. Doesn't Scab realize that he's spouting off in front of a cop—about something that's supposed to be illegal?*

A thicker than usual cloud of smoke came wafting past, making her cough. *Oh. Right.*

Scab deflated a little and shook his head. "No, they're with my friend. I think he's gonna make a big killing—" He broke off with a glance at Will. "I mean, make a lot of money. If he took all the guns we got down south to Massachusetts, he could get twice as much as he paid, maybe more—"

Val brought her lips close to Scab's ear. "You know what else he'd get?"

Scab looked a little dazed. "No, what?"

Val's voice hardened. "A federal rap for illegally

transporting guns across state lines." She reached under her coat and produced a leather case. "Know what this is?" She opened it up to display her badge.

The sight of that left Scab a little short of words—and maybe breath. He managed to squeak out a no.

"That's a federal marshal's badge, as in federal rap. Now, do you want to go in as an accessory before the fact?"

"Think!" Scab gabbled. "I said I *think* he was going to go there and sell them! I don't know! I don't know nothin'!"

"Tell us how it went down," Will said, his voice as hard as Val's.

"This guy comes in here, asks if I want to make an easy fifty bucks. He's got two carloads of people going up to Vincentville for this show. A couple of guys from here, and some of his drinking buddies from a bar down by the waterfront. We go up there, he looks over the different tables, then he sends us around to make purchases." Scab snickered. "He spent so much, he had to go to the ATM and withdraw money to pay us."

Blowing his whole alibi to do it, Sunny thought.

Scab's skinny face tightened. "Then, when I came back, this Bear guy threatened to take me apart."

"Why would he do that?" Sunny asked.

"I dunno," Scab whined. "I thought I'd spend some of the money I made here. When Bear found out how I got it, all of a sudden he was on my case." His face took on the same sullen look Shadow got when someone picked him up against his will—a large human against a much smaller cat. "Yeah, big, bad Bear, with his stupid motorcycle tattoo—didn't know how to spell Satan, had a big mother *Y* in the middle of it."

Will leaned in. "Satyn's Guard?"

"Yeah. I never heard of them. But he acted like a big man. Big *Y* on his arm. Stupid."

Will stood silent for a moment, then nodded. "That's it then. We can go."

Val looked suddenly serious. "I guess so."

Will turned to Scab. "And you'll keep your mouth shut, if you know what's good for you."

"Yeah, right, I'm going to tell that jackass." Scab turned back to the bar and his drink.

As she followed Val and Will to the door, Sunny said, "Y'know, I'd like to know what's going on, too."

"I'll clue you in," Will promised, glancing around. "Outside."

When they got back into his pickup, the beer-scented interior smelled like mountain-fresh air compared to the sludge they'd been breathing in O'Dowd's. "So what's the story, Will?"

"It goes back a few years ago, when I first joined the state police and wound up in Troop F, up by the Canadian border. A local tattoo artist turned up nearly beaten to death. He'd annoyed some clients by making a typographical error in some tattoos. They were supposed to mark the formation of a new gang, but he'd done three guys before they caught the mistake. He inked in Satan as S-A-T-I-N."

"Satin?" Sunny had to choke down a laugh. "Sounds like he depended on spell check."

Will shook his head. "The three guys stuck with it didn't think it was funny, and the beating began. The only thing that saved the guy was that his partner suggested putting wide horns on the offending *I* to make it a *Y.* So they became

Satyn's Guard. The other members got their tattoos with a regular-sized *Y*. But the three with the typo had to make do with, as Scab described it, 'a big mother *Y*' in Satyn."

Val nodded. "Of those three, one died in a shootout with federal officers, one is in jail, and the last is Yancey Kilbane, chief enforcer for the Satyn's Guard biker gang."

"A biker gang up by the Canadian border," Sunny said slowly.

"You got it," Will agreed. "A biker gang that specializes in smuggling anything from cigarettes to assault weapons. . ."

17

"So now we have a new motive for the murder of Charlie Vane," Sunny said. "Good, old-fashioned business get-up-and-go—in this instance, getting up and going to eliminate the competition." She looked from Val to Will. "Is it really such a big business?"

"You heard Scab talking about people getting twice as much as they paid in Maine for guns they sold in Massachusetts," Will told her. "In Canada, where the gun laws are even stricter, a gun can go for ten times the price you'd pay here in the States. People build special panels in the doors of cars and trucks to bring them across the border. One bunch was targeting cars with Canadian plates, sticking guns in the bumpers along with a GPS. Unsuspecting drivers would go home, bringing the contraband in for them, then they'd track down the cars for a later pickup."

"Yipes," Sunny muttered.

"I know." Val frowned. "Does that count as slick or sick?"

"Actually, I was thinking I must be in the wrong business." Sunny shook her head, echoing, "Ten times the price."

"Sure," Val pointed out, "if you don't mind having the ATF after you, not to mention the customs authorities of two countries—and competitors ready to shoot you dead."

"Yeah." Sunny sighed. "That part of the business sounds more like our pal the shark of the fish market."

"The biker gangs up north are way more vicious than Deke Sweeney ever was." Will looked a little sick. "I've seen things—it's nothing you'd want to talk about."

Val shifted suddenly in her seat, her elbow digging uncomfortably into Sunny's ribs. "You've got to give this scheme top marks for ingenuity," she said. "Rather than driving into Ontario or Quebec, Vane could take his fishing vessel and make a bulk transfer to the Canadian Maritimes. I just have one question. How does a fisherman, even a somewhat shady fisherman like Charlie Vane, have the connections to start gun-running in the first place, much less become competition for an outfit like Satyn's Guard?"

Will sat silent behind the wheel for a long moment. "We'll have to take a serious look at his friends and associates."

"There can't be that many—" Sunny began. Then her voice died down. "Oh."

"Yeah, 'oh,'" Will chimed in.

"Uh-huh." Val's voice was dry. "One associate comes to mind, with criminal connections."

"A former mobster, in fact," Sunny said. "Neil Garret, formerly Nick Gatto. Maybe you should be checking his associates, to see if someone wound up in Canada."

"To hell with that," Val said flatly, all trace of her earlier party-girl persona gone. "I vote we go up and get some answers from the horse's mouth—or whichever end of the horse he really is."

Will nodded, started the truck, and headed out of town.

"There are still a lot of holes in this theory," Sunny said as they drove along quiet streets. "For instance, how did these Satyn's Guard people know to come here to Kittery Harbor?"

"Biker gangs have been recruited as muscle by some of the old-line crime families in Canada," Will suggested. "Maybe they were able to leverage their position with the Montreal mobsters to track down the Canadian end of the gun-running pipeline."

"So Garret's connection talks," Sunny said.

"No doubt with lots of persuasion," Val put in.

"And this Kilbane character comes to town to take care of the American end," Will went on. "He goes to the fish market to take out Neil and finds Treibholz breaking into the place. Maybe Treibholz tries to bargain with him, maybe Yancey shoots first and asks questions later."

"That explains one thing—why the body was left in the freezer," Sunny said. "Jasmine said her guy came to town on a big Harley. No way would he try transporting a dead body on a motorcycle."

That got a laugh from Will and Val. They got out on the county road that led northward to Sturgeon Springs. The town was more countrified than Kittery Harbor. Houses stood farther apart, but unlike the ritzier suburbs, most of that land was scrub forest rather than the elegantly manicured grounds of the new developments.

Claire Donally

A graveled drive led through the trees to the place that Neil Garret rented. At least it was supposed to be graveled. Will's pickup hit a lot of bald spots as he jounced his way to the clapboard house.

Val jumped out as soon as Will stopped the truck, strode to the door, started ringing the bell, and then swore. "Neil told me the stupid thing didn't work." She pounded heavily with her fist.

"All right, all right, keep your shirt on." Neil's voice came from the rear of the small house. A moment later, he opened the door while still tying the belt around his bathrobe.

"Oh. Val. And, uh, Will. And Sunny?" His voice went up, and so did the corners of his mouth. But Sunny saw the way Neil's eyes darted among them, trying to figure out the reason for this late-night visit and what he might say to them.

Val didn't give him a chance to speak. "Considering all the trouble I've kept your sorry butt out of, I think it's really lousy that you decided to play me."

"P-p-play you?" Neil echoed, somehow maintaining that phony smile.

"Look, Neil, keeping up the dumb act is only going to make me angrier with you," Val told him. "We've figured out the little scam you had going with Charlie Vane—the guns going to Canada."

That wiped the last traces of a smile off Neil's face. "I—we—it was—"

He sounds even worse than he did trying to sell those skate wings to that woman, Sunny thought.

"Just tell it straight, and don't insult our intelligence." Will spoke over Neil's babbling.

For a second, Neil seemed to develop a slow leak. His

shoulders slumped, his head went down, his gaze drifted to his feet. "I put every dime I had into the shop, and it wasn't enough," he said quietly. "I just didn't figure on how expensive things would be. And how could I raise any cash? The ways I knew how to make money were closed to me."

He shook his head. "Then I remembered this guy who'd been in the joint with me, Gino Lodestro—they used to drive him crazy, calling him G-Lo for short. He used to tell me the stock market was nothing compared to the gun market."

"Like making ten times the original price in a single transaction," Sunny said.

Neil spread his hands. "That's what Gino said. He used to run guns across the border into British Columbia. But then he headed east, working for one of the old-style families in Montreal. I managed to track him down, gave him a call. He took the cream off the top—offered six times the price so he'd make a handsome profit. All I needed was a way to get the guns to him. Charlie Vane had been moaning about money ever since I met him, so I put the proposition to him. We'd go in fifty-fifty. I scraped together every cent I could and gave it to him. He took care of the buying, going to gun shows. That's something I couldn't do. We packed the merchandise in waterproof containers, and Charlie took them for a boat ride."

"Where was the transfer made?" Will asked.

"A cove somewhere in Nova Scotia," Neil replied. "Gino had a van waiting, took the whole delivery, Charlie got the cash, and he brought it in with a load of fish. It was supposed to be a one-time thing, to get us back on our feet. Then Deke Sweeney dropped the hammer on us, banning us from the Portsmouth market. Money got tight pretty fast. And when Phil Treibholz showed up . . ." Neil took a deep breath.

"I gave him everything I had left, but it wasn't enough. Treibholz wanted more. That's when he went after your cat, Sunny, to show he meant business. I took Charlie Vane out to breakfast, suggested we try another load. He told me no way, just the one time had been too dangerous. He could lose his boat and put his boy in jail. So I had to try and find some other way to raise the money."

He glanced at Sunny, but she kept quiet. *No need to bring Dani and Olek into this,* she decided.

"So how did you feel when you heard about Vane getting killed—with a house full of guns?" Val asked.

Neil looked as if he'd just taken a bite of something vile. "I realized he'd been playing me. He must have made a deal of his own with Gino, probably even hauled a couple of shipments without me even knowing. When I think how he gave me this pious song and dance, all the time screwing me over—"

"You could have killed him, huh?" Will said.

Neil's eyes snapped in Will's direction. "No, that's not what I meant," he said quickly. "I never killed Charlie—or Treibholz. When Phil turned up dead, I figured maybe somebody trailed him from California, and I sweated bullets. Then Charlie got it, and I wondered if it involved our deal with Gino. When I set things up, I got a burner phone and did a little traveling. I didn't want things to trace back to here, so I gave Gino the impression that I was in Boston."

"But Charlie Vane may not have been so careful," Sunny said.

"Maybe not," Neil admitted. "When Charlie got shot and

I realized what was going on, I tried to get hold of Gino. But his number keeps going to voice mail."

"Not a good sign," Sunny said.

"Does the name Yancey Kilbane mean anything to you?" Will asked.

Neil shook his head. "Who is he?"

"He's an enforcer for one of the biker gangs running guns across the border. We think he's the one who dealt with Treibholz and Vane—and you're next on his hit parade." Val thumped Neil's chest with a forefinger. "Get your go bag. I'm pulling you out of here."

"But my store—my money," Neil protested.

"You won't enjoy either if you're dead." Val turned away, got out her cell phone, and hit something on speed dial. "Get your bag," she told Neil, glancing over her shoulder.

Neil slouched away while Val identified herself over the phone. "I need a pickup, and someplace safe to keep a witness," she said. The arrangements were made by the time Neil returned with a small travel bag. "We've got a quiet place where you can lie low until local law resolves this thing with Yancey Kilbane," Val told him. "Depending on the results of that, we make a decision as to whether you stay in this area."

Sunny and Will stayed with Val and Neil until a big SUV came grinding up the gravel path. A pair of men were aboard, and the driver got out, holding up his marshal's star as he advanced toward the house.

"You Overton?" he asked Val. She produced her own badge. "I'm Kirby, and that's McDonagh in the passenger seat. Where's our customer?"

Neil bent and picked up his bag.

"I'll be riding with you," Val said. She turned to Will and Sunny. "Well, this has been an exciting evening, but I've got work to do."

Will nodded. "So do I—after I get Sunny home."

Sunny fought back a yawn. *Wouldn't look good, with all the forces of law and order set to start marching,* she thought.

They watched the SUV disappear into the night and then climbed into Will's pickup. "So what are you going to do?" she asked.

"I'm going to bring in Yancey Kilbane," Will replied.

"Alone?" Sunny couldn't keep the worry out of her voice.

"No, this is too important," Will said. "I'll arrange for backup." He sighed. "Even though it means going through the chain of command."

"Is that such a bad thing?"

"It will take time, and I have a feeling the clock started ticking the moment we walked into O'Dowd's." Will frowned. "It's not a good feeling."

"Well, Neil is safe," Sunny pointed out. "Val just spirited him off to the proverbial undisclosed location."

"She did her part," Will agreed. "Catching Kilbane is mine. And the longer we wait, the more chance he realizes we're on to him and disappears."

He drove Sunny home and kissed her good night—good morning by that point—but she could tell he was distracted. "You know where I'll be tomorrow," she told him. "Let me know how it's going, okay?"

Will nodded and drove off. Sunny turned to open the door and sneak inside—and encountered an accusing pair of gold-flecked gray eyes.

"Sorry, buddy," she whispered, leaning down to scoop Shadow up. "Things happened."

Shadow's nose wrinkled and he wriggled out of her arms, landing on all four feet and stalking off, his tail lashing.

Guess I still have a good whiff of O'Dowd's all over me, Sunny thought. *That counts as two strikes to Shadow.*

She crept upstairs and took a quick shower, mainly to get the stink of cigarette smoke out of her hair. As she sat on the edge of the bed in her pajamas, a towel wrapped turban fashion around her head, Shadow shouldered the bedroom door a little farther open and came in, making a big production out of sniffing all around her.

"So, do I pass inspection?" Sunny whispered to him.

Shadow responded by making a leap into her lap. Sunny gently stroked his fur until he lay boneless, purring up at her.

"I'd love to keep doing this, but I have to get up—" She looked at the clock radio and winced. "All too soon."

She wiggled around to lay on the bed and tuck herself in. Shadow burrowed through the covers and into her arms, a warm and comforting presence as Sunny quickly drifted off.

*

As soon as Sunny started to breathe deeply in sleep, Shadow carefully disentangled himself. He dropped quietly down to the floor, crept out the door, and headed down the stairs. The house was dark and quiet. It was time to patrol.

I should have done more to let Sunny know she did a bad thing, going off and making me wait like that, he thought. But what? This wasn't something to scratch and bite over, even play-biting. *I should have stayed away from her. The way she smelled, that would have been easy.*

But then, when she was in her room, slightly damp with all the bad smells washed away . . . Shadow remembered her hands gently petting him and gave a little quiver. No, that was too nice to pass up.

I'll think of something to make her feel sorry, he decided, padding along the darkened hallway. *Next time.*

*

Sunny dragged herself out of bed the next morning, winced at her tangled hair, washed her face and brushed her teeth, dressed, and headed down the stairs. Mike had breakfast ready. "I heard you go out with Will. Late night, huh?"

"We may finally have gotten some things straightened out with the case," she said.

Mike nodded. "That's his job, though. What about yours?"

"Just the usual Friday rush for weekend bookings," Sunny said. "I should be able to keep my eyes open."

She finished eating, went to get her parka, and stopped, shaking her head. The coat still stunk of cigarette smoke from last night's visit to O'Dowd's. Sunny picked it up and brought it back to the kitchen. "Guess I'll have to hang this outside and let it air out."

Mike waved at the air in front of his face. "Yeah. And maybe knock off smoking all those cheap cigars."

Shadow appeared in the doorway. But, instead of making his usual beeline to his bowls, he ostentatiously circled around Sunny and the offending coat.

"I guess that makes it unanimous." Sunny sighed and

took the parka outside, hanging it on a wrought-iron curlicue that came down from the light beside the kitchen door.

"I'll keep an eye on it," Mike promised, "and occasionally use my nose to see if the fumes have dissipated."

"Thanks, Dad." Sunny got another coat and headed out to her Wrangler. She drove carefully in to work, arrived at the office with no problems, and settled into the daily routine.

But she found she couldn't keep still. She'd be working on e-mails, when suddenly she'd get a vision of Will walking up to an apartment door and a gun battle erupting. Sometimes there'd be uniformed cops with him, and she'd see someone she knew like Ben Semple fall to the ground bleeding. Other times it would be Val Overton. Worst of all, though, her mind's eye would see Will getting hit by a flying bullet, falling, and then lying motionless. She'd shake her head to bump that image away, but it kept coming back.

Sunny bent over her keyboard, trying to keep her thoughts on work alone, when the door abruptly swung open, making her jump. Will strode in.

"Is it over? Do you have him? Kilbane?" The words fairly burst from her lips.

But Will shook his head. "Ingersoll stuck his oar in, and he wants to dot every I and cross every T before we try to do anything."

Captain Dan Ingersoll was the second in command in the Elmet County Sheriff's Department. As a newly elected sheriff, Lenore Nesbit depended heavily on him for proper police procedure—maybe a little too much in this case, Sunny suspected.

Ingersoll wasn't happy with the way Will tied up the last murder case, she thought. *He's got Will pegged as some sort of glory hound, after a high-profile arrest, whether it's justified or not.*

Will must have been tuned into her mind, because he said, "The captain thinks we're reaching too far, that we don't really know who this Bear is."

"We suspect we know who he is," Sunny tried to argue, but she knew that wouldn't move an editor, much less a police captain.

"So I've tried to find out more," Will said. "Your friend Jasmine has had a visitor in her apartment for the last couple of weeks, a guy with a motorcycle. He hasn't been seen since the ice storm, when he apparently had an accident. The Harley has been under wraps, and Jasmine has hit several pharmacies for medical supplies."

Sunny frowned, trying to call up a memory. "Jasmine said something last night about Bear being banged up."

"At least he wouldn't have road rash." Will broke off when he saw the look of incomprehension on Sunny's face. "Usually when a motorcycle goes down while it's moving, the biker keeps on going and can scrape away a lot of skin on the pavement. On ice, the cyclist is usually more padded, and the ground is more slippery—that's why the bike goes down in the first place."

Sunny waved that image aside. "So we know Bear was out the night that Charlie Vane died."

"So were a lot of people who wound up in hospitals—and a couple in morgues." Will pulled out a sheaf of papers from inside his coat and put them on Sunny's desk. "I managed to get copies of Kilbane's file from a friend in the state police."

She laid them flat, examining the mug shot appearing on

the first page. The markings in the background showed that Yancey Kilbane stood several inches over six feet, and his shoulders were wide and husky. He had a surprisingly snub nose with shaggy brows and a shiny shaved scalp above and a big, bushy Fu Manchu mustache below.

"He doesn't look very bearlike to me," Sunny said. "Except for his build."

"From what I've been able to find out, he let his hair grow back and sprouted a full set of whiskers now," Will explained. "Don't know if he did it for this job, but it certainly changed his look entirely."

Sunny turned a page. "At least you have his fingerprints."

"Yeah, but they won't help until we've got him in custody." He blew out an exasperated breath. "The problem is that Ingersoll wants to hedge his bets. If Bear doesn't turn out to be Kilbane, we're only asking him to assist in our investigation. If he is Kilbane, we might be stepping into World War Three, and the captain wants more than a few patrol officers trying to bring him in."

Sunny blinked. "So where does he figure on getting this extra help? From Val and the federal marshals?"

"Ingersoll wants the state police tactical team. Which means additional hoops to jump through." Will shook his head. "And more delay. Now I'm hoping we can get this operation underway before the kids start coming home from school." He reassembled the papers on Sunny's desk. "Wish me luck."

"All of it in the world. And be careful, Will."

He nodded and left.

Sunny couldn't eat lunch. She got on the state police

web site and saw pictures of the tactical team, feeding new and unpleasant daydreams. They looked professional as all get-out, in helmets and camouflage uniforms, assault rifles at the ready. One photo showed a guy poised with some sort of one-man battering ram beside a door. In Sunny's mind, however, things kept going wrong. The Yancey Kilbane whose blurry mug shot she'd seen kept appearing in the doorway, wearing what would have been a ridiculous wig and fake beard except for the big handgun he was aiming, making even bigger holes in any things or people who got in his way.

Finally, Sunny couldn't stand it anymore. She used her computer to get the live stream from the local all-news channel.

Might as well hear it as it happens, she thought.

But there was no news. Oh, there were politics and sports, traffic and weather, and a feature on Seasonal Affective Disorder, but no reports of police activity in downtown Kittery Harbor.

The sky was beginning to darken when Will reappeared at the office door.

"Thank God!" Sunny jumped up from her desk and went to him. But the look on his face stopped her. "The tactical team moved in perfectly. They woke Jasmine out of a sound sleep and probably scared her into a lot more gray hair. But Yancey Kilbane wasn't there, and Jasmine doesn't know where her Bear could be. He was in bed when she came off her shift at O'Dowd's and went to sleep. But he and his stuff were gone. So was her car, by the way."

He smacked a frustrated fist onto the top of a desk. "I couldn't keep the place under surveillance without tipping off that we were interested. So while I was doing a lot of paperwork, Kilbane—or whoever—skipped."

Will took a deep breath. "I apologize, Sunny, but there's no one else I can talk about this with—at least no one that I'd want to. I'm off to headquarters with the head of the tac team to give a report to Ingersoll and Lenore Nesbit." He managed to summon up the ghost of a smile. "At least nothing else can go wrong today."

As if on cue, his cell phone began ringing. Will took it out and brought it to his ear. "Price," he said. "Hi, Val. I guess news about our foul-up must have traveled fast." His expression changed as he listened. "What? When? Is there anything we can do? Yes. Yes, I can see that. Keep me posted."

He clicked off his phone and looked at Sunny. "I know it's no fun listening to only one side of a conversation. Trust me, you wouldn't have enjoyed the whole thing. I was wrong. Things could get worse. Val Overton just told me that Neil Garret has disappeared from the motel where the marshals were keeping him under wraps. Apparently he got a text and a little while later was in the wind."

18

"**Neil ran off?** Why would he do that?" It didn't make sense to Sunny. Neil hadn't been happy when Val told him he had to go. But he had to realize that with Yancey Kilbane out there, he wasn't safe: "What are you going to do?"

"Nothing much we can do. WitSec is a voluntary deal. People leave it all the time." Will shook his head. "Of course, that decision doesn't help their life expectancy. And practically speaking, putting a BOLO out on Neil would just make him more conspicuous."

"What does he think he's doing? Did he take his bag?"

"No, he left that. Used the old out-the-bathroom-window routine," Will said.

"So he's got the clothes on his back and whatever money is in his pockets." Sunny frowned in bafflement. "I know Neil didn't want to let his investment in the shop go. But

I don't think he can arrange a quick turnover sale late on a Friday."

"Val said she was going to check out his house and the store," Will said. "For the rest . . ." He shrugged. "This is one I'll happily pass along to the decision-makers in Levett."

He gave Sunny a perfunctory kiss on the cheek. "I'll catch up with you later this evening. After all this stuff has been hashed out." On that melancholy note, he left.

Sunny plunged back into the rush for last-minute reservations on quaint Maine bed-and-breakfasts. When she surfaced, it was time to close down the office. She drove home to find a welcoming committee by the door—Mike as well as Shadow.

"What's the matter, Dad?" She could tell Mike was worried—he couldn't stand still. And his mood had communicated itself to Shadow, who stayed so close underfoot, Sunny was in danger of tripping with every step she took.

"We don't want to sound like jittery old people, but—well, Helena gave me a call. She took a nap this afternoon, and when she got up, Abby was gone, and so was the car."

"She could have gone shopping—getting something for supper," Sunny suggested. The sky had been fully dark when she walked from her Wrangler to the house, but that was just Maine in winter. It wasn't even six o'clock yet.

"Maybe she's making a big fuss over nothing, but Abby's been gone—" He looked at his watch. "Almost an hour and a half. And usually she leaves a note." Mike bit his lip. "I was wondering—maybe if you gave Will a call—"

Yeah, that would be just about the topper for his day. His third missing person, this one gone an hour and a half. But she kept that thought to herself.

"I think it's a little, um, premature to go to the police quite yet. And I know Will is tied up right now." She looked at her father's worried expression. "But I bet that Mrs. M. is pretty upset, too. What do you say we go over there and keep her company?"

She turned to get Mike's coat off the peg by the door and encountered a furry body just about wrapped around her ankle. Shadow's gold-flecked eyes met Sunny's in a full-on guilt stare, sending the message *You're not leaving me again, are you?*

Sighing, she reached down and picked up the cat. "We'll all go. Maybe Shadow can distract Helena until Abby comes home."

Soon, I hope, she silently added.

They walked the few blocks to the Martinson place and rang the bell, eliciting some disconsolate woofs from the basement. Mrs. M. opened the door. "I put Toby downstairs in his crate. He was getting a little—let's call it high-strung. And what's worse, he was getting it from me. I hope you don't think I'm being a silly old woman, Sunny."

Mike stepped forward and took Helena in his arms for a comforting hug. "Nobody's saying that."

"Well, I'm certainly thinking it." Helena Martinson stepped back to usher them into the house, finally noticing the additional member of the group. "Well, hello, Shadow. What brings you over here?"

"I've been running around a bit lately, and I didn't want Shadow to think I was ignoring him again."

Helena brought her hand forward for Shadow to sniff. "It should be safe," she said with a crooked smile. "I washed up after getting Toby settled."

Shadow lay quietly in Sunny's arms while Mrs. M. gently stroked his fur. "Abby would probably say you're spoiling that cat, but I think it's all right."

They moved into the living room, seating themselves on the couch. Sunny arranged Shadow in her lap so that Helena could keep petting. "It's better with company," Mrs. M. said, relaxing a little. "Waiting alone, all sorts of things pop into your head."

Sunny nodded, remembering her unpleasant daydreams about Will throughout the afternoon.

"It's just that Abby is more thoughtful about letting me know where she's going. At least she has been since coming home on this visit."

And discovering that her mother is a bit older and, yeah, frailer than she remembers her being, Sunny thought. *Been there, done that.*

"I'm sure she just popped out to get something, and then—maybe she met a friend from the old days," Sunny said.

Although most of the people our age left town to find careers somewhere else, that annoying reporter who lived in the back of Sunny's brain commented.

"Or if not a school friend, there are plenty of parents around who might recognize her. Especially after that nice story Ken Howell put in the *Courier*." Maybe Sunny was grasping at straws, but Helena Martinson nodded.

"Yes, we have a couple of people—parents of schoolmates—who commented on that. They said how nice it was to see her around town."

Helena smiled, but anxiety crept back into her eyes. "Mike wanted to call you when I first told him that Abby wasn't around, but I thought if I asked you for help, it should be face-to-face." Her smile wobbled a little bit. "You have a friend on the police force."

"And I'm afraid he's up to his neck right now." Sunny tried to make her voice gentle. "He was expecting to make an arrest, and the person he's after got away."

Her voice trailed off as she remembered the other missing person of the afternoon. "Helena, could we go upstairs and take a look at Abby's room?"

Mrs. M. stared at her. "Whatever for?"

"Well, she may—" Sunny fumbled for a reason. "She may have left a note for you there. Did you look?"

Hope appeared in the older woman's eyes. "I didn't think of that." She led the way upstairs. "I know I often get distracted in the middle of something and leave it where it was instead of where I was going to put it."

She opened the door to a room that looked pretty much unchanged since Abby's college days. A framed poster from the summer Shakespeare festival she'd worked on held pride of place over the bed.

Mrs. M. checked the small student's desk and the spread on the bed. Sunny edged open the closet to make sure Abby's travel bag was still in place. She spotted the wheeled carry-on immediately.

"Sunny?" She turned, silently cursing herself, to find Helena staring at her. "What are you doing?"

"I wanted to make sure Abby's things were still here," Sunny said, trying to figure out the nicest way to put what she had to say. "Neil Garret has apparently taken off."

"Is that who Will expected to arrest?" Mrs. M. asked.

"No, this is another thing altogether," Sunny replied. "But you remember that Abby said she had . . . known Neil back in California."

"This is the first time I'm hearing about this," Mike said.

"There are reasons, Dad," Sunny told him. She turned back to Helena. "Anyway, I remembered their friendship, and it struck me that maybe Abby would help him."

And maybe their relationship was a lot more than Abby let on, and that Neil either called her here, or maybe she contacted him after spotting him in his shop. However you slice it, Abby might just be the girl a fugitive would turn to for help. Neil has no money. At least Abby has access to an ATM.

Sunny tried for a reassuring smile, but she wasn't sure she managed to get her face quite right as she led the way down the stairs. "Anyway, I've changed my mind. I think maybe it would be a good idea to give Will a call."

She stopped in the middle of the flight when she realized someone was standing in the hallway downstairs. Neil Garret.

"What are you doing here?" Sunny burst out.

Mrs. M. looked over her shoulder. "Mr. Garret? I'm afraid Abby is out."

"I know." Sunny had never seen Neil Garret look more miserable. "And it's my fault. She's been taken, Mrs. Martinson. Taken by a man who wants to trade her for me."

"Taken?" Helena said the word as if she couldn't quite grasp the meaning.

"The man who's after me, he got hold of a file. It told about my background, my associates, and it included a picture of your daughter. Apparently there was a picture of her that appeared in the local newspaper, and this guy put two and two together . . ."

Neil gave his head a violent shake. "Abby didn't deserve to get mixed up in this. I'm going to get her out of it. I've got an hour to show up at Charlie Vane's boat. As soon as I get there, this man will let her go."

"Can you trust him?" Mike said. "I think that sounds more like a job for the police."

"If this guy sees police, Abby gets it." Neil's voice was rough. "So I can't let you call your friend Will."

"And how are you going to stop us?" Sunny asked.

Neil brought up the hand he'd kept hidden behind his leg to reveal a gleaming pistol. "Abby told me about her dad, how he was always hunting and fishing, about his fishing gear and his guns. This was in a nicely engraved box from the Kittery Harbor Sportsman's Club. I don't trust the word of the man who took Abby. This will be an equalizer."

"Neil." Sunny tried to keep her voice calm. "You told me you never touched a gun in your life."

"Yeah, but I watched other people take care of them," Neil replied. "I know which end the bullets come out of."

He gestured with the pistol. "So let's all get on the same level here."

Step by unwilling step, Sunny, her dad, and Mrs. M. joined Neil.

"Turn out your pockets."

"What for?" Mike demanded.

"I want to get all your cell phones," Neil explained. Once that was taken care of, he gestured toward the kitchen. "Now—into the basement."

"What are you going to do down there?" Mrs. M. asked.

"I'm going to lock you in," Neil replied. "It will just be for a little while. If everything goes right, Abby will be back here to let you out."

And if it doesn't go right . . . Sunny pushed that thought aside. It didn't pay to argue with a man holding a gun. He herded them down the basement stairs, standing over them with his pistol. When they were down in the cellar, he slammed the door shut. A second later they heard a click.

Mike charged up the stairs like a much younger man. He grabbed the shiny new lever he'd helped install and tried to twist it.

Of course, it didn't budge.

"Locked," he said, pointing out the obvious. "I—"

"Shhhh." Sunny had joined him at the top of the stairs, pressing one ear against the panel and holding her hand over the other ear, which was being assaulted by barks and whines from Toby. "The front door closed. He's gone."

"We've got to get out of here!" Mrs. M. moved over to Toby's crate and let him out. The dog danced around them in a dithering run.

Pretty much the way I feel, Sunny had to admit.

"There have to be tools here, something we can use to jimmy the door open." Mike flicked the switch to turn on a dim bulb on the ceiling.

"Vince kept his workshop and his hunting stuff in the garage," Mrs. Martinson said. "He redid it as a den."

"Maybe one of us could squeeze out a window," Sunny suggested. Mrs. M. was petite. If they could boost her up—

But Helena shook her head. "They've been seriously winterproofed. Nothing's getting in—or out."

"We could get something to use as a battering ram," Mike desperately suggested. "The three of us—"

"Wouldn't have much room on those stairs," Sunny pointed out.

"There has to be something we can do." Mike pounded a frustrated fist against the wooden panel.

"Wait a second." Sunny listened carefully—she'd heard a noise outside. A sort of high-pitched mew. The sound of a curious cat.

"Shadow!" she called. "Are you there?"

The answer came as a scratch, Shadow's claws on the wooden door.

"Great, the furball is out there," Mike grumped. "What are you going to do, slip a note under the door for him to take to the neighbors?"

"I'm hoping—praying—he can do something more useful." Sunny took hold of the door lever and rattled it. "Hey, Shadow, you hear that? Come and get it!"

*

Shadow stared up at the door, not sure what kind of a game this was. He'd been kind of annoyed when Sunny put him down on the floor and all the two-legs climbed the stairs, so he hadn't followed them. Instead he'd stayed in the room with chairs, wrinkling his nose. The whole place smelled of Biscuit Eater. At least the big yellow dog wasn't there to annoy him.

Then he heard other footsteps coming in. Maybe this was Good Petter. Shadow peered around the big chair and got a surprise. It was the Generous One, moving in that funny way the humans did when they thought they were being quiet.

Voices came from above, and then Sunny, the Old One, and the Old One's She were coming down the stairs. Obviously, they were surprised to see the Generous One, too. Shadow stayed where he was. He didn't like it when friends fought, and whatever the two-legs were saying, it wasn't friendly. Some of it sounded sad, some angry.

Then the humans began moving toward the room of food. *Maybe this is better,* Shadow thought. *Maybe the fight is over and they're going to eat.*

But, no, instead the Old One opened the door to the dark place below, and he, Sunny, and his She went down the stairs. This didn't look like a good thing. It didn't look like a game, either. Shadow watched in puzzlement as the Generous One slammed the door. Then he put a shiny thing in his pocket, went down the hall to the front door, and left.

Shadow crept into the kitchen and sat in front of the closed door. He could hear agitated voices on the other side. Couldn't the two-legs get the door open? Shadow thought humans could do that.

Now you know how it feels to be a cat, he thought as he heard banging from the other side.

He put a curious paw out to push against the wood. It didn't move. He gave it a quick scratch, but he could see claws wouldn't work, either.

Then he heard a rattling noise. He looked up to see a metal thing moving slightly—not a knob like most doors, but a squarish thing kind of like the catch on the screen door that he was able to jump up and work. He heard Sunny's voice calling him, like when they played the Chase the String game.

Shadow crouched down, then sprang up, his paw batting at the metal thing as he passed it. But the door didn't open.

He landed on the floor, staring up, as Sunny called him again. He jumped, but again the metal thing resisted his efforts, for that try and two more.

It doesn't move when I hit it, Shadow thought, examining the thing above his head. *But it sticks out enough. Maybe I can catch it . . .*

He gathered himself for another leap, but this time instead of batting at the recalcitrant thing, he hooked a paw around it. A sharp vibration went through his leg, and then the metal thing twisted beneath him, trying to dump him to the floor. Shadow spun in midair, getting his legs under him and springing away from the sneaky thing—just in time.

The door almost flew open, and Sunny came running out, calling his name. She swooped down to him, gathering him up in her arms and planting her lips to the top of his head. She didn't do that very often. Shadow had learned that two-legs didn't like to groom.

He settled in her arms as she hugged him close and put her lips on him again.

This is pretty nice, he thought. *But I wouldn't want to play that game again. It's kind of stupid.*

19

Sunny blinked away tears as she kissed Shadow again on the top of the head. "You did it, little guy," she told him. "You saved us."

Shadow's eyes slitted and he purred with pleasure. Then his eyes went wide as a series of barks echoed their way up the stairs, and Toby came galumphing into the kitchen, capering around Sunny's feet at all the excitement.

Shadow's expression of pleasure disappeared. Now he gave Sunny a look as if he'd just received an awful surprise, like the time he'd tried to jump onto the hood of Mike's car while he was washing it and had slid all the way across to land in the pail of soapy water. "You know Toby lives here," she whispered to him. "I'll make sure he doesn't bother you."

By now, Mike had brought Mrs. Martinson up the stairs

and installed her on a kitchen chair. Sunny shifted Shadow around her neck like a stole and scrambled down the hallway, retrieving her cell phone and calling up Will's personal number. *Don't go to voice mail, don't go to voice mail,* she silently chanted as the phone rang.

"I'm at Helena Martinson's," she told Will when he picked up. "Neil Garret was just here."

"What? Why?" he instantly demanded. "I figured he'd be out of town by now."

"He stopped off to pick up a pistol from Vince Martinson's old gun collection," Sunny told him. "The reason Neil gave Val the slip is because Yancey Kilbane kidnapped Abby Martinson. If Neil wants to save her, he's got to turn up at Charlie Vane's ship in less than an hour now."

"Neil got a gun." Will sounded as if he wanted to make sure he was hearing correctly. "I don't suppose Mrs. Martinson gave him one willingly."

"No, he got hold of the gun first, rounded us up, and locked us in the cellar."

"Is that where you are now? Should I send help?"

"No, we got out," Sunny said. "I'll save the story of how. You won't believe it anyway. But maybe you should send some cops to Vane's boat—try to cut Neil off before he does something stupid."

"If he felt that he needed a gun, he doesn't trust Kilbane very much." Will sounded worried. "I'll call it in, but the nearest patrol cars are probably up in outlet-land. Do you have a car model or description I can pass along so we can maybe intercept Neil?"

"Sorry," Sunny apologized. "We didn't see him come up, and we were down in the basement when he left."

"Too much to hope for," Will muttered. "I'm on my way back from Levett, so I'll head for the dock directly."

Alone, Sunny thought. But all she could say was, "Be careful."

"Definitely," Will replied.

They hung up, and Sunny turned to Mike. "Will's calling it in—I figured he'd get farther than we would dialing 911. But it's going to take a while before the cops get there." She took a deep breath. "I think we need to catch up with Neil—slow him down until some help arrives."

She glanced at Helena Martinson's worried face. "We'll need to beat the clock, but I'm betting on Will."

Sunny unwound Shadow from around her neck and passed the cat to Mrs. M. "Can you take care of Shadow? I don't want to leave him alone after all of this."

Shadow did not look happy, clinging to Helena's arms and glaring down at the barking Toby. "Thanks," Sunny said. "We'll be back with good news, I promise."

She headed for the door with Mike in tow. Her dad looked frankly dubious, but he kept quiet until they were out in the street. "Sunny, it's not a good idea to make promises you might not be able to keep."

"I know, Dad. But I'm going to do my darnedest to make sure things turn out okay."

She started rushing back to their house, to find Mike speed-walking right beside her. "*We're* going to do our darnedest," he told her.

They just about flew up the driveway to Sunny's Wrangler. She got behind the wheel, buckling into her seat belt. Mike did the same. "I suspect it's going to be one of those kinds of rides," he said.

Sunny started the engine, and they were off. She negotiated the local streets at as fast a speed as she could safely
manage. Mike glanced at his watch. "He has quite a lead
on us. How do you figure on trying to catch up with him?"

They hit a county road, and Sunny pushed the speedom-
eter a little more. She'd been sorting through options as they
drove and had finally decided on one—not the best choice,
she had to admit, but the only chance to cut down their travel
time to town. "I was thinking of taking Ridge Road."

"Ridge Road!" Mike burst out. "Are you crazy? You
want to take an unpaved goat track in the dark?"

"It's the one shortcut that might put us ahead of Neil,"
Sunny said.

"Yeah, if it doesn't put us in traction." He paused. "The
last time you tried that shortcut, somebody got killed."

"They sure as heck didn't mean me any good and got
what they deserved." She gripped the steering wheel
tightly. The turnoff for the disused road would be coming
up soon on their left. "Have you got a better idea?"

Mike stayed silent for a long moment. "I don't, damn it.
Just don't go racing downhill. The ruts and washouts are bad
enough, but there may still be ice along the way." He put his
hands against the dashboard. "And brace yourself."

Sunny downshifted and angled off the pavement onto
Ridge Road. *One good thing,* she told herself, *no traffic to
deal with.* The car dropped heavily into a rut. *One very bad
thing—there's no way to see other cars get in trouble —no
advance warning.*

They thumped and bumped down the incline. Even
though Sunny was sparing with the gas, they picked up

speed. The jouncing view in the headlights looked like the surface of the Moon. Great pools of darkness hid potholes that seemed to go to China. Sunny tried to stay in the ruts, following the route where generations of teenagers had gone joyriding. *So far, so good.*

Then they hit a washout, and the truck went airborne. Sunny gripped the wheel as they landed heavily, her body flung against the restraints of the seatbelt. But she managed to guide them back onto what was left of the road.

The hillside steepened, and they picked up more speed. Sunny carefully applied the brakes. *No racing,* she told herself. *You don't want to bottom out.*

Even so, they suffered a couple of bone-jarring rattles and crashes. Beside her, Mike grit his teeth as he tried to keep his grip on the dashboard. Every once in a while, she saw his foot pump in the air—trying to use a nonexistent set of brakes.

Maybe I should have put Dad behind the wheel, Sunny suddenly thought. *He was the professional truck driver.*

Mike stifled a gasp—or was it a groan?—as they took a bump that pitched them far over to one side.

On the other hand, Dad's also the one with the heart condition.

But it was a little late to be considering that. She had to devote all her attention to keep them from flipping onto their noses or their sides as the Wrangler battered along, bucking like a live thing. The frozen ground was unyielding, and they took quite a pounding. *We've got to be three-quarters of the way down . . .*

Their nose flew up again, landed heavily, and rebounded.

The bouncing cone of illumination from their headlights showed something Sunny hadn't encountered before on this thrill ride.

Somebody had abandoned a car in the middle of the ruts. The old beater must have bottomed out and died in a sort of hollow along the route and apparently had just been left to rust. Now Sunny had to gun the engine and get the Wrangler out of its ruts, or they'd end up rear-ending the dead car. She managed to get the Jeep up and out, only to discover that the depression had also collected a pool of ice.

The Wrangler was going sideways almost as fast as it was going forward. Sunny yanked her right foot back, fighting the instinctive response of tromping on the brakes. That wouldn't work if the tires couldn't get traction. She gripped the steering wheel until her hands hurt, but she didn't try to yank them into some sort of course correction. Most likely, that would send them spinning out. Her breath seemed to freeze in her throat. Was this what her mom had gone through in the last instants before that fatal crash? All she could do was hang on.

Their skid seemed to last forever, but it had to be only seconds. At last they slowed as they came out of the sunken area, Sunny gently working the steering wheel to get the tires set in the direction she wanted to go. Pebbles rattled under them, and Sunny cautiously gave the engine a little gas. Two of the tires bit into dirt, slewing them around a little, but then they were out of the ice patch.

Sunny picked her way around the derelict car, slid as gently as possible into the ruts again, and proceeded down the rest of the way. The incline slowly leveled out, with only a few more bumps to rattle everything loose in the car—not to mention their teeth.

Mike let out a long-held breath as Sunny finally climbed onto the pavement of a county road. "Good driving," he said, and then, "Well, I can see where your raise for this year is going to go—to Sal DiGillio."

Mentioning their mechanic after she'd just given the shocks such a workout should have annoyed Sunny. But in the exhilaration of having survived the wild ride and the skating pond experience, she laughed. "Like you never took a hot rod down this way," she told her dad.

"Not in the middle of winter," he replied. "Those ancient days might have been a time when men were men and seat belts hadn't been invented, but we weren't out-and-out stupid."

They continued onward towards Kittery Harbor's old downtown area with Sunny crowding the speed limit and sometimes going well past it. *If there were cops around, we'd have heard the sirens,* she told herself as they barreled along. It was well after the town's version of rush hour, and traffic was thin.

The dock area, when they got there, was pretty much deserted. Fishermen were early risers— and just as early to bed. There weren't many cars on the street or even parked. The only sign of life was the Dockside Diner with its broken neon lights.

"Keep going," Mike directed as they rolled past. "That's the pier where Charlie used to tie up his boat."

"Not exactly in heavy use," Sunny muttered.

The dock wasn't totally dilapidated, but it was certainly lonely. About halfway out, a fishing boat lay moored.

"There's the *Ranger*," Mike said. "People think it's named after the ship John Paul Jones took out of port here. But Charlie told me his buccaneer ancestor had commanded a ship by that name sixty years before the Revolution."

"Nobody around," Sunny said, coasting to a stop. "No police, and no Neil. You figure he'd have left his car here, and there's nothing."

"This Kilbane fellow picked a pretty good place for a meeting." Mike peered along the length of the pier. "There's no cover, and he'll see anyone heading for the boat long before they get there."

"Yeah, we're a little too obvious here ourselves," Sunny said. "I'm going to pull back to the diner. We should be able to catch Neil as he passes through there—"

She broke off as a figure stepped out of the shadows and into their headlights. He was a big guy, bearded, with a thatch of hair receding from his forehead. Only the snub nose and the wild eyebrows gave Sunny a clue to his identity. That, and the pistol he aimed at her.

It was Yancey Kilbane.

"Out of the car," he said. "And don't try anything stupid, or one of you gets hurt right now." He moved to cover them both as Sunny and Mike exited the car. "Onto the dock. We'll join your friend Abby on the boat."

Walking onto the pier at gunpoint, Sunny glanced longingly back toward the land. The sign from the diner flashed its mangled message: DOCKSIDE DI E, DOCKSIDE DI E.

I really hope that's not an omen, Sunny thought as she walked along.

20

"You must be the redhead who came with the cops to O'Dowd's last night," Yancey Kilbane said to Sunny from his vantage point walking behind them. "Made me move this up sooner than I wanted to."

She could see that Kilbane moved stiffly as he herded them onto the boat. But he had no trouble keeping the gun on them. "So who are you?" he asked Mike.

"I'm her father," Mike snapped.

Gun or no gun, Dad's not about to roll over, Sunny thought, caught between pride and worry for her father. *I just hope he doesn't get himself hurt.*

But Kilbane laughed at Mike's feistiness. "Boy, you keep an eye on her, the cops keep an eye on her, it must be hell to date your daughter." He poked them along up to the bow of the vessel, where Abby Martinson sat slumped behind the gunwales, silver duct tape wrapped around her wrists and ankles and forming a gag over her mouth.

Her eyes went wide when she saw Mike and Sunny, but all she was able to manage was a muffled "Mmmmmph!"

Yancey Kilbane tossed a roll of tape to Mike. "You see how it's done," he said, nodding toward the tied-up Abby. "Now do the same to your daughter."

I'm getting heartily sick of duct tape, Sunny thought as Mike began to wrap the stuff around her ankles. She nervously licked her lips. *Especially the taste.*

"Look, Bear—Yancey. You have to realize you're on borrowed time," Sunny said as Mike finished with her wrists. Anything to keep from being gagged as well as helpless. "The police are on the way."

"Kind of figured that, especially since you know my name." Yancey took the roll of tape and motioned for Mike to lie down. "And you must have talked to your buddy Neil to turn up here. Why you jumped the gun before the cops arrived, I don't know. But as long as Neil gets here before they come, I can do what I got to do. When I first arrived down here, it was just business as usual, a two-fer to cut out the competition. But now it's a question of earning." He shook his head, a greedy glitter in his eyes. "You won't believe how much some mob guy out in L.A. will pay for a picture of good old Neil—dead and done."

The sprouting, receding hair and the full beard certainly softened Kilbane's image from the hard-faced biker in his mug shot. But obviously he'd abandoned whatever act he'd put on to win Jasmine's heart as Bear. He efficiently trussed up Mike and then checked Sunny's bindings to make sure they'd make her stay put. At least he didn't gag them—yet. Apparently, he wanted some entertainment as he waited for Neil.

"So why did old Neil come and tell you about our little meeting? That's a definite no-no."

"He needed money," Sunny lied easily. "He couldn't get to his stash when the marshals dragged him off."

"Yeah, Neil is all about the money. At least he was back when he was Nick. If you know about the marshals, then I guess you know he was Nick, too. Abby here was actually pals with him when he was Nick, back in California."

Abby made another noise through her gag.

"I thought I'd blown my chance when I realized the cops were onto me." Kilbane shook his head. "I got away from that old bartender broad I was squatting with before the big raid. But when I went looking, Neil's shop was locked up, and his house was empty. Then I sat in a diner, reading this throwaway newspaper, and I saw a picture that looked familiar. It matched an actress' head shot in this briefcase full of stuff on Neil that I—picked up."

"From Phil Treibholz," Sunny said. *After you killed him,* she silently added.

Kilbane shrugged. "He didn't need it anymore. And it turned out to be useful. It put me on to Abby here. A nice, quiet town like this, I was able to find a home address for the Martinsons in the phone directory. Then all I had to do was watch until she took Mom's car out for a spin."

"After which you got in touch with Neil."

"I found a couple of phones when I went through the detective guy's pockets, getting rid of his ID. One was obviously a burner, a phone Tribe-whatever had picked up after he arrived here. And there was just one local number on it. Pretty easy to figure out. So I reached out and touched old Neil, told him his little friend here would be in deep trouble if he didn't get his butt over here."

Kilbane frowned. "Now I've got to wonder if you gave Neil enough money to skip town and leave me holding the bag here until the cops come." The look on his face promised that no good would come of that.

Mike tried to get a look at his watch—impossible, with all that tape around his wrists. But Sunny understood his anxiety. *Neil should be turning up soon,* she thought, *if he's going to show up at all. Let's face it, he doesn't have a history of being a stand-up guy. Like Charlie Vane, he put on a big song and dance about being the victim of circumstances. Maybe he'd persuaded himself that this was just one more circumstance he couldn't change and moved on.*

She swallowed, hard. The police didn't seem to be in any rush to put in an appearance, either.

Boy, wouldn't it be ironic if we got ourselves killed trying to save Neil from doing one good deed in his life— because he decided not to do it after all?

A car came past the diner and rolled to a stop at the foot of the pier. The driver-side door opened, and Neil Garret stepped out. He squared himself up, but it was hard to look heroic in a cardigan sweater.

He must be freezing, Sunny thought. But then, she realized, he wouldn't have been able to bring a coat along if he escaped by bailing out a bathroom window.

"Good old Neil." Kilbane chuckled. "Somehow I knew I could depend on him."

Sunny strained her ears. No sirens. No police. Kilbane

was going to kill Neil, and then he would turn on the rest of them. Inconvenient witnesses. Collateral damage.

She twisted her wrists, testing the duct tape bonds. There was a little give—Mike had managed that much. But she didn't think she'd be able to get free before this dirty business was all over.

Kilbane rose from behind the gunwale when Neil was about halfway down the pier. "Hey there, Neil, step right up," he said.

Neil stopped. "Not until I see Abby."

"Sure, buddy." The biker leaned down and hauled Abby into view. "Here she is, alive and—well, not exactly kicking. But breathing."

Neil took a few hurried steps forward, then stopped. "You've got to let her go. That was the deal."

Kilbane brought up his gun. "It's a little late to start negotiating, friend. She'll go after we finish our business."

Neil shook his head. "No. Before." He managed a smile, even if it was more of a death's-head grin. "Afterward, I don't think I'll be able to protect my interests."

"Hey, look. I've got lots of hostages." Kilbane hoisted Sunny and Mike to their feet.

While he was doing that, Neil suddenly ran forward.

"Everybody down!" Sunny yelled. She dropped to her knees as Mike and Abby went flat.

Neil brought up the gleaming gun he'd kept hidden behind his leg. Kilbane aimed his pistol. Their shots went off almost at the same time, a brutal blow to Sunny's ears. The biker jerked a little, letting out a startled exclamation. But Neil was flung on his back, his borrowed gun clattering on the wooden planking.

Kilbane pocketed his pistol and brought a hand to his other arm, wincing a little. "Huh. Grazed me."

Moving his injured arm carefully, he brought out a cell phone, transferred it to his good side, and raised it to take a picture. "There's one. But I guess I should go for a little more insurance."

He replaced the phone and got out his gun, carefully making his way to the dock. For a moment, he stood over Neil. "Head shot is sure, but that would mess up the picture." Kilbane brought his pistol down, aiming for Neil's chest.

"Police! Freeze!" a harsh voice shouted.

Kilbane twisted, snapping off a shot at the figure running up the pier.

Two more shots roared out, and the biker reeled, an almost comical look of astonishment on his face as he looked down, his free hand plucking at his chest. He tried to bring his gun around, but it dropped from his fingers. Then his knees gave out, and he toppled onto his back.

"Everybody all right?" Will ran forward, kicking the pistol farther from Kilbane's hand.

He knelt beside Neil, feeling his neck for a pulse. "Everybody on board, I mean."

Sunny poked her head a little higher, succesfully heaving up onto her knees. "We're okay. Just tied up," she said.

Will nodded and started back down the pier. Sunny managed to get to her feet, waving her taped-together wrists. "Hey, aren't you going to cut us loose?"

"After I call in for backup—and an ambulance," he shouted over his shoulder.

Will was back in a few minutes, clambering onto the boat, then freezing for an embarrassed moment when he realized he still had his pistol in his hand. Will quickly holstered it under his coat, then reached into his pocket to pull out a folding knife. With the help of that, he quickly sliced away the tape from around Sunny's wrists.

As soon as she was free, Will pressed the knife into her hand. "Take care of the others. I'm going to do what I can for Neil."

He dropped back to the dock, took off his coat, folded it up, and put it to Neil's chest, both hands on top.

A pressure bandage, Sunny realized.

"What about Kilbane?" she called, cutting her ankles free. Will just shook his head.

Now that Sunny could move around, she got to work getting the tape off Abby and Mike. She was especially careful getting the tape gag off Abby's mouth. Lips are always more fragile in wintertime, and the sticky stuff from the tape could pull off skin and turn a mild case of chapped lips into a bloody mess. Sunny succeeded in getting Abby ungagged without any terrible consequences.

Abby grimaced a couple of times, trying to get the taste out of her mouth. Then she said, "That man kidnapped me right out of the supermarket parking lot! I never even managed to get in and do my shopping." She peered down at the dock. "Is he—?"

Mike took her by the arm. "Some things you just don't want to see."

As he spoke, Sunny slipped over the side of the boat to land on the pier.

Mike sighed. "And then there's my daughter the reporter."

She walked over to where Will was working on Neil Garret. "How's he doing?"

"Losing a lot of blood." Will's face was pale. "I knew there was trouble as soon as I spotted your car there—empty. So I drew my weapon and advanced while these two were playing Gunfight at the OK Corral." He glanced toward the landward end of the pier. "It's just as well. Where the hell is that backup?"

Actually, the first reinforcements to arrive weren't police, but Val Overton and the federal marshals. Her lips thinned to a tight line as Will and Sunny brought her up to date on why Neil had slipped away—and what he'd done since. "The news vultures are going to be all over this story—sorry, Sunny, but you know the people I mean."

"No offense taken," Sunny assured her. "Some of my best friends were vultures."

"So, unless you want to deal with them, Will, I'll take over here."

Will breathed a sigh of relief. "Gladly," he said. "As it is, there are people in the department that like to think I'm too fond of the media spotlight."

Like Captain Dan Ingersoll, Sunny thought.

The second wave of first responders to put in an appearance was the ambulance. Paramedics immediately took over from Will and went screaming off with Neil on a gurney and a deputy marshal riding shotgun as a bodyguard.

"Executive decision," Val said. "Neil may have left our custody, but I'm ruling he didn't actually leave WitSec."

After that, it was a dead heat between the first police cruisers arriving and the onslaught of the TV news vans. Will got Ben Semple in his blue constable's uniform and several deputies in sheriff's department green to run interference, keeping the media people at a reasonable distance while Val's people made a few preparations, like covering Yancey Kilbane's body with black plastic sheeting.

Will paid no attention, having other things on his mind. "Where were you guys?" he hissed to Ben, who shrugged in reply.

"The first I heard of anything going on was a report of shots fired. So I hauled butt away from outlet land and came here," Ben said, but he looked troubled.

So much for bypassing 911 in hopes of getting a jump on things, Sunny thought. *Apparently some folks in headquarters must have decided Will was telling tall tales.* She pursed her lips tightly to keep those notions from spilling out. *That could have gotten him—gotten all of us—killed.*

The cameras had assembled by now, and Val stepped forward, showing her silver star. "I'm Deputy U.S. Marshal Valerie Overton. We had a shooting incident here tonight, an attempt to murder a person in the Witness Security Program—what's commonly called witness protection."

She made a brief statement, not mentioning Neil Garret nor his previous name, but identifying Yancey Kilbane, or rather, tentatively identifying him subject to fingerprint evidence. Just as she was finishing up, a screaming police cruiser arrived and Captain Ingersoll and Sheriff Lenore Nesbit arrived.

"We'd like to thank local law enforcement for their help and quick response to keep this attempt from becoming a tragedy," Val said as the sheriff and the captain hurriedly huddled with Will, trying to catch up on what was going on. That was something Sunny wasn't let in on, but from a distance, she watched Lenore Nesbit's expression as she listened and then saw her talking sharply to Ingersoll.

However, Lenore was graciousness itself when she joined Val to face a pack of reporters rabid for answers to their questions. "We're still ascertaining all the details for this incident," she told them. "We'll need statements from several witnesses and from the officer involved." She softened a little to seem a bit more human. "We're also dispatching an officer to reassure the family of one of the witnesses that she is all right."

Sunny saw Ingersoll whispering to Ben Semple, who jumped into his cruiser like a shot. *Off to Mrs. M.*, she thought. *Good.*

After the usual media hoedown was concluded, Sunny, Mike, and Abby were escorted to the sheriff's office in Levett to give statements about what happened. Will, of course, was expected to write a report.

They arrived to find Helena Martinson already there, courtesy of a ride in a prowl car by Ben Semple. Mrs. M. wrapped her arms around Abby. "Safe. Safe. Thank God she's safe." She opened one arm to embrace Mike, who quickly pulled Sunny into a group hug.

"We're all safe," he said, "all of us."

*

In the end, Abby had to extend her vacation by a few more days, waiting for the media frenzy to wear down. But at last they were yesterday's news. Sunny took a day off herself to organize a farewell dinner. She wanted to make something that Abby was unlikely to find in California, the land of light food. Finally, she settled on pot roast with ginger snap gravy, mashed potatoes, and glazed carrots.

Delicious scents came wafting from the kitchen to fill

the whole house as she worked with Mike to set the table with the good china. Five places—for Helena and Mike, Sunny and Will, and Abby.

The Martinsons arrived first, Mrs. M. bearing the usual coffee cake, Abby with a bottle of red wine. "I know this feast is supposed to be the opposite of West Coast cuisine, but I didn't think that would disqualify a California wine."

Sunny got to work with the corkscrew as the doorbell rang. Mike went to answer and returned with Will, who also carried a bottle. "I thought of stopping off and getting a box of O'Dowd's house special," he joked, "but then Gene Avezzani slipped me a bottle of the good stuff."

They settled in the living room with glasses, and Shadow's inquisitive face poked in from the hallway. "There's our hero," Helena Martinson said, and Shadow was coaxed in for a lot of petting—not that it took all that much persuasion. Sunny smiled at the look on Will's face as the former hostages made much of the cat. *After all, he probably deserves a little credit for shooting the cold-blooded killer.*

Soon Shadow lay in a boneless little heap on Sunny's lap while small talk flowed overhead—a little neighborhood gossip and Abby's travel plans. "My return tickets may have taken me all over God's country, but at least they weren't nonrefundable. I'm taking a much more direct flight from Boston."

"That's a long drive," Mike glanced at Helena.

Abby shook her head. "I've already booked a car service—for an ungodly hour in the morning." She grinned mischievously at Helena. "Knowing Mom, she'll be up to wish me bon voyage. But then she can go back to sleep."

A timer buzzed in the kitchen, and Sunny rose to her feet. "Just a couple of last-minute things, and then we can eat."

The feast tasted every bit as good as it smelled, and conversation suffered for a while as everyone concentrated on eating. "It's a shame Val Overton wasn't able to accept your invitation," Will said. "I think she'd have enjoyed this."

"I suspect you never passed it on to her, trying to guarantee yourself a third helping," Sunny mock-accused him.

"The thought never crossed my mind . . . much," Will assured her. "But Val was out of town as soon as she recovered Phil Treibholz's briefcase from where Kilbane stowed it on the *Ranger*. I think she's trying to track down the leak that allowed Treibholz to find Neil in the first place."

"How is Nick—Neil? I'll never get that straight in my mind," Abby said. "He was taken off to the hospital, and that was mentioned in the news. But afterward—nothing."

Will hesitated for a moment. "Officially, Neil is dead."

Abby's fork clattered to her plate. "D-dead?" Tears appeared in her eyes. "He tried to save me, and I never got to thank him. When we were together, I wondered about Nick. There was this seed of doubt. He always seemed to take the easy way out, and—well, that kind of colored how seriously I took the relationship. He was kind to me, good, but when he got me that job in the Valley, there was this question—did he do it for me, or was he just breaking things off? Then, when I got kidnapped, he put his life on the line for me—and I guess I got an answer."

"Hey, I didn't mean to upset you," Will apologized. "As I said, that's the official story. The truth is, I don't know. Neil was in pretty bad shape when they took him off. I certainly couldn't say whether or not he'd pull through. But remember, the first thing they tell people in witness protection is that their old life must be dead to them—and they have to be dead to their old life."

Abby stared. "So when they're saying he's dead, that might be a cover to protect him?"

"Maybe." Will spread his hands in a helpless gesture. "The only thing that's sure is that you'll never get an answer from the WitSec people."

"And some people don't care about answers, only assets," Sunny said. "The lawyer that put Treibholz on Neil's trail turned up in town this week. Neil's ex-wife wants everything of his that isn't nailed down. They're fighting with Ollie over the walk-in freezer Neil installed in the store."

"That's terrible," Helena said.

Mike shook his head. "Vultures."

But Sunny stayed silent. *If Neil did survive, he's starting his new life without any of his "buzz off" money,* she thought. *No more being his own boss. I wonder what kind of scheme he'll wind up involved in to keep from being a greeter at Big Box, Inc.?*

She glanced at Will and put her hand over his. *It doesn't matter anymore. Alive or dead, Neil is out of our lives. And I know who really saved us.*

Sunny leaned toward Will, keeping her voice low. "Are you all right?"

He looked at her for a moment, a slow smile appearing on his lips. "What, are you expecting a galloping case of PTSD?"

"You shot Yancey Kilbane," Sunny pointed out.

"After he shot at me," Will replied. "It's not the first time I pulled out my gun—or used it. In the heat of action, you're usually too busy—and yes, a little scared—for any deep thinking about what's going on. That comes afterward. Yancey Kilbane was no saint. I'm not going to lose any sleep—or peace of mind—over what happened to him."

But I bet poor Jasmine is going to miss her Bear, Sunny thought. *The guy who was going to change her life.*

"So, no regrets?" she asked Will.

"One," he said. "That nice tie you gave me for Christmas got pretty messed up while I was trying to help Neil. And I don't think Abby's get-out-the-spot trick is going to work on a big bloodstain."

Sunny patted his hand. "Then I'll have to get you a replacement. After all, your birthday isn't that far away."

*

Shadow looked up at the humans gathered around the table, enjoying the aromas from their plates. *His* humans, he liked to think of them, his clan. When two-legs sat around like this and ate a lot of food, they were usually celebrating something and acted happy. They certainly left him purring earlier. So he was surprised when Good Petter started making sad noises with water coming out of her eyes. That eye-water was a specially bad sign.

Often, when two-legged Shes made eye-water, either they or their mate went away. Good Petter didn't have a mate, but Shadow had the suspicion she'd be going soon. It was just in the tone of voice she used talking to the others.

That would be too bad. He'd miss Good Petter.

But it wouldn't be as terrible as if Sunny were to go away. Cats were supposed to wander, but two-leggity people, ones close to a cat's heart, should stay where they could be found. A cat wanted to be able to depend on them.

Some humans, though, were just undependable. Take the Generous One, for instance. He'd been friendly and a lot of fun, playing with Shadow and tossing him delicious tidbits. But now it seemed he was gone. Shadow had caught rides with Sunny several times when she went to that place where she spent her days. But when Shadow went next door, to the store where he figured the Generous One lived, it was always closed and empty. Even the scent of fish was disappearing.

Maybe the Generous One was more like a cat and went off wandering, Shadow thought. The two-legs were always getting crazy ideas, making things, doing things that didn't make sense. Shadow had learned early that he certainly couldn't hope to understand them, even though he'd grown attached to a few.

All he knew was that the Generous One was gone.

That was too bad.

Shadow would miss the Generous One.

Especially, he'd miss the fish.

Also from
New York Times Bestselling Author

CLAIRE DONALLY

Hiss and Tell

A Sunny & Shadow Mystery

Political heiress Priscilla Kingsbury is about to marry
Carson de Kruk, son of business mogul Augustus de
Kruk, at the Kingsburys' waterfront compound. For
reporter Sunny Coolidge, an assignment from the
Harbor Courier to cover the event is like catnip.

But when Sunny photographs men pulling the body
of a dead woman out of the water, the Kingsburys'
private security isn't happy. They claim the woman's
death was an accident, but the story seems fishy. Now,
with a little help from her police officer boyfriend
and her cunning cat Shadow, Sunny is determined to
get the scoop on a killer.

Praise for the Sunny & Shadow Mysteries

"Applause for paws—Sunny and
Shadow take Best in Show!"
—Susan Wittig Albert, *New York Times* bestselling author

Also in the series:
The Big Kitty
Cat Nap
Last Licks
Catch as Cat Can

facebook.com/thecrimescenebooks
penguin.com